BEWITCHED AND BE DITCHED

BEWITCHED AND BE DITCHED

KAREN MOLLER

www.blkdogpublishing.com

Unlucky as you or maybe I!
The fool was stripped to his foolish hide,
What he might have grasped when he cast love aside
(isn't on record that he even cried)
Some of her lived but some of her died
As he let the vampire suck him dry
as carelessly as you or maybe I!
Only God can reason why

Poem Inspired by Rudyard Kipling

Chapter 1

The lover who just walked out your door
Has taken all his blankets from the floor
The carpet, too, is moving under you
And it's all over now, Baby Blue
Bob Dylan

Karen Moller

The world mocks the old fool in his last gasp, who runs off with a young floozy, so this tale is pretty much a classic laugh. Yeah, whatever age men are, they tend to believe they are still young cockerels and up for a hump if a young chicken comes on to them. And it's true, you could gob-smack me with a hundred reasons why an old guy might dump his wife for a younger model, but few men would be quite so foolish as my husband Arthur, who after a four-day sex orgy with a Columbian gold-digging groupie dumped his ever-loving, clever, wife. Yeah, I prefer to think about myself as the ever-loving, clever, wife—it makes me feel less humiliated.

And dear reader I hear you asking, *why wouldn't Arthur, an 84-year-old, and not a dumbo, be suspicious of the motives of a 42-year-old floozy who had a reputation for sucking up to old guys for financial gain? Why would he convince himself she was consumed by love for his brilliant mind and his sort of still functioning appendages rather than his pocketbook?* It seems a greenie optimist would. But then delusions are not just a masculine weakness, plenty of rich old ladies have been deluded into believing guys half their age were mad with love for them. And some don't care, and some don't mind paying. It all depends on how they want their cookies crumbled.

I certainly would not, at my ripe old age, be deluded into believing a forty-year-old guy, who dropped into my lap, was attracted to my scintillating mind rather than my comfortable lifestyle. A bearded dinosaur, not even as old as Arthur, had tried to kiss me when I was in my forties. To kiss him seemed like trying to make out with Santa Claus. Give me Santa now and if he has a fascinating mind and sense of humor, I'll kiss him with pleasure. Don't know about anything beyond that.

Here's the spoiler so you'll know what's coming, so you will be prepared. This is the legacy I give to you. I wasn't given that courtesy. I wasn't prepared for the soul crushing agony that tore my life to shreds. I had been living in some happy bubble walking along the beach of destiny with Arthur, the love of my life, when in truth I was off with the fairies drowning in the surf while a

3

groupie lifeguard latched onto Arthur's brass balls and plotted my demise. This romance I thought I was living was a bogus flyover, an elaborate fairy tale. Not only had I been played for a fool, I *was* the fool. A dumb dreamer or what? You guessed it, more a dumb schmuck who discovered love was Russian roulette.

Do I sound bitter? So would you be bitter if a few months into the recent virulent Covid-19 pandemic, your life was shattered by horrific changes in everything you had taken for granted! Something died and the thing that died was my marriage. Arthur's sudden departure sent me into a flat spin; it was, however, his second dumping of our freshly murdered but still warm marriage that caused the real kick in the gut. It was then my mind went blank—the place where memories should have been—emptied. According to my therapist, memory loss is mostly a refusal to face reality; in truth, I wanted anything but that! The reality was senseless, unthinkable. Not only did I get dumped but Arthur acted like the cat who had bagged all the cream. How could twenty years of creative union be so disposable?

Having read this far you may be wondering where I am going with this story, which isn't far from my own thinking. All I can say is six months after being dumped I decided to tell the tale, in the hope of gaining some sort of understanding of human actions. I would have preferred to write a different story with an ending to tickle the mind and warm a romantic heart. Who needs to read this raw stuff about female rage and inappropriate curse words?

You may think the laughs in this story would be far and few between and yet even I found myself laughing hysterically. Who wouldn't? This tale of an aging husband going slightly mad over a fake religious groupie is truly mind boggling. Kind of sloppy and unreal especially when he claims he was bewitched into believing she was his spiritual guide with a direct connection to God.

When I met and fell in love with Arthur, I'd semi-retired from my fashion company and taken up writing a memoir, not just about the fascinating 1960s and my successful career in the fashion world but also about my less successful series of relationships with men of my generation. Of course, hanging out with artists didn't help but as well my young mind was irreversibly marked, or rather distorted by reading *Jane Eyre* at a vulnerable age. Jane, the poor governess, feels she must leave the owner of the manor when she believes he is about to marry one of the local ladies. She tells him if she had beauty and wealth, she would make it as hard for him to leave her as it is for her to leave him. That made me question: *is beauty and wealth what it takes to have someone's love?* Yeah, I was dumb and innocent, but we all know great weights hang on thin wires.

I don't have a clue whether it was my looks, success and wealth that frightened off many a successful man. Certainly, successful men viewed independent women, interested in their own work and creations, as both unpredictable and uncontrollable. Sure, they wanted to screw me but as a life companion they wanted a compliant woman who would look after them and the children. Not a carefree nocturnal scamp or a woman as clever as they believed they were.

Being creative helped me heal but it was writing my memoir that gave me the valuation and the courage to give my heart to Arthur, a quirky poet with a complicated love life and a multitude of curious hang ups. Mostly my previous lovers had been self-obsessed, hopeful navel-gazing unsuccessful wannabe artists who thought they could suck up what I am and become me. Yeah, I know, they wanted to hitch a ride on my bandwagon of success without the hard work. It's human to want a short cut.

In 2020 as we headed into the Covid pandemic I'd just finished corrections on my latest manuscript and sent it off to the publisher. Not exactly with a hula hoop, more a sigh, like, what am I going to do now? I am not one to sit around thinking beautiful thoughts even though you probably think it enough to be content with family and reading books or visiting museums, but here's the kicker. Where's the pleasure in doing it alone? Which of course brings up the next question—what happened to all those fun girlfriends who once filled my empty spaces before I hooked up with Arthur? Apparently in our patriarchal world, when you get together with a guy, he takes over your life and—bam—you got only him. And twenty years later, it is likely you have him only when *he* has time for you. Yeah, I know - my own fault. My mother would have mocked sarcastically—*so the little miss know it all, who thought she was so clever, ended up just another domestic slave.*

No doubt as you read this tale you may begin to question if I am making this story up for a hoot. Let me assure you this story is mostly true, like 98 percent. The other two percent would probably get me sued. There are a lot of uptight, easily offended people out there. Of course, I'd love it if the man-eating groupie/vampire who enticed Arthur with porno photos of her privates would sue me. That would be the real kicker and it would certainly let all those other vulnerable Sugar Daddies know to avoid this Columbian witch out to strip them of their goodies.

Chapter 2

If you give me back my baby, I won't worry you no more,
Give me back my baby, I won't worry you no more,
Don't have to put her in my house, Lordy, just lead her to my door.
Bob Dylan

Karen Moller

A ll this happened a couple of months earlier, before I was shaken awake by a dreadful nightmare. I'd lain in a sort of aftershock of fear, sucking down deep breaths as I waited for the walls to stop pulsating. The clock said seven minutes past midday. Midday! Why was I in bed? I blinked and tried to focus but an in penetrable fog blocked my thinking. My next thought was—where is Arthur? Was that him running water in the bathroom, bare feet on the hardwood floor? No, just slight sounds from the street creeping in through the windows. Arthur's closet door lay open and empty, as if everything had been vacuumed out, his belongings gone. There seemed no rhyme nor reason for this. Suddenly, my lungs cramped as a sickening thought crept over me—this implausible nightmare wasn't a nightmare, this was the real nightmare.

A sudden noise gave me proof I was awake. I called out and my daughter Sarah popped her head around the door. "Good morning. How are you?"

"Not sure, everything seems strange. Where's Arthur?"

She looked uncomfortable, which gave me a partial answer that something dreadful had happened. Her face was smiling and full of what seemed like hope but more *something has gone horribly wrong* look. "Arthur is gone. He's been gone for over two months. Everything of his has been removed from the house and sent to him as you requested."

"What do you mean? How can that be?" A roaring in my ears split my head with a collision of opposing thoughts.

"You've been ill. Not yourself. Everyone has been worried."

"What day is this?"

"It's September 18th." Her eyes stalked my every glance. "You lost your memory after your return from Venice. A protective mechanism the doctor said. Not wanting to face reality."

Empty areas of blanks flipped back and forth in my mind. What should I remember? What had I forgotten? Suddenly a memory hit me like a thud square in the gut. I'd returned home tired and exhausted, looking forward to seeing Arthur and having a pleasant chat. I poured myself a glass of wine to pass the time and opened the iPad lying on the table to glance at the news. My heart had flipped and juddered to a halt, one, two random beats as my eyes focused on pornographic photos exchanged between Arthur and a vulgar groupie who had been tracking him since the previous year. A million questions scorched my brain like gut rockets, one after another as if a dog was pissing misery juice all over my brain. Rage stormed my mind with hallucinations of committing assault and battery on the guilty parties. I would have shrieked if I could have but everything froze.

This memory caused a pain so sharp, so overpowering it racked me with nausea. Dizziness soon joined the party, almost blinding me. I lurched out of bed and collapsed on my knees beside the toilet bowl in time to relieve the rush of bile. I swallowed or tried to, but the lump in my throat stayed put like the worst case of indigestion on the planet. I could hardly breathe as sweat trickled down my back. I brushed aside my matted hair and lay my head on the cold marble floor. An eerie quiet surrounded me, the kind of quiet that permeates the air after something dies. It left me picking my heart out of the trash.

The profound words of my pals, the Existentialists: *life is meaningless, and nothing happens for a reason* should have prepared me for the shock of Arthur taking off into the neverland in search of a new thrill with a primitive Columbian savage. But it didn't. Which pretty much sucks.

I pulled out my computer and began to read through the months of email exchanges with Arthur that I had no memory of writing or receiving.

July 7, 2020.

Dear Arthur,

I am in shock. I have been sick for hours. Not even a note to tell me I have been dumped and replaced by this groupie! Anything would have been better than the horrible jolt of discovering on the iPad you had been exchanging masturbatory photos with this groupie since January. Am I to believe you left me your iPad full of porno photos because you could not face telling me you were dumping me? How could you stoop to such ugliness. Have you lost all sense of decency?

Did you purposely include copies on the iPad of the Antwerp apartment rental and the airplane tickets you bought for her—one for four days in January, Madrid/Paris, and another Madrid/Antwerp for two and a half months with extra baggage. Not a week but two and a half months with extra baggage!! Was that to let me know I have been completely and totally dumped without explanation. I've never thought of you as a callous man, but I cannot believe otherwise. Obviously for months you methodically made plans, then without a word packed my car and drove off to your prepared love nest. It is your right to leave me if you no longer wish to be with me, no one could argue with that, but to leave me in this brutal way without a word after twenty years of complicity and shared love is beyond comprehension. I am saturated by a deep sense of failure; tortured by delirium of guilt. My head spins and spins with self-accusations. What did I do wrong? Was it simply our love had become fragile like bones grown brittle with age? Had I stopped showing you how much I love you, or how important you are to me? Had I been so focused on what was working in our partnership that I didn't notice what wasn't working? I have searched my mind, and I honestly don't know how I failed. Perhaps I should I have interrogated you after you left the sofa bed opened out in my studio in January, or when a woman came back asking my assistant to search the bed for her earring? Should I have made you confess when you went around with a puzzle look in your eyes and no kisses on your lips? Was I a fool to believe that, if I were patient, if I gave you time to yourself, in what you called your spiritual crisis, you would come back to me?

Katherine

xxx

July 15, 2020.

Dear Katherine:

Something you wrote—and is on my mind and since this may ease your mind, although I do not want to get into a discussion of the whole thing, I feel I should bring up. You say, "what did I do wrong, how did I fail?" You did nothing wrong, and you did not fail; I acted spontaneously as I have all my life, as I acted with my family, with Ciguapa, with Paula, with Fiorelle and with you and finally, with I. Impetuous, without restraint, I liked, I lusted, my emotions in turmoil, I seduced immediately! Remember how I was with you. I made it clear right away that I wanted you. Nothing stopped me. I had earlier proposed marriage to Fiorelle in a thoughtless moment, ridiculous as I was still married to Ciguapa, but that did not make me hesitate. This has been the pattern of my life.

I am not cynical, I am not a 'seducer' in the normal understanding, no pleasure in 'conquering' a woman, no vanity as you suggest (flattered), it is more a weakness—some huge psycho-sexual imbalance in my emotional make-up. It is just 'the music of chance', just the way I am. This obvious arrogance on my part does not mean I am not filled with doubt like a man who assumes he's in occupied territory. Maybe there is still more that I can tell you. It is very hard to spit it all out. Still, nothing I have told you is untrue. For the first time in my life, I felt the full weight of my careless and irresponsible behavior, not just with respect to her or you, but throughout

12

my life. I examined my conscience and realized how impulsive and selfish and reckless I had been over decades. I plunged deeper into my soul than ever before. I went through a dark night of the soul. I felt I had to act with responsibility and live with transparency.

I feared to discuss it with you because I could not face your emotional reaction. I put it off hoping to find a solution. My mental world made a 360° revolution and I promised myself not to lie to women anymore—so I left you. From now on, I will not hide anything from you so you can count on my being transparent. Straight. Not confessional, but honest. This obvious lesson I have at last learned. Vis à Vis Woman. Nothing I have said or say will be the result of any idiotic emotional calculations. I am sick of that.

I am now consumed by regret for my heedlessness. I now repent it. I was overwhelmed by passion... But this is not just about sex. You asked for the truth. I simply could not resist and now it has ended. I want to live without the flesh. I need to live on my own to go more deeply into my own mind and soul. I used to meditate on my work, on the next step, now, all I think about is being divided down the middle—drawn and quartered. I feel I need to break one way or the other. My efficiency and productivity has taken a hit—yes, the fatigue is more than emotional because I am constantly being reproached for time-spent working. I need to pour myself into work, it is the mark I will leave on this earth. Ultimately, all I have is time.

I blame myself bitterly for the way you learned about this. I meant to do it gradually. Please try to forgive me for that. I ask forgiveness from God every day for the pain I have caused you. I do care about you and love you more than you realize. Believe me,

if I could be as kind and as generous as you,
I would be. The twenty years we had together
left an indelible mark on my soul. You are
central to my life's experience, and to lose
you would be a deep sorrow. I find it difficult
to think about anything else.
  Love Arthur

Rereading these emails, memories slipped back, one after another like bumps on a relief map, each too brief to be experienced fully. I'd grown comfortable with the idea of being with Arthur, like wearing a pair of shoes I loved. Arthur wasn't perfect. He was at times an exhausting companion, yet I deeply loved him. When I met him, I realized he was a flirt, ready to lay a rag on many a bush. I'd worried that he might give in to a whim, but this is not a whim, this is not just falling into bed with someone. He meticulously planned to leave me. That thought ricocheted around in my head like popcorn exploding in a microwave oven. A black loop of horror straight out of a Stephen King novel or Edvard Munch painted scream: "He is sick! Unbearably sick!"

I was halfway through leaving a weeping message on Arthur's phone, before I realized it was the middle of the night. I fled to the garden; I needed air. The sky was dense and impervious like a gray carpet; it pressed down on me, suffocatingly claustrophobic. I hunched my shoulders against the wind and sucked in steadying breaths.

My eyes filled with tears, but instead of weeping, distraught laughter overtook me. It was all so stupid, so nonsensical and unbelievable—he dumps his perfect working environment and then complains *to me* about being reproached by this groupie for time-spent working. *He hadn't thought this through. He never thought anything through! That was his problem.* He cannot even go out and buy himself a pair of socks let alone turn on the dishwasher. Why would he think an ignorant groupie would slip into my role of paying his bills, cleaning up his messes and fighting his battles to get his fair share.

I cried, "Woody, where are you?" my voice rising an octave as I looked around for my six-foot kangaroo. In an instant he was there, quieting all but the wind that rustled the leaves scattered on the paving stones. He looked at me the way one might look on having discovered a fast-food order was everything one hates and long past returnable.

"Calm down. Arthur is a pushover of inescapable senselessness! Passions are a form of madness. He met her, felt entitled to have her, so he humped her. And in the end the hump became more important than anything else."

If you have read this far you are likely to agree with Woody. Arthur is a confused, crazy mixed-up son of a possum. Not only is he unable to weigh cold facts, he now lies and cheats, then justifies it by saying it is just 'the music of chance', just the way I am. What kind of nonsense is that? He says he couldn't go on lying to me, so he left me. But he did carry on lying and would have continued if I hadn't seen the porno photos? Then after a mere week with this floozy, he says: "I simply could not resist and now it has ended. I want to live without the flesh." I ask you what does that mean? Was I seeing regret where there was only guilt? Does he think telling me this will somehow ease my pain? What would I answer if he asked to come back? Could I actually reconcile with a man who acted with such contempt for my feelings?

I re-entered my house and returned to the emails.

July 26, 2020.

Dear Arthur:

Kerouac got it about right when he said marriages begin as fabulous roman candles which explode like spiders across the stars but as the years pass the magic become mere shadows as insubstantial as ghosts reflected in a window or dreams that disappear upon waking? Your love is as insubstantial as a ghost reflected in a window or dreams that disappear upon waking? If there is a caring person inside you, I deserve an explanation. I deserve to know why you dumped me.

Some friends excuse your going off with a woman half your age as a *folie du cœu*, especially the men, but most of them think of you as a foolish old man seduced by an 'interested' groupie. It is ridiculous to say it is not just about having sex with a new woman. What else would make you walk out on a happy marriage? The iPad shows this departure well planned: you rented an apartment, applied for special work papers for her to travel during the pandemic, then prepacked my car and went off to pick her up at the airport. I want my car back and I want it back now.

Katherine

xxx

August 13, 2020.

Dear Katherine,

I'm sorry. Everything, I say seems to end up having the opposite impression than I thought it would. You have been in every way all that any loving woman could be... If anybody could have saved me from my rashness it would have been you. Nothing has been wiped out as far as my feelings for you are concerned. I have loved you all these years and still love you. When I spoke of it not being about sex, that was hyperbole, I meant that I have recovered a religious-spiritual concentration with her that I have neglected, abandoned, for years. Yes, I am talking about recovering my Christian identity. I have been going through a conversion and recovery of prayer. I imagine you will not take this seriously, but it is for me. You ask me if I have a plan. I may end up alone; I just don't know anything now with certainty.

I want desperately to rebuild our partnership—to be open-minded and loving. Seeking to forgive, even if you aren't ready or able to do so yet, is a way to grow. The only question is whether you are willing to recover something I hope to recover. Let's live and find a way to be in communication. If you choose, you can say good-bye and be rid of me. Whatever happens between us, it is very important to me to know you are okay. I know you suffer, and I bleed for you. Whatever you may think, physically I have aged,

16

my cheeks have caved in, my cheekbones make me look a bit like an El Greco. Old age, like a frost, has taken me by surprise. I have fully assumed my age of 84 instead of the 60-year-old artifice I stuck to so long. I have grown a beard, which I always swore I would not do until I sensed life ending.

Love Arthur.

xxx

August 20, 2020.

Dear Arthur.

Perhaps your potential success made you feel entitled to a bit on the side, but this isn't a bit on the side. I could forgive and understand that. What I can't forgive is your walking out the door after a four-day sex session with this far from presentable creature from the swamps of Columbia. Why dump a working, creative marriage as if twenty years of love and creative union meant nothing to you?

For years I was your main support (artists always need support). I helped you with your work. Canadians are handymen so it was natural for me to help you with my physical and mental skills which you simply took for granted. You can sandwich it any way you please, but it is humiliating that people now assume you used me, you pimped off me until you had some money of your own. Take it from the horse's hind leg there is no possibility that I will ever forgive. Not only have I been shamed and betrayed, but trampled, punctured, and broken as well. I weep for the helplessness into which you have plunged me. Your passion for another woman has created an empty space in my heart which is unlikely to ever again include the person who caused that hole.

You excuse your leaving me as weakness, due to your upbringing and years with your ex Ciguapa mentally corrupting you. Certainly, you cared little about ruining our life for a roll in the hay and an orgy of sex. Only a fool would think it okay to bugger off without a thought of the consequences to a partner of

17

twenty years. Your responsibility was to be straight with me, to tell me unreservedly what was going on inside your mixed-up brain. Sure, I know—as you say, you feared my reaction. That makes you a coward.

You are right to refuse the word flattered; there is nothing flattering about an old guy paying a groupie for sex. Everyone who knows her knows that's exactly the situation. I never thought of you as a fool but even a demented fool would know this is a sadistic enterprise, employed for the sake of her gain. Ludicrous! Asinine! Friends call you an innocent fall guy with a big ego, and they are right. Only a very big ego would believe this ignorant, avaricious floozy with the intelligence level of an octopus (likely I am insulting octopuses) is after anything but a meal ticket. *Love lasteth long as the money endureth.* Never forget that!

You say you will from now on be transparent and honest with me. Well, it is about time! Had you been honest with me I could have made my own choice, and it would have been my choice! You claim you took a long and painful look at yourself, and recognized the wrongs, deceptions, and lies you were guilty of throughout your life. Your regret has its own inelegant symmetry which has to be a joke. Aren't Christians supposed to be kind and well... Christian? Does a priest absolve you of your sins and evil acts when you confess? Is that how Christians live with the broken bits they leave behind?

You tell me this groupie has a Hot Line to Heaven which helped you find your Christian identity. That has to be another joke. How do you reconcile this renewal of religious faith with the fact that you committed the crime of leaving me the gift of an iPad full of pornographic exchanges typical of squalid Internet porn. Just take a long and painful look at that. And then you ask yourself why would I want to rebuild our partnership? What partnership? The person I thought you were, is nothing more than a lustful Billy Goat eaten up by obsessional passions.

Katherine.

xxx

August 21, 2020.

Dear Katherine.

You cannot understand why I left you because you trivialize what happened. You always use an expression with me, I suppose also with friends—how could I leave you after a couple of fucks with a groupie? Of course, if you think of it like that, it is incomprehensible. The reality is I was 'bewitched'. I would not have left you for a trivial little thrill. Since you press me endlessly, I am telling you—I have told you this before—I have been emotionally vampirized. I am shocked to recognize my impulsiveness and the continuation of this type of behavior in myself. A behavior I thought I had left behind fifty years ago. It is a kind of sickness.

I understand you think it would be healing if you could understand why I left you, but I don't understand this myself. You are hurting yourself by endless questioning why. For me it is unbearable. I have said this before, I do care for you deeply. I want to keep a deep channel of communication open between us. If I live alone and independent, can we rebuild our relationship?

Love Arthur

Chapter 3

As I walk this land with broken dreams
I have visions of many things
But happiness is just an illusion
Filled with sadness and confusion.
Jimmy Ruffin

Karen Moller

I'd like to say I had a perfect childhood: an older brother who cared for me, a beautiful loving mother, and a superhero father who believed women were worthy human beings. Would it be that was true—when it was almost the opposite. I know it is typical to deem oneself a damaged child; it makes one feel special. In truth, most people are uniquely damaged—it's just part of the crap of growing up. Don't get me wrong. I'm not talking about anything serious like physical or mental abuse, alcohol addiction, depression, or uncontrollable anger. Just everyday upsetting stuff. Just the usual kind dished out by incompetent and uncaring parents, and rank amateurs like Arthur's mother who had no flair for child rearing.

Growing up in a dysfunctional family created many doubts about the institution of marriage, doubts that surfaced somewhere around the time I was a teenager. My parents, who seemed for the most part to be mortal enemies, had by then assumed their fate, and as was the custom in those days, stayed married. Two characters as mismatched as God and the devil, they disagreed on almost everything except socialism.

Andrea Dworkin, a much-admired feminist, said: "*Lonely kids are exiles who found books to be their church, even more than their native land. It was their place of refuge, their DP camp where they felt they most belonged.*" Books *saved me. Alice in Wonderland* whispered the secret that a magic world existed where one could disappear down the rabbit hole to have tea with the Mad Hatter and a chat with the Cheshire cat. Arthur gave my ego a boost when he claimed he had been seduced, not only by Alice's magical world but by Alice herself, a gutsy girl heroine rather like me. Enough to make anyone want to fall in love.

You think I'm romancing? I'm not! Not only did books provide my essential education, they were a portal to the imagination. I spent whole days walking in the shoes of odd characters I encountered in books and many of those characters became my friends. To have friends was a miracle. It gave me hope that everything might work out for a lonely, optimistic bookworm born in a dysfunctional shit pile.

In Holden Caulfield's *The Catcher in the Rye*, his protagonist says right off that he is not going to go into all that David Copperfield crap about where he was born, his lousy childhood, and how his parents were straight out of Dickens. Like Caufield I was rebellious and independent, the kind of kid who doesn't take no for an answer. Ditching the rules was in my DNA and my rule-breaking likely planted the seed of who I am today. However, unlike Caufield it was Dickens who offered me truths and encouragement, as did Walt Whitman:

Then courage revolter, revoltress!
Resist much, obey little,
Beat the gong of revolt,
Symbol of my soul, its dearest hopes.
Revolt! and still revolt! revolt!
Abate not one jot of your fullest radicalism

Curiosity is the most useful gift a fairy godmother can endow a child. But authorities, and parents have a hard time putting up with either. Often, they do their best to suppress inventive minds. And yet, imaginative does survive like mushrooms growing in decay. Bearing the cross of being different was something both Arthur and I wrestled with from our earliest days. We sought refuge in other people's stories; a way of understanding, but not joining, a way of moving through difficulties by retreating behind books, a way to create a physical barrier.

Arthur and I spent much of our young years in detention and being beaten for misbehavior. The authorities in Arthur's strict Catholic school were convinced there existed a cause and effect between medieval punishment and academic success. Arthur often angered the priests with his pranks and absentminded ways, they frequently humiliated him by locking him up in a dark closet to give him time to repent his sins. To correct his flaws, and to the shock of nuns and early morning sinners, a priest had grabbed him by his cassock and thrown him face down on the altar in punishment for his reading behind a tree instead of participating in sports.

After an episode of his heating doorknobs with a cigarette lighter he was sent to the Dean's office. The Dean asked, "Do you know who I am?" Arthur said he'd been confused and laughed. If he didn't know who he was why didn't he check his driver's license? The Dean shouted, "Don't sass me. When I say to you, do you know who I am, I am asking if *you* know who am." Arthur admitted he was even more puzzled. At that point the director gave up and simply said, "I've let your undisciplined nonsense go on too long. Why did you heat the doorknobs?"

"To surprise the students because they were warm ..." He'd stopped midstream because it seemed obvious.

"We've had enough of your troublemaking," the Dean shouted. "It's about time you learned you can't go around upsetting people. Your next misdemeanor will be more than a rap over the knuckles. Now get out!"

Arthur admitted that two things were clear to him: with his ramped-up imagination and his inability to follow the rules, he was headed for disaster. A few months later disaster arrived when he'd set fire to paper gliders and sent them down the central stairway. In answer to the Dean's question why, he'd answered, to see if they would reach the ground before the fire was extinguished. An inappropriate answer apparently and he'd been expelled much to the despair of his mother.

As a dreamy, somnambulant child, I admit lacked the mechanics on how to conform to the status quo, how to gain love or be popular. I was socially at the bottom of the ladder, even off the ladder before I even tried. I probably wouldn't even have wanted to hang out with myself given the option. What was more insane—and my mother should have known better—was her endless badgering, her endless phrase: "Don't be a sheep, be a leader." How dumb is that? No way can you be a leader if you don't fit as a sheep, and you have zero followers.

Of course, I now realize this adolescent desire to fit is the insanity; it would have meant giving up who one is; it would have meant my being shoved into a box labeled for girls who need to be silenced for their own good! No way could I accept being treated as a powerless, worthless girl. My refusal to conform to my predestined role didn't endear me to my brother's friends. Someone should have warned me: don't eat Eve's apple, don't try to be stronger, smarter; don't try to be what a boy is supposed to be but mostly isn't. Boys would watch me play their games in the hope I would fail and when I didn't fail, they criticized me for imitating a boy. "Don't be dumb!" I would shout. "I throw a ball like a girl who knows how to throw a ball. So, smarten up."

Hudson my brother adopted the role of Batman and his naming me Robin allowed me to hang out with him and his friends. That allowed me to do all the risky things girls aren't supposed to do. We swung on ropes high in trees, jumped in the icy stream that ran by our house, scaled rocks with no preparation, and dug tunnels that managed to hold up despite their lack of supports. We disregarded all dangers and lived in the deluded belief we were indestructible. You think I'm joking? I'm not.

At the age of fourteen Hudson was into boy things and discarded me like yesterday's newspaper. He bought a car before he could drive and dynamited the upper part off the chassis with the intention of rebuilding it into a fancy racing car. Our mother accepted his activities as normal, even ignoring his practicing his racecar driving by stealing our father's car or someone else's and driving like a maniac around the back roads. When he smashed flat his little pug nose, the doctor merely pushed it into a sort of shape and taped it up.

Hudson's dumping me, a girl who believed, behaved, and dreamed differently than other girls, wrong became a daily word, a word almost my nickname. I didn't miss Hudson all the time, only the days when the sun came up. His never-ending taunts, and thrashings had fired my imagination and made me determined to win. We fought incessantly, but we were soulmates. My bond with him was stronger than with anyone else.

Lonely afternoons in my treehouse watching the flocks of blackbirds swooping over the stark and sober Douglas firs, before flying off like black dots on a scarf trailing in the wind, were meaningless without Hudson. The booty of having breasts gave me some sort of new attention and power over boys but not as friends they became boyfriends. The reality of my situation ricocheted from one befogged synapse to another. I was about to despair until I remembered a film, about a man who had an imaginary mate called Harvey, a six-foot rabbit who accompanies him everywhere. As I lay watching the vibrant hues reflecting off the creek under a sky hung like a watercolor, I began to pray for a six-foot rabbit of my own. Suddenly like some Edgar Allan Poe phantasm a six-foot kangaroo materialized. I blinked several times not sure he was accessible. He returned my look with what I can only describe as deadpan realness.

"I was hoping for a rabbit," I squeaked.

With a chuckle he put a large paw around me and gave me a hug. "There is a big demand for rabbits these days. So, you got me. I'm Woody."

"You going to stick around?"

"I'm here for as long as you need me."

"Seriously? Where have you been till now?".

He laughed softly. "Around, waiting for you to see me."

"Let's celebrate," I said to provoke him. "Aren't you just dying to dance across the treetops in this autumn air?"

His chuckle was a refreshing change from the uncomfortable laugh most people gave me. "Only if this rebellious dame is dancing by my side." He tossed in a last-minute cough then did a few cartwheels on the narrow floor, nimble as could be.

This amazing miracle was no miracle for my mother, already a puddle of nerves. She had limits and refused to set a place for Woody at the dinner table. She called it precarious. I could not imagine the slightest thing precarious about a six-foot kangaroo enjoying our undisciplined dinner table riots. Apparently, it was my run-away imagination that was precarious. Not surprisingly, my mother came to prefer Woody over me. Well, it was mutual. I'm sure she would have preferred Arthur to Woody when he partly replaced him in later years.

Chapter 4

Ring the bells that still can ring,
Forget your perfect offering,
There is a crack, a crack in everything,
That's how the light gets in.
Leonard Cohen

We all have our secrets so before I get into the sad-eyed side of this tale let me explain a bit more how I got to be almost sixty before I fell in love. I admit my career and my daughter tended to take precedence which inhibited many a romantic prospect. A good choice, since a career is more sustaining than a subpar spouse and will never dump you for a last fling with a groupie. The saying goes, *Let not women remain unwed lest they grow to prefer the state...* and I did enjoy it. Women are rarely central characters in human history, which frequently reminds there is no greater sin a woman can commit than to take great pleasure in creating her own life and not to feel bad about doing so.

Future generations with look back on these years as normal but it was an exceptional epoch because we got the right to make choices even if it was a fight. I haven't quite figured out if this is a blip in progress, or just a narrow strip of time in a never-ending story before patriarchy manages to crush women and drive them back to where men preferred them: behind closed doors where every action and decision requires male permission.

The cliché is: men fall in love with their eyes; women fall in love with their ears, which is true for me. Certainly, a curious and creative mind is the first thing that attracts me to a person, whether male or female. After reading Albert Camus' many intriguing books, I'd fallen madly in love with his mind, which meant every man paled by comparison. On my arrival in Paris, I'd optimistically hoped I might catch a glimpse of Camus in his favorite café drinking his morning coffee and lighting his first cigarette.

While working as a waitress to finance my art studies, I'd occasionally overhear couples engaged in an intellectual conversation about books, philosophy, or art. Wow, I thought that's what I want. A guy interested in intellectual things. Of course, I also hoped for a breathless passionate affair and memorable sex, with an intelligent, interesting man. This happened occasionally, actually mind-blowing when it did—as it did with Arthur. More of that later.

The men of my generation were mostly a bed of roses with prickles. For years I lived a type of serial monogamy, drifting from one man to another like a busy cloud rarely wanting more than conversations and fun cuddles. Sarah, my daughter, being a sharp-eyed kid, and more perceptive than I am, thought my diet of men primarily interested in art and literature were men completely superfluous to life's necessities. These creative, childish, unusual, bizarre artist friends and lovers, who drifted through my life, were according to my daughter mostly *hopeless unreliable men.* Yeah, but an hour of their company was often more stimulating than the yawning abyss in the minds of guys whose idea of a night's entertainment was beer in hand and TV football game going full blast. Yeah, I know, macho stuff, which of course didn't always exclude artistic interests.

Wouldn't we all like to be sensible, responsible women picking the right kind of suitable, faithful, guys with interesting well-paid jobs. Yeah, men who would allow us the freedom to get on with own creative lives? Do they even exist? Maybe today, but certainly not back then in the 1960/90s.

I'm not claiming I don't have my faults. I fall over them every day. Sarah criticized, rather accurately, every man I'd ever dated or had anything to do as guys not completely sane with raging egos, and generally unable to support themselves. For Sarah's sake, my choice of men should have been better, but it couldn't have been too different, nor so far-fetched as to fall for some wall street investment guy or street cleaner. Hey, I'm not that off my rocker. Yeah, I live on planet Z but that is not exactly a recipe for disaster, so I just chuckled whenever she accused me of being a collector of hopeless men few women would put up with. Arthur is a good example, one of his previous lovers had said: the only way to live with Arthur was if he had an apartment next door. Arthur is a little cuckoo. Not clinically crazy but his reactions often far from what is considered normal. Sarah often saw the humor in his delusions. When a strong wind broke a blade off my decorative wind detector. Arthur, not a do-it-yourself kind of guy, ended the noise by breaking off the other blade. Sarah looked at me with a twinkle in her eye: "I hope you never break an arm."

Arthur stuck his foot in his mouth so often he may have acquired a taste for feet. When the hairdresser asked him what he wanted, and he said, "Wash, cut and blow job." After he congratulated the family at the funeral of a friend, I quickly pulled him away on departure, in fear he would reply "anytime" when they thanked him for coming. He gave his worst enemies hugs, not out of forgiveness, but because he'd forgotten they were enemies. He often spent hours looking for where he'd left my car when he hadn't come by car. Mostly I was relieved when he arrived home without having had another accident. It least until now he hadn't tried to start the car with a jack hammer but maybe that was only a matter of time.

I'd first seen Arthur on one of my visits to Shakespeare and Co, my favorite bookstore, now revamped and renamed in honor of Sylvia Beach's bookshop of the 1920s. A magical place full of fairytale spells and booklovers, a must stop for writers and expats passing through Paris. I'd often taken Sarah there in the hope of enriching her life and awakening a love of reading. Apparently, a goof ball idea—no way did my passion for reading seem normal to her. No way did she accept that books are the heart and core of understanding the past and ourselves. Sadly, she is convinced that the only reason to read a book is to learn something practical: like cooking or gardening or bricolage. Bill Gates said the internet and iPhones have replaced bookshops for lonely kids who once read books. The internet is now their new town square and global village.

On that day in 1998, as I waited to pay for the books in Shakespeare, and Co, I'd glanced out the window at the overcast sky. It held an energy as before a thunder and lightning storm. Everything was paused by an invisible force, force one feels but cannot see. In that glance, my eye caught the eye of a handsome man, with a thought-provoking face, sitting outside in the shadow of Notre-Dame, engrossed in a book. Occasionally he raised his eyes to look off into the distance with a blank, unfocused gaze, as if he was memorizing the text. Exactly the sort of man to catch my attention. Well, the sort of man who might stop anyone if they saw his photo while flipping through a magazine.

The books I'd chosen were the *Dream of a Ridiculous Man,* Dostoyevsky's short story. It is similar to his earlier novel, *Notes from the Underground,* a book which had a profound influence on the Beat writers. The other book was *The Stranger,* by Camus. I've already read all of Camus's books by the age of twenty, but his books remain rainbows of fascination well worth a second read. In *The Stranger,* Camus argues that absurdity is the search for answers in an answerless world—where for no reason humans do things, for no other reason than circumstance. Meursault, the book's protagonist, kills an Arab for no reason and is condemned, not so much for this crime as for not playing the game society demands. Meursault's ultimate crime, a sacred cow, he did not cry at his mother's funeral.

What does it mean if you do not cry at your mother's funeral? Did I cry at my mother's funeral? I can't remember. I suppose I did. Did I love my parents? Love is only meaningful if it is reciprocal and, in my family that would have meant shifting gears. When Camus, who I knew only through his words, died in a car crash, my sense of loss was as deep or deeper than my grief at the deaths of my parents.

On my way out of the bookshop, the intriguing man, who I came to know as Arthur, sat up straight; brushed back his unruly hair and looked at me as if I was some sort of surprising apparition. If I hadn't found him intimidating, I might have smiled and said hello, but his look unsettled me, like a cloud of butterflies let loose in my belly. If you believe in fate, then I suppose you accept it was normal that I bumped into him a few days later at a party, but the international artistic world in Paris was a relatively small world.

The festivities had scarcely begun in Jessica's large, newly painted pink and orange salon when I arrived. Even though 1960s had long passed, the girl in a fuchsia Pierre Cardin outfit sitting on a sofa still turned the scene into the film *Space Odyssey.* Remember that film? It was earth shattering at the time. A distant piano tinkled with unresolved notes and equally uncertain chords one might hit by accident. My curiosity aroused, I made my way tentatively towards the sounds where a lot of paunchy guys were craning their necks in search of something to chew on. Before I reached the source of the sounds, I spied the man from the bookshop. His scrutiny hadn't altered. He gave me a simple one-second glance with a ridiculously sexy smile. Not a full-on smile, but enough of one to send a quiver through me like a mosquito bite, just the sort of bite likely to be a total pain if it flared up later.

The sounds changed to Celine Dion's song, *That's the Way*. As it burst through the air, swaying couples moved to the dance floor. The intriguing man took my arm, his touch as unsettling as a slap on the face. "I'm Arthur. Shall we? You look like a good witch I want to capture before you float off on your broomstick." The lilt in his voice, a husky American Humphrey Bogart type, was the sort often described as straight out of an aged bottle of whisky. There was something attractive about his hazel eyes, the color changing with the light like the eyes of a cat. The curve of his cheek as it dimpled at the corners of his mouth made him appear vulnerable. His flowing white hair and erratic zeal gave him an air of agelessness.

Some people are well turned out badly and then there is Arthur who was badly turned out well. He had the panache of a European/American bohemian as artlessly physical and stylish as Fred Astaire. In his rumpled beige suit with its missing buttons, and fraying cuffs, he was the sort of guy who could have worn a burlap sack and look incredibly elegant.

"What are you doing in Paris?"

He bowed his elegant head, his expression crinkling into the smile of a man who wanted to be liked, if not loved. "I'm a poet,"

"Have I just met one of those long dead poets I've read about and always wished I could have met?"

"Dracula more like!" he'd said with an offhand shrug. I thought he could well have replaced Leslie Howard had Leslie Howard ever chosen to do an interpretation of Dracula.

I suggested he show me the bar, I needed a drink to kickstart my heart. It was rare for me to be prone to flights of euphoria or to feel instant kinship to an obvious flirt who likely tried to get into the knickers of all attractive women. And yet it felt like the connection I had been waiting for. Well not exactly waiting, I'd given up waiting; who likes waiting? You might as well wait for a werewolf to emerge from his closet.

By the end of the evening, I was swimming pleasantly in the gentle grip of intoxication wondering how long it had been since I'd felt so titillated by a guy. The feeling wrapped its powerful yet gentle fingers around me like a python encircling a bunny. No doubt everyone has met someone, where neither pretend what they feel is comradeship and nothing more. I kept nudging the thought to the sidelines, yet this feeling of instant closeness hovered like a vague, erotic, hyper-kinetic undercurrent not unlike the sensation of having drunk too much wine. When he insisted on seeing me home, we wandered through a fog of tobacco smoke in search of the exit.

By the time we'd climbed my steps, we were both trying to outdo each other in silliness, laughing and giggling helplessly at our own jokes. Were we drunk? Not really, but then again, I had a lot of trouble opening my door.

"Might I ask for a kiss?" Arthur's grin softened his features endearingly as a look of desire slid into his attractive eyes.

"What would you do with it if I gave you one? Put it in your pocket?"

"That's not a safe place so I'd probably lock it up for future use."

"It would go stale, so you'd probably come back for more."

"Only if it was worth it. Not every old peck is worth locking up."

I'd laughed, shrugging to recall the last time I'd kissed a man or when a man had made me feel so wobbly on my feet. His kiss slow, soft, and delectable spread the taste of wild honey across my tongue and triggered a sensual earthquake of sparks, like fireworks to whip through my body at a bewildering rate. This was something entirely unexpected. Not a prelude to sex, more a total collision like falling in love with a character in a novel.

I slid my hands down his chest, then brought them up under his shirt, where they became lost in silky hairiness. I whispered. "I want you." This lustful whisper seemed to act like an aphrodisiac on him and he stepped back, unbuttoned his shirt; his belt was next and in one swift movement his trousers fell with a soft thud at his feet. He stared at my dress, willing me to take it off. With a nod I pulled the straps off my shoulder, and stepped out, pushing aside my heels. He clamped his hands around my waist and lifted me onto the bed. His breath mingled warm and wet and danced across my face as his lips brushed my mouth and then the soft side of my neck before moving down to my breasts. His insistent hands were everywhere, as if he was trying to map my body. His touch made my skull explode and my skin tingle with electrifying sensations from head to toenails.

I knew next to nothing about this man who was making love to me in a slow, intense way like some sort of Don Juan, who having just escaped from prison was out to make the most of this moment. A hunger united us and raged in harmony as in one easy movement and to my utter amazement, he slipped inside me. His moans long and low heightened my own gratification as he exploded inside me. I rode his undulating spasms till they broke the final barrier, and I climaxed in a wave of pleasure that fluttered through me like a minor heart attack. Arthur showered me with kisses then gave me a slow lazy grin.

I was surprised by this unexpected familiarity, but it was too late to do anything but revel in it. Sex, after my initial disappointment at the age of sixteen, had always been easy for me. My body reacted with an enthusiasm that left my mind behind. It allowed me to rise to the grand finale, not only with somebody I liked, but with just about anybody.

Arthur was asleep in an instant, his chest rising and falling gently, like the ebb and flow of waves on a gentle sea. I'd smiled at the look of peace on his handsome face, full of lines like a well-used haunted cave. I lay reveling in the feel of his skin against mine, then coiled into his warmth and drew the covers over us.

The next morning it was raining. Not a quick thundershower, the here now and gone, but a heavy, remorseless rain set to pour steadily all day. Arthur wolfed down his pancakes with bacon and eggs. An enthusiastic eater of what he called safe foods I soon discovered that meant nothing fancy like asparagus or mushrooms. His Catholic school had formed his undeveloped palate, and he happily ate anything over-cooked or mashed up like baby food.

Over a second cup of coffee, I realized he was studying me, speculating, what happens now? He cleared his throat.

"You look...lovely. When I first saw you outside the bookshop, I was in a trance all day wondering why I hadn't run after you to offer you a coffee, just to spend a moment with you." A bubble of laughter rose in his chest when he admitted he hadn't laughed after I'd disappeared. "I can't believe you're here now on this dull morning when nothing was remotely planned." He leaned over and kissed me, murmuring soft words as our lips parted and met again. A tremor of desire rose and passed through me like water rising through the stems of a plant nourishing my wilted limbs back to full vigor.

His lips brushed my jaw stopping near my ear: "Come, let's cuddle. I want to feel your breasts on mine, you skin against my skin, and when the sun begins to set, we'll talk of many things: of shoes and ships and sealing-wax—of cabbages and kings and why the sea is boiling hot and whether pigs have wings."

"A pleasant walk, a pleasant talk, along the briny brew and how like oysters in the sand we'll miss a word two." I giggled. "Sorry bad call."

"It's very rude of you to spoil the fun! So, join me in the oyster bed, we'll have a pleasant run."

This poetic invitation bordering on the obscene spread a warmth though my abdomen. "I thank you much for that and hurry to oblige. Let's strip and stand in underwear naked of disguise."

His palms skimmed across my breasts and back. His sinuous arms encircled me as desire like molten lava flooded through me as his lips devoured my body and squeezed the air out of my lungs. Pleasure spiked inside me, deep, hot, and intense, with the potential of a grenade only less stable. More a Molotov cocktail that had short-circuited. This wanting him felt like forever, a kind of desire that goes beyond the flesh, the stuff of best dreams. Together we hovered in mutual exultation, teetering on the edge till his chest heaved, his muscles contracted, and we climaxed in sudden wild fury. In stunned silence, I wept. Tears streamed down my cheeks with dizzy exhilaration till laughter washed over me like cool water.

Arthur totally captivated by me. He seemed ready to engage in a no-holds-barred fight for my undivided attention, but promptly lost my telephone number. That was puzzling, well, actually, insulting. More to the point, if we women are interested in someone, we don't lose their telephone number, do we? Women often reminisce about the first kiss with the guys they have loved while men seem often to have forgotten the last kiss. Some of my friends can summon up what every man was like as a lover while some of my lovers seem to have forgotten that we even had sex. I hate to think I am so forgettable. Let's just say women are romantic while for men women are just so many a sex numbers notched up on their bed posts, if they even remember to do that.

Love might light us up and show us ourselves, or it might feel like being smacked in the temples with a cricket bat, but that doesn't mean we are reborn without unhealed layers. Soulmates aren't always what we think they will be, nor does finding a soulmate mean happily ever after. Of course, fate sometimes does the dirty work for you. It's called karma. As a tactic for survival, I am usually ready for worst-case scenarios with artists— their lives of chaos often dependent on fate. I did meet Arthur again and he invited me to dinner. It was no surprise that he had to borrow the money from me to pay for it. Paying for the first date is like saying *I want to look after you.* Not that I needed someone to look after me, it was more I would have liked to believe he was a giving sort. In fact, he is a giving sort, but he apparently lacked funds because he was giving what money he had to other women—supposedly they had priority. As it turned out other women would always have priority, presumably because *I had money, and they didn't.*

Arthur, an ambitious embracer of the world, called himself a shifty-eyed softy with no money and turmoil written all over him. This very seductive description made him sound lively and cool, like someone out of a romantic novel. His excuse was he bumbled along his path of tunnels and cul-de-sacs, lost but optimistic that he could squeeze out a pimple of relevant creation before it all collapsed in a welter of commas and wrong notes. "I try not to think about my lack of funds and the number of books, poems, and songs written each day, each month, each year, because it makes me question if the better option would be to get a job driving a truck."

"You'd be good at that!" I'd said with a smirk. I was super

Karen Moller

impressed he thought he could make it as a truck driver when he couldn't find his way to the post office even after numerous trips. He was the most navigationally impaired person I'd ever met. Ask him directions, he would surely send you off to Neverland—the sort of person who would blindly follow his GPS even if it maneuvered him straight over a cliff.

Arthur said he'd never been interested in the commercial art world, the sort of dumb thing people said in the 1960s after being brainwashed by the idea of not selling out to the commercial market. The art world is not only commercial but is conducted on very shady terms with few rules or ethics. Bob Dylan, younger than Arthur by only five years, had with the effortless quality of his words created the opportunity for poets to reach people who no longer read poetry. He opened the doors for other poet/singers, by transforming the poetic boundaries that made it possible for poets like Leonard Cohen, and those who followed, to make a buck in a straightforward commercial way from their art.

The thing that separates successful people from the those who aren't, is their willingness to work very, very hard at their passion. It is a bit late for Arthur to finally concentrate on his career in the belief he could still achieve the worldwide success he craves. His early poems were particularly touching, their meandering consciousness, much like prayer. They were influenced by the descriptive poetic language of Keats expressing his love for the moon goddess, imaginative longings of an ideal love. When I mentioned I thought this particular quality was missing in the later poems, he screwed up his eyes and threw me a quizzical look. He admitted he'd felt orphaned, abandoned amid the flow of Beat poetry, the stars of his generation, his poetry too literary, too establishment type, too old hat if you like. This had made him want to be freer in his writing. He said he didn't consider himself a great singer, but he knew how he wanted his poetry to sound, or at least how he didn't want it to sound. "I appreciated the view you show me of my work, it adds a force to our friendship. But don't think I'm raw material that can be manipulated towards a goal."

I shook my head. "We want the same thing. A loving companion who gets on with his work, and a partner who cheers

40

us along occasionally."

He sighed as if that was understood. Then suggested I cheer him along by accompanying him to the recording studio the following week to pick out the phrases for the chorus, the magic trick which made the song.

Later that week as I'd waited for Arthur to join me at our favorite café before heading off to the recording studio, I saw him moving towards me, obviously lost in his own world, his head hatless, his tall form dressed in a lightweight black suit which hung gracefully over his lean body. I loved the gentle slope of his nose, the curve of his jaw, the arc of his shoulders and even the way he gazed about in his short-sighted way. Most of all, I loved how his tense expression would soften into a broad smile when his eyes focused on me. I'd never known a man who could communicate so much with a smile.

"Come," he'd said, putting out his hand. "Sorry to keep you waiting. I had to go back as I forgot my notes, then I left them in the taxi. I'll just have to do the best I can without them."

I'd had expectations that Arthur would pick up a few regular practices, if I stopped aiding and abetting his careless habits, but he never did. Perhaps attractive men expect others to take care of things for them or more likely he had decided not to encumber himself with such incidentals when others were ready to do them for him. His gaffs which he readily admitted, weren't monumental, but certainly annoying. If I gave him a list to pick up a few things at the supermarket, he lost the list or bought anything that caught his eye. He would spent ages looking for his glasses and misplace money he said he'd had ten minutes earlier and hidden somewhere. Maybe not hidden; more likely forgotten on the bus if he had the money in the first place. If he found what he was looking for he would say, *At least I left it in a logical place.* What had logic to do with it, if the wallet or whatever ended up in the fridge and the groceries in his desk, eventually found because of the smell of rotting food.

Chapter 5

I've been hit too hard, I've seen too much
Nothing can heal me now, but your touch
I don't know what I'm gonna do
I was all right 'til I fell in love with you

I did not drift into love with Arthur in the classic way as one drifts into sleep, I fell madly, passionately in love. I opened like a new leaf unfolding in the sunlight. No joke, I fell so hard, and so completely, not because love is blind, but because it is blinding. Had I been asked if I'd wanted to fall in love with a poet and take on the burdens of a lover/companion who had all the complexes of a quirky self-centered artist living in his own ego-centered imaginary world, I would have unhesitatingly said no. Who needs that? Who needs another trip around the moon with a cash short artist, only interested in his own work but not above complaining loudly if other people did not show enthusiastic interest in his artistic creations.

As a feminist I was never comfortable with women not pulling their weight financially on expenses nor the reverse. So, Arthur not being self-supporting never sat well with my feelings that things should be equal between men and women. I tried never to mention his few and far between earnings in fear that reversing of the male/female role, of who brings in the bread, might crush his self-esteem. Arthur was not one to throw my money about as if he was a ponce, yet he did not hesitate to treat my money as if it was his own. He even offered to send his previous girlfriend and sister on holiday with my money, without mentioning it to me. A good script for a comic act to say the least.

His occasional reproach, "I don't need this. I could happily live in one room," made me feel my financial support offended the Petite Prince's masculine pride. I know it is unkind of me to say, but I can't help a tiny bit of satisfaction that with his present foolish ways, he will likely not only end up living in one room but on benefit as well. The long and the longer of this story is that love, complicity, and financial help cannot prevent a train wreck. Nor can it prevent a slightly mad artist abandoning his home and comforts for a last fling with a pathological narcissist masquerading as a religious fanatic. I ask you: how does one understand that? What had I missed? Was I incapable of accurately seeing the whole picture? In truth there are some fundamental gaps in my ability to understand men, that's for sure. I am no genius in that area, more a dumb-assed female who can't figure out how guys got to oversee the human race when a lot of men are incapable of getting out of a paper bag or following a shopping list. I ask you, how could Arthur learn all those complicated musical techniques from the computer and yet be unable to follow a simple freaking grocery list his wife carefully wrote out for him? Even if he managed to buy everything on the list, he invariably made wrong product choices on things he ate every day.

These generalizations might anger a lot of men. I'm sure there are a few who could get out of a paper bag. Certainly, it is a pretty good description of Arthur: a man who wanders about lost in his labyrinth and likely to shoot himself in the foot if given a gun. This is no joke. As a lieutenant in the Belgian army, he led his troops on an exercise, only to discover he had them firing on his own men. Luckily, he did not own a gun when cellphones were invented because he would probably have mistaken his gun for his cellphone and shot himself in the ear.

As I sat pondering past events, I noticed a few of Arthur's old journals on the bookshelves that had been missed by the packers. I regretted that I'd thought it dishonorable to read people's private writings. These scruples are long gone. I would advise any woman who suspects infidelity to do everything to find out the truth before it was too late. I picked out a journal Arthur had marked 2003, the year we had taken a trip to the south of France—the year Arthur had asked me to marry him.

Sept 19, 2003.

This morning I thought about a line from *On the Road* which described how Kerouac had, all his life, danced down the streets like a dingledoodie and shambled after people who interested him. *The only people for me are the mad ones, mad to live, mad to talk, and mad to be saved. People desirous of everything, people who never yawned or said commonplace things.* Now I am tripping after

Katherine: smart, kind, and utterly fearless as she strides through the world, her creativity giving her license to shoot the dragon. She is quick to laugh, and fun to be with. An impressive, formidable friend who sees beyond the surface, which carries the promise of her seeing me as I want to be seen. Her warmth of affection adds depth to my feelings like wearing warm slippers. Not only do we balance each other's inabilities, but our artistic and literary culture connects us. My production has doubled as my ideas ferment like rising yeasts which create poetic songs uniquely my own.

What more could an artist want than a woman who professes belief in my talent and leaves me to create while she brings in the bread. I feel no need be gallant when Katherine picks up the tools and stepladders and trundles them upstairs to paint my room and make my space more comfortable. It pleases me she takes over all the unpleasant tasks and competently organizes the shopping, cooking, cleaning, and washing while her young assistant looks after my appointments and taxes and other simple office tasks. This is true liberation; a true breaking down of traditional gender roles in a joint undertaking where each of us does their part.

More than once, I have looked up from my work and found the day has ended and it is time join Katherine for a drink at the kitchen bar, to open a bottle of excellent wine and relaxed in the exuberance of our conversations which are like never-ending poems, a kaleidoscope of past and present thoughts.

That last line brought tears to my eyes. Life with Arthur had been messy but agreeable. Our marriage was wacky, filled with laughter and complicity. I'd loved his wit and intelligence, his respect for my opinions and ideas. He rarely corrected my mispronunciations although maybe he should have. With his unsophisticated palate, he appreciate the delicious meals I prepared and yet happily ate my occasional burnt food which I'd left cooking while I got on with various jobs. Multi-tasking was my ability to screw up several jobs simultaneously, but he rarely noticed.

Our trip to Aix-en-Provence in Southern France had been a trip down memory lane to visit the studio of Cézanne, my first art love. It was almost the only holiday trip we had ever taken as he resisted time away from work. After climbing the hill above the city, we entered Cézanne's house, surprised to find no one there. Not a soul. The caretakers off having coffee I suppose. We'd peeked into various rooms and took a nostalgic spin around the studio. In the vast garden that surrounded Cézanne's home, the hawks circled in slow arcs before vanishing towards the Mont Sainte-Victoire which Cézanne had painted many times. A cool breeze had sprung up and it pushed the cloud shadows over the villages along the coast which must have been virtually empty of tourists in Cézanne's day. With a sighed for those lost intimate days with Arthur, I returned to reading his journal.

Oct 21, 2003:

After the *visit* to Cézanne's studio, we'd climbed the hill that overlooked the bay and took a rest in the nearby park. The emptiness and serenity, like a cool breeze transformed that moment into a dream like sequence. The murmur of water trickling down the mountainside from stone to stone mingled hypnotically with our voices and lulled us into a restful sleep. I had awakened when a strawberry-haired angel had bent over me and brushed my lips with her burning red mouth. The intoxicating ecstasy of that dream lingered as I gazed at Katherine, still asleep by my side. Her expression at peace, her eyelids heavy with long lashes, her skin tanned but paling below her shoulder, turning white as it disappeared beneath her thin red shirt, her teasing nipples just visible, rose and fell with her regular breathing. I stroked her hair as it fell out on the grass and let it gently wrap itself about my fingers. The physical sensuality of women's otherness and their incomprehensible and their all-absorbing difference always made my heartbeat at a frantic pace.

Recently I had been captivated by a painting attributed to Fragonard, depicting misbehaving children; a boy and girl in an ivy-covered grotto near a waterfall, overhung with bronze tinted foliage, the kind of voluptuous and tender stuff of the Rococo masters. The figures had magically transformed with as me the boy bent over the nymphet Katherine. On her neck a few damp strands of hair curled about her ears, her long auburn hair glowing gem like in the sun.

I tried to remember the exact quote from Shakespeare that invited me to pull her out of the painting and cover her mouth with kisses: Who is this marvelous creature? Who is this woman who has become all women for me? Who is this woman who lingers in my thoughts like whispers in my mind? Nothing is what it appears but exactly what it is. That thought made me question if Katherine would have been as interesting or original, had she not been drawn into the artistic community so early in her youth?

A tremor of anticipation touched me, the kind that presaged a poem. About to leap up to find a pen and paper in my bag, I stopped myself. Why cut this moment short I questioned? A sense of peace settled over me, a sense so natural I wondered why I'd taken so long to accept this gift of love and friendship. Why had I avoided admitting my feelings for Katherine as one might avoid the evitable note that ends a symphony. The drawback to the fulness of my sentiment wasn't her independence and strength; it was our inequality of finances.

A nearby leaf, crisped and curled to brown, lifted in the breeze, and flipped across her cheek. In that instance her eyes flew open. I brushed the leaf away and brought my fingers to her mouth. I told her I loved her smile and the way her eyes lit up when she had a new idea. She'd laughed and said her smile had been the bane of her young life. I'd whispered, the bane of my life had been women trying to possess me.

My smile was the bane of my young life because of my mother's habit of saying she was so ugly she was lucky to get a husband. Said perhaps, in the hope people would disagree. Kids do believe their parents. I have her smile and whenever I smiled the busybodies in the town would say, "Oh donna you be lookin' just like your Mommy?" Enough to make me stop smiling or become a Buddhist monk.

I knew by the way Arthur looked at me, he no longer feared to love a new kind of woman, an independent, irreverent, and headstrong kind of woman. "I don't want to live without you," Arthur had whispered as we lay cuddled under the shade of those umbrella pines. Elation coursed through my veins that he was ready to come to me as my fellow traveler. I'd clapped my hands and cried, "You are my Paul Auster, the writer I've fantasied about all my life!"

"Well, I hope you'll fantasize about me now," he grumbled, not at all liking to be in competition with one of America's best-known postmodern novelists.

I pulled out one of my old sketchbooks and flipped through it until I found Arthur unfinished poem, the one he'd written that afternoon: *For whatever souls are made of /our souls are as different as moonbeams are from lightning / as frost from fire / in our difference we completed each other / when I hold you close / we draw strength from the stars and terrors are no more.* Below his words I'd scribbled: *From the innermost depths of our being / we dream our dreams in separateness / our needs like cries, our wishes like sighs / nowhere are our souls at rest.*

Later in the hotel shower, large enough for us both, he'd eyed me with a combination of lust and wicked intent. He cautioned me not to open my eyes as he'd palmed my hair with peach smelling shampoo. I could tell from the tone of his voice he was smiling, almost laughing as his fingers rubbed and prodded my scalp, as if I was a toddler. He'd scrubbed my back, soaped my feet, and tickled me in unexpected places, then nuzzled his face in my wet hair, twining his fingers in it, as he drew it aside and traced my shoulder with his tongue. Pulling me to him he'd said, "If I put a finger in that little cockle, promise not to snap it shut."

"Why not? Then I could keep you prisoner to my pleasure forever."

Amid low gurgles of laughter, and little gasps of discovery his caresses intensified. "I want this moment to last." The soft touch of his lips, all sensation made me care for nothing but nestling into his body. My body leapt to him like a pin to a magnet. His fingertips slid over my breast and damp thighs as his tongue followed. Soft sounds mixed with murmurs of encouragement escaped my lips and intermingled with the unspoken pleasure of letting our flesh merge and overlap to a rhythm of, he is here to have and hold, he is here not just figuratively, he is here literally, and he loves me. The scent of heat on skin set our rhythm and carried the force of his rhythmically thrusting. I'd grasped him firmly and pulled him to me as we moved slowly but surely toward climax. His forehead against mine, his moans long and low heightened my own gratification until the dam burst, like being swept out to sea.

Heartbreak squished into a single moment made me long for those lost days of enchantment when the world had seemed complete. I went into the kitchen and poured myself a large glass of wine, then returned to read what else Arthur had written.

Oct 22, 2003.

Back at the hotel, after making love we'd lain entwined, wet from our exertions, too awed to do anything but cling to each other and watch the half-light filtering through the window, throwing tattooed shadows along the wall. Katherine said she loved a lot of things about me but was not going to tell me because she was trying to play it cool. With a giggle she said she liked the respect I had for her ideas and capabilities. She thought it rare for a man to treat his lover's ideas as seriously as his own. I told her my favorite thing about her was the way she sowed seeds in others in the belief the seeds would take root and their lives would be fulfilled.

Katherine my muse, she seduces and stirs me. Since time immemorial poets have described love, religion, and philosophy as both profane and sacred, and sexual union the closest glimpse of the Godhead. Fool that I am, it has taken me till now to understand how physical attraction acquires a broader power with the love of the whole person. What Plato refers to as Mature Love. My original fear on meeting Katherine, a fear of being attached to someone independent and financially successful is no longer relevant. I want to wake up every day beside this authoritative female, this sexually charged loving companion who is passionate about my poetry. Whatever her feelings are for me, I am ready to beg, literally beg her to marry me. In that moment of infinite possibilities, I said, "Marry me."

I admit I'd shuddered at that moment—like being in a cinema with the screen flashing a warning: *All the exits are jammed*. My hands fluttered, frantically flying this way and that like a pack of startled crows as I tried to shape the air and brush away the idea of marriage. In truth, the only aisle I wanted to walk down was an aisle which sold something I wanted to buy. A woman's wedding day is touted as the greatest day of her life, yet it is little more than a deed of ownership: the bride as property and the marriage contract indenture between master and slave. Why, I ask you, would any sane female voluntarily choose to lose half her rights by entering a prison controlled by men and a government basically against freedom for women? In France until the 1970s, married women could not have bank accounts in their own name; they could not borrow or have credit cards without a husband's permission. Yet if the little old hubby ran off without paying his debts, guess who was held responsible? It went against my instinct of survival to even consider it.

Joseph Heller, who wrote *Catch 22*, invented the term *Catch 22* to describe an impossible situation. One evening as I dined with him, in Venice he'd said: "I wasn't sure I wanted to be married but I was always sure I wanted a divorce." My sentiment exactly, well not exactly, because I'd never contemplated marriage nor even if I wanted to be married. It flattered me that Arthur wanted to marry me even if there were precedents to his fickleness. But his unromantic statement – *Marry me* – was about as unromantic as one could get.

Women suffer from lack of romance because most men don't see the need for it. Romance for them seems to be only in songs, movies and literature, not in real life. And yet any spontaneous gesture that let me know the man in my life was thinking about me, warmed my heart. When one of my lovers bought me a seawater nose spray, I was incredibly touched. He was not just saying *I love you,* he was showing me, he'd actually thought about me. It touched me as if he had bought me flowers or pulled the car over to share a romantic moment in the moonlight.

Arthur was disappointed by my lack of enthusiasm to his proposal. The next morning, he was even more taken aback, when I said I had to discuss the idea of marriage with Woody, my six-foot kangaroo before making any decision. He'd looked puzzled, then laughed. "You are joking! A grown woman can't be having imaginary conversations with a six-foot kangaroo."

"And why not?" A therapist once told me self-dialogue was an officially recognized creative practice in the world of coaching and therapy. Most people talk to themselves, Agatha Christie talked to her imaginary friend throughout her life. Different parts of the brain talking to other parts of the brain is less abnormal than one thinks. Of course, that relies a certain extent on my ability to suspend reality and place myself in Woody's large shoes. Probably exactly what people are doing when they pray but a lot more satisfying because one gets a good chance to chat. "How often does God talk to you?"

"Not often, but when he does it is earth shattering. Prayers are mostly monologues, but I do get showers of intuitive fragments from a spiritual source when I compose my poems. I'm often amazed to discover what I've written."

As usual, Woody gave me a lot of sensible advice. He reminded me Arthur was kind and funny and clever and endearing, but also a self-centered egoist who didn't lack the ability to sell his ideas to a promoter but with his raw narcissism he thought it was beneath him. Likely he would expect me to do that as well as organize his artistic activities and comforts.

As the months passed, I'd felt a transforming as Arthur and Woody began to unify. Not in a gentle gradual way but like two bricks smashing a fictional barrier trying to become whole. Sometimes I wasn't sure which one I was talking to.

I'd almost forgotten Woody's warning against marriage and my own terror when I told Arthur that if I painted a psychological portrait of him, I would show him more spiritual than how people saw him. Arthur had given me a roguish grin. "Would you now? So will that portrait allow you to marry me?" Perhaps that was the moment he breached my resistance, the moment when I questioned: what is wrong with me? After three years together we were like two plants sharing independent plots of soil but our roots growing around each other in a creative union. So why I asked myself, why not marry my chosen soulmate, the person I wanted to be near for the rest of my life? Yeah, I know that is very unromantic acceptance to a very unromantic proposal, a sort of total romantic cop out.

When the day came, and we exchanged vows he twirled me around like a bird he had captured. "I wanted to marry you because you are my very favorite person."

xxx

So much for believing in a man who dished out smiles as false as his lies and pathetic promises. So much for my being Arthur's favorite person, so much for his claim I was the only woman with whom he had ever been happy. So much for *everlasting* love and complicity. As false as he turned out. I might as well have hoped to go to the moon.

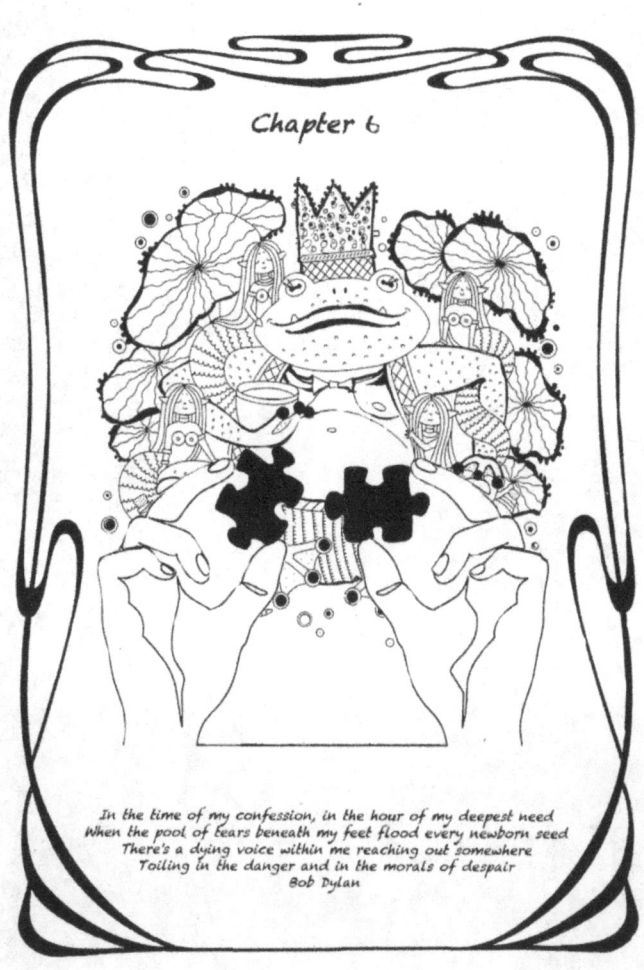

Chapter 6

In the time of my confession, in the hour of my deepest need
When the pool of tears beneath my feet flood every newborn seed
There's a dying voice within me reaching out somewhere
Toiling in the danger and in the morals of despair
Bob Dylan

Hélène, my assistant, informed me that the therapist, who'd previously visited me, was waiting to see me. Good God, why did I need a therapist? My vomiting wasn't a compulsion, it was a reaction to indigestible stress. Any sort of food was as unpalatable as the so-called lies my husband had been spouting.

The therapist swept into the room and stood checking me out with the look of a pompous attack hamster. "I've heard your memory is returning. That's good. The mind literally ceases to function when one is in a state of flight except for the necessities of survival. Tell me what you do remember."

I sighed. Everything in my mind was foggy apart from the relentlessly negative and cruel inner voice that repeated over and over: *You are thrown away like an old shoe.* Tears came in a deluge, and I sobbed: "I just want to know why he left me."

"There will never be an answer to that question. There never is just one reason. He probably doesn't even know himself. The most painful goodbyes are the ones never explained. The only person who can give you that answer has a strong reason not to tell the whole truth. Arthur has surely roughed together some sort of story for himself, but it's not the whole story. It's likely his childhood experiences wired his brain to walk away when wrestling with chaos, rather than face up to his actions." She paused a moment as if checking my reaction then added, "Cheaters cheat because they feel entitled to cheat. They often lack Christian morals or their moral compass misfunctions. Sometimes it's simply a lack of empathy for their partner."

I was astounded by her trite explanations. Same old crap. Just blame childhood or lack of Christian morals. I'd read enough of Arthur's emails to know this fake religious groupie, who had Arthur by the short hairs, had somehow convinced him she was his route to salvation and recovery of his Christian identity. How the hell did he lose his Christian identity in the first place? Had he forgotten it on a clothes rack? I mean, it's not something you hang in the closet or put on when you feel like it. He would have been better off thumbing through the lists of prayers for sale on eBay. He could have then asked the Supreme Being where he'd left it.

The therapist's penetrating brown eyes regarded me closely over her wire-rimmed glasses. "There's a physiological reason for everything which is often related to early wounds. You, for instance, this being unexpectedly treated without worth from one day to the next likely reopened your old wounds that had never healed and sparked a reaction of extreme stress which caused the memory loss."

I gritted my teeth. Yeah, all the fault of my childhood issues. "I didn't dump myself."

"I'm not an analyst, I'm simply here to encourage you to put this trauma behind you. Let's look at it this way. Unless something dramatic happens to psychologically break us, we remain relatively stable. Each and every one of us has a model inside our skulls but everyone's model is flawed. When chaos strikes, our ability to control the external world breaks down and further chaos echoes. Arthur's fact-checking senses likely went offline and caused a state of temporary paralysis. Specific situations can overwhelm inherent predispositions. The key word here is situation. In certain situations, people are swept away. Call it a smash-up."

"That's kind of banal. I want the skeleton key to unlock this sordid tale?"

Her wary but pleasant eyes implied I was being puddled-headed. "What is clear is a cheater's values are not aligned to support a healthy relationship. If a cheater gives the old half-crazy response, 'I went mad', he obviously lacks serious self-awareness. I am not saying cheaters don't care, they just don't care as much about the other person as they care about themselves. They prefer not to be discovered, but once they are, they often revel in being wanted by two women. A catfight over his fabulousness. All attention on him!"

"I'm not in a cat fight." I spat out the words. "She can have the lying, cheating frog that she's handcuffed and plunked in a pot of soon-to-be-boiling water for all I care. His calling this idiotic bag woman his perfect fit is his way to avoid the humiliation of being labeled a foolish old man running off with floozy for sex, a role he often mocked. I cannot believe he left me the iPad of porno images intentionally; that would be too cruel."

She sighed. "I'm sorry. What we often think are unintentional acts, are in fact intentional. A way of letting someone know the truth without taking responsibility for their acts."

My gut contracted and I doubled over in pain unable to breathe. The therapist moved closer, as if to soothe my rising frenzy, which made it even harder for me to breathe. I lay back on my bed and thumped the heel of my hand against my breastbone till my lungs released tiny coughs.

Finally, when I could speak, I said Arthur was obsessed with pornography. "I'd never objected to it. Why would I? It seemed harmless enough until the months of the pandemic when his porno addiction took him over and he spent hours in the bathroom looking at porno, or so I thought. I now know he was ogling this groupie's sexual bits and sending her porno photos of himself."

"The internet changed our world with sex addiction mutating to the internet which is just as unhealthy as actual infidelity. A man addicted to online pornography has little time or thoughts for his primary relationship. As you probably realize, pornography depends on objectification, it reduces human beings to things. Suzan Sontag, best known for essays on modern culture claims: *Pornography is a theater of types, never of individuals. The attraction is the private being made public, the forbidden being revealed in a pornographic theater in which people cast themselves in the role they wish to play.*" She hesitated then added, "And it's not just men corrupted by Internet pornography, women have added even more conspicuous come-hither moves by sending sexually explicit emails and porno photos to get male attention."

I was taken back and gasped out: "You mean this groupie knew what she was doing, she had done it with others?"

"Most likely. The consensus is that pornography can affect or even supplant real encounters. People become lost in their own fantasy and end up believing they know the person. In Arthur's case, it's more complicated because he'd had sex with her. It is likely Arthur's sex and porno exchanges with this woman triggered obsessive feelings that became additive."

"Hey, wait a minute. You think months of masturbating to her porno photos made Arthur believed he was in love with her. Even made him believe he could make a new life with her?"

"It's likely he could no longer tell the real from the unreal and had convinced himself *she was in love with him*. Men are as prone as women to acting out sexual daydreams and projecting feelings onto a romantic interest they barely know. Falling for a porno star happens frequently, just as casual sex can trigger feelings of passion and attachment. It's not unique."

In that gut-wrenching moment, I had a flashback of Arthur the morning I'd left on my January trip. He'd had a smirk on his face like the cat who had swallowed the canary. A look of having done something naughty and being deliriously happy to have got away with it. That memory threatened a new round of vomiting, so I quickly flicked the memory away like a fleck of dust and changed the subject. "Do you think there is something intrinsically wrong with humping multiple people?"

"It's wrong and can be forgiven but not if that person sets up a whole new life with another person and tries to hang on to his wife as well. That is just being greedy and not realistic. Infidelity happens every day, ad nauseam. Arthur should be condemned and forgotten as a self-indulgent egoist who has no idea what it is to love. It's well-established unfaithful men often lack the ability to be truly intimate with their partner because they suffer from sexual narcissism and an inflated sense of their own sexual ability. This encourages them to pursue extramarital affairs." She looked at me questioningly. "Why would you want a man who dumps you after twenty years to shack up with a woman half his age without having the kindness to mention it?"

She was right. Why would I?

xxx

The next morning, my brain see-sawed between extreme distress and rage like a supercharged pressure cooker about to explode. I needed superhuman strength to throw back the covers, struggle out of bed, shower, and dress for a normal morning. Normality was what I needed and a stash of hot chocolate. Only when I looked in the mirror did my resolve sink. The fluorescent light revealed a forlorn, sad face, a testament to my tortured nights and a youth long past.

Sarah brought me a coffee. She was obviously confused about what to do with a sobbing pseudo widow whose digging into past events might bring a relapse. In an angry moment, I showed Sarah the dozens of porno photos the groupie had sent Arthur. She waved them away as too horrific.

"They aren't pretty, I know, but I would love to spread them all over the Internet, which would be too bad for Arthur as he didn't bother to cover his face while she hid hers. Few people would recognize this Columbian's sexual bits, but each photo has her name, email and date sent so everyone would know what kind of whore Arthur got mixed up with."

"Don't do that! You are better than that."

"Still, threatening revenge on this gold-digging Columbian might stop her trying to manipulate Arthur into getting everything I own once she realizes his funds are minimal."

Forget it. Arthur may be weak but he's not immoral. His meeting this woman was an accident that should never have happened." She sighed. "Your being endlessly accommodating made it possible for you to live with Arthur, but being accommodating does not include accepting his infidelity. It's time to forget him."

xxx

By mid-October 2020, my trying to focus on what had happened and what it all meant was like watching an endless film with the sound off. The scenes played over and over, all night long in my brain as I'd recovered many more ghastly memories. One memory in particular stuck around long enough for me to get a handle on it. Patasola had shown up at Arthur's concert in the north of Spain the previous year, acting as if she had some sort of priority, a special invitation from Arthur. Every nerve in my body had gone wacko, as she moved into his territory, circling him not twenty meters from me; a freaky, disheveled brunette in a skintight mini skirt and puffy pink jacket. She'd sidled up to Arthur, a true feat in her badly fitting stilettos that reminded me of Cinderella's evil sisters and their attempt to squeeze their feet into Cinderella's shoe, in the hope of making off with the prince.

Patasola gazed coyly at Arthur, fingered his arm, tilted her head, batted her eyes, giggled, and raised her puckered lips, signaling, *I am here, you can have me.* The scene caused the hair on the back of my neck to rise like cat fur when it senses a viper infiltrating its nest. Later at the reception dinner I gave for our friends, I'd refused to invite Patasola, then relented when my dear friend said, "Come on, she's a sort of gypsy bag woman that hangs round for scraps. Arthur could not be interested in such a silly, vulgar groupie, the sort any sane man would flee." But he didn't flee, which is pretty much proof that our brains cannot be trusted to gauge accurately how an old fool can be an old fool.

Rereading Arthur's emails, I kept tripping over the same thought constantly until the truth hit me like Dostoyevsky facing the firing squad, the tip of the gun barrel on his temple. I knew that *Arthur had not only encouraged her to come to the concert, he'd fucked her after his concert in Madrid. And during his questionable disappearance, while I worked finishing up the details for the evening event, he'd probably been off with her.* Yeah, right, real dumb. A clever git would have told the groupie straight off that I would string her up like a dead rat if she didn't lay off Arthur. If Arthur had objected, it would have confirmed the devil was sitting on his shoulder.

I returned to reading the emails sent in the first weeks of being dumped curious as to what memories they might recover.

August 11, 2020.

> *Dear Katherine,*
>
> *I want to write you with an open heart—I want to talk to you in the same way. Everything I say seems to offend or hurt you, so I hardly have hopes it will be different now, but I still do hope. The situation has changed, but why does that mean we cannot continue in a different way? There are men who have had a mistress and their love for their wife is unchanged. You have read Montaigne. There is nothing exclusive here, why should there be? Let's live and find a way to be in*

communication! Our life together has not been a lie. I have always loved you. I have failed you. But it is not just sex. That is easy to get and does not need to upset lives. I could live without sex.

Of course, I understand those private photos were revolting and shocking to you, and perhaps the worst thing that has happened in this misery, but they were not of two persons together—they were solitary, masturbatory, so to speak. As to not telling you right away about my leaving you, it was not an on-going deception since I planned to tell you after a few weeks. I thought it was better to tell you gradually, with time, but never imagined never telling you! I thought it would be preferable, and honest, if I were going to have this relationship, to leave and have it openly. I never considered asking you if you would object to me having an ongoing relationship and us staying together. I would have thought that was impossible to accept. Although now I wish I had, it certainly would have been more worthy as a man. You asked me how I would have felt if the shoe were on the other foot. Devastated, mourning, yes, but I would not have been so bitter. What you don't understand is that I love you and still do love you and want to reopen a channel of deep communication with you.

Love Arthur.

I gasp. What kind of a dream world did Arthur live in? Did he really believe he could hang on to both of us? Coupling with a floozy yet wanting me, his help mate on the side? A plural wife or what? I'm surprised he didn't ask me to support the two of them. Any comic genius could turned Arthur's underhanded grotesque farce into wacky one liners likely to have an audience rolling in the aisle in riotous laughter. Friends could hardly hide their amusement when I told them my 84-year-old husband had lost his brass balls to a groupie in return for her offer to help him recover his Christian identity. Yeah, truly hilarious if you aren't the dumped wife. Human foibles make us who we are, and few people have their stuff together, least of all Arthur. His sin is he wants it all, his wife, and his fantasy of having found the perfect fit to his neurotic self. Only a retard would claim it was not an ongoing deception because he planned to tell me about his 'new situation' in the future. How? By email? Truly horrifying! Like a Kafka fun house of distorted mirrors. I almost threw up in disgust. It was insane to compare today with Montaigne's time, a man who lived in the sixteenth century, a different world with different moral codes.

The secret key to messing up his cozy little love nest was surely to change the lock. Yeah, right. Arthur staying in communication with me will expose her fears and drive her into coocoo land because everyone knows pathological neurotics want complete authority and control over their victims.

August 12, 2020.

> Dear Arthur,
> Montaigne lived in the 1500s and as usual you got it wrong—he lived with and supported his wife and had the occasional mistress on the side. You threw me away as if my usefulness to you was finished when you had some money of your own. Now it appears you don't want to finish with me even though you have set up home with this groupie. If, this is not about sex but about recovering your Christian identity there would have been no reason for you to dump me. I could have forgiven you for humping her, for jerking off to her porno photos, for lying and being deceptive. But I cannot forgive you for exchanging me as easily as changing your brand of cigarettes for this lightweight neurotic with the intellectual capacity of a pot plant.
>
> You say I blackened your name to our friends by saying I opened my heart and my purse to you. Truth does not blacken a name. All artists need help until they are successful. Nobody questions that. You obviously thought the brutal way you dumped me was okay, so why does it bother you that our friends know the truth? You complain they don't write to you with sympathy. Huh? Ask yourself—why would they? You acted disgracefully. Of course, if I had not told

anyone about your shitty behavior it would have avoided turning you into a laughingstock, stigmatized by a mad passion for an 'interested' groupie after a four-day fuck session and months of porno exchanges. Your Monty Python skit is full of illogical surreal insanity and an unapologetic lack of glamour full of cowardly back-alleys communications, porno exchanges, and debauchery.

Grief is a whole gamut of awful emotions; confusion, regret, anger, and loneliness, all wrapped up in that one little word. Some people grieve; some are grief-stricken. You behaved badly and then have the nerve to tell me I should overcome my grief, be open-minded and move on from the obsessive question of why. You say it hurts you to see how hurt I am, then you ask: why all the fuss? What did you expect? That I would quietly disappear into my humiliation? You excuse leaving the iPad of porno images by saying passion drove your every thought and decision. Certainly, it drove out all decent behavior. *A wise man rules his passions, a fool obeys them.* Your saying, "things happen!" is enough to destroy mentally and physically the strongest of human beings.

I am furious you didn't love me enough to stick around, furious for my being so easy to leave, furious that you didn't have the decency to tell me you were buggering off with this floozy. What the hell was going on in your mind on our last evening together. Why did you tell me how much you loved me. Was that some sort of insurance policy, like riding two horses, in case your floozy fling didn't work out? You now claim our years together made an indelible mark in your soul. That has to be a joke, however, the crueler joke is your saying you intended to tell me later. How? By email? Could anything be more brutal, more insensitive than to dump your lover and helpmate of twenty years by email!

Katherine

xxx

August 15, 2020.

> *Dear Katherine.*
>
> *While I understand your anger, I wish you would not refer to the party concerned as a groupie. Patasola, whatever impression she may have made on you, or whatever you may have heard, is a strange and exotic human being born in the high Andes on a dirt floor. After the first erotic encounter with this woman, I learned much about her intense devotion and religious dimension. That is why this encounter became a spiritual awakening. By not practicing my religion I had been living a deceptive life. I was not lying when I told you it was the irresistible intertwining of eros and religion that dominated. For the first time in 40 years, I went to a priest and confessed.*
>
> *I imagine you will not take this seriously, but it is serious. I went through a 'dark night of my soul'. Although it is true this erotic encounter split us apart, it is not as you say, 'a fuck'. This spiritual dimension is more important than sex. The reality of this affair, even if I had at first thought of it as temporary fling, I now recognize I have been emotionally vampirized as in Benjamin Constant's novel, Adolph. The main protagonist Adolph is emotionally vampirized because of his pathological need to convince himself he is lovable. All that and more.*
>
> *Love Arthur*

Arthur's absence wasn't emptiness, which is final, it was incompleteness with a thousand tomorrows empty of whatever promise they once held. The words of the writer C.S. Lewis', who had influenced my youth with his *Chronicles of Narnia,* echoed around in my brain: *You grow more and more a stranger to me at each word. And I had loved you so...You were my nest before you locked me out and left me to wander.*

Woody eyed me as if I needed a good talking to but what I needed was a good hug. Yeah, all discarded muses need hugs for all the crap they put up with. Cultural critic and feminist

Germaine Greer, a woman of many talents and minor faults, wrote an enlightened description of the modern female muse: One *who engages in a reverse penetration of the male artist's mind and helps bring forth his creativity from the "womb of his mind".* Sounds sexual and I guess that was her intention.

Most egocentric artists who dump their muse on achieving some sort of success, usually upgrade for someone they believe can be more useful to them. Ian McEwan the much beloved English writer had once described his wife Penny as his muse. "She is the single most important influence on my work. I suppose I was lucky, I married a woman who fascinated me, and I remain fascinated by her." These words were very similar to what the poet T.S. Eliot said about his wife Vivienne. "I owe her everything. She is central to my life and art." These amazing men in the lamest of gags both dumped their muses. With Arthur it was more taking the easy option: a *man too lazy to climb the tree, gets the rotten apples lying on the ground.* Not only did Arthur downgraded, one might even say he scraped the bottom of the barrel. But at least he hadn't tried, so far, to lock me up in an insane asylum and live off my money as T.S. Eliot had done.

August 16, 2020.

> Dear Arthur.
>
> There is a rumor going around that you think you found God. That seems unlikely since you mostly can't even find yours keys, and there is plenty of evidence that they exist. People with courage can live without self-respect, *cowards* can't. Those who lack courage will, like you, always find a philosophy to justify it. As you put it: *Eros sex sessions helped me recover my Christian identity.* Wow, you sound like a guy trying to prove the unprovable by unproven conspiracy theories. Everyone knows Patasola is a bipolar groupie who suffers from OCD, a compulsive obsessive disorder, which manifests itself in obsessive praying, all to avoid punishments for her sins.
>
> To call her a groupie is complimentary compared to what other people call her. Some of

your best friends call her a Bag Woman looking for scraps. She fits the category of groupie because she sucks up to men for what she can get out of them. In other circumstances, I might have a sneaking admiration for a primitive Latino female, who never got a proper look-in from birth, yet managed to her pull herself up from the Columbian gutter, even if it was by flaunting herself and screwing old men.

You tell friends you are doing the maximum to rekindle our relationship but what have you done apart from saying you love me and asking if I am sleeping and eating properly? If that is the maximum, forget it! If you want to rekindle something, straighten your life out, decide what you want. Cheaters have a nasty habit of trying to keep a foot in both worlds. Stop gaslighting us both and playing us false.

Katherine

Chapter 7

If today was not an endless highway
If tonight was not a crooked trail
If tomorrow wasn't such a long time
Then lonesome would mean nothing to you at all
Bob Dylan

A Mack truck didn't slam into whoever said life doesn't give you more than you can handle. Much as I try, I can no more get over my grief than change my eye color or trade in my tin ear. Even while I try to hate Arthur for being a rotten fish that no amount of tartar sauce can disguise, I am disturbingly aware that he was once the man of my life.

Marc, Arthur's best friend, had warned me when I met Arthur that he was complicated, and that it would be a miracle if he ever faced up to Ciguapa's manipulations and divorced her. "He is separated from Ciguapa but tied to hand and throttle. He clings on to a young uneducated, childlike sickly Fiorelle, who he complains about constantly but is reluctant to give up.

My friend Julia told me firmly to wake up to reality. She said Arthur was as unstable as uranium: both an unreliable man with an unreliable penis. With a charming tilt of her head, she'd softened the comment by adding, he is trouble. Think carefully, fluffy feathers are what you get with an unstable artist. I would advise against taking on a man over sixty who lacks finances and unresolved romantic complication. Arthur is exactly the sort of artist we love to drop in on for a visit but not to take home. Creative people are great as friends but make lousy life companions. Arthur is a people-pleaser and presents the parts of himself that he thinks others will like. Endearing to say the least if it wasn't that he despises himself for giving in to other people's demands."

Julia sniggered and cast a glance around the room. "Voicing this makes me sound like a man hating feminists while I think of myself as a humanist. I love humans especially humans like Arthur who allow women the same rights and consideration as they allow themselves."

Dreams of love are like waves and when the right one comes along, the one you think has your name on it, you grab it even if it is less than that fifty-fifty proposition. With hindsight, Julia's keen-eyed early forewarning should have dragged me out of my beatific state or at least prepared me for the barbed wire suppositories of Arthur's rocky swan song. But who in the throes of early romantic bliss believes the man they love will go whole hog and become a lapdog to a malicious spirit who he claims has caught him in a vampire's nest? Escapism at its most fanciful or what?

Despite Arthur advanced age and his being a clever, talented artist when I met him, he was still having concerts in backwater, worthless venues where he was paid in pennies like a beginner or student. "I have to admit penniless artists have pursued me for all the things I'd become then rejected me because they couldn't suck me up and become me."

"Have your success you mean?"

I nodded.

At least Arthur was not Bluebeard with a basement full of ex-wives' severed heads, although the absence of them didn't guarantee he hasn't a trunkful of them somewhere. Art history is littered with abusive, larger-than-life painters, sculptors, poets, writers, musicians who used and abused women, then excused their behavior as keeping their artistic freedom. Critics laud Picasso's work as an expression of man's virility and power rarely mentioning he was a self-mythologizing monster of toxic masculinity who extracted their essence, then disposed of them. The women he called goddesses were doormats. Picasso's granddaughter Marina Picasso said the seven women he'd claimed to have loved had all been subjected to animalistic sexuality and their lives made miserable. Much as I admire Picasso's work, I cannot excuse his behavior.

xxx

On my first years in Paris, I'd frequently camped out in Café de Flore on Boulevard Saint-Germain in an effort to avoid the hellishly cold of my unheated room. How the French managed without central heating or any kind of heating was a mystery. Winters in France are not nearly as extreme as in Canada, which would freeze the balls off anyone navigating a Canadian blizzard, but they were still wretched. Albert Camus and French existentialist writer Jean Paul Sartre obviously suffered from similar lack of heat as they also camped out in Café de Flore for the warmth. That Café had taken on a special magic when Ken

Sturdy, my art professor in my Canadian Art College, told me, he'd grown a beard and had hung out there. I imagined him surrounded by all those famous guys, recounting his stories, his thin face alive with energy, his hands flying in all directions. Years later, when he dropped in to see me in Paris, he admitted it was only for two weeks after his military service. A glorious myth, nevertheless.

Paris had been every bit as transformative, disorienting, and uncharted as I could have wished. It had lived up to its reputation as an Alice in Wonderland quixotic haven of artists, poets, designers, and reclusive misfits. The city was like a good book, the further I got into it, the more it made sense that I was there, where success, even for a woman, might be possible.

I'd discovered Simone de Beauvoir, the only woman in the existentialist movement, while studying works by the Danish Existentialist Soren Kierkegaard, to impress my father. Which did, sort of, because of my father being Danish. With the passing of years, Kierkegaard's message about the meaninglessness of existence has become clearer to me but unfortunately, at the age of sixteen I'd been unable to grasp why Kierkegaard thought life absurd, or to understand what he meant when he said: 'Life can only be understood backwards; but it must be lived forwards.' That did somewhat limit discussions with my father.

I knew what Simone de Beauvoir meant when she said that women would never feel free until they could walk down the street alone and be left in peace. In Paris that was impossible. French guys and creepy Arab guys followed me along the street, making aggressive vulgar suggestive movements with their mouths and hands. It dampen my enthusiasm for Paris as I stroll the city. Apparently my *allez vous en* was much too polite. Now I've learned *fous moi le paix* is more effective.

I pulled out my old sketchbook to reread the notes I'd written about my first encounter with Julia in 1960.

January 26, 1960:
    Today at Café de Flore a young girl at the next

table, leaned over and snapped me out of my stupor by pointing to my book: "Simone de Beauvoir lives nearby. She is often here or at Les Deux Magots." I stared at her trying to get my gravity together.

"You mean the woman who wrote *The Second Sex*?"

"Yes! Simone de Beauvoir." The dark-haired pretty girl got up from her chair, reached over the table and shook my hand. "I'm Julia. Simone De Beauvoir said women must, among other things and beyond their natural differences, unequivocally affirm their *brotherhood*. I welcome you to the brotherhood of female fraternity!"

I was elated. I'd always wanted to be part of a brotherhood, even the brotherhood of Beats. Pretty dumb, as the Beatniks were a male fraternity and chicks were there to be fucked. Yeah, I know it's called being fucked over. That is not a substitute insult, being fucked over was exactly what was going on. I told Julia I was re-reading *The Second Sex* because I was flummoxed as to how men got control over our society and why women had not rebelled against their lack of rights and their restricted freedom. Why hadn't they rebelled with the suffragettes or protested when clever women were burnt as witches?

Even women who attained power did little for women's emancipation, some even hindered it. In the mid-1800s the famous French novelist George Sand, a rich and unhappily married woman challenged feminine norms and received critical acclaim. As the only female member of the 1848 second French Republic, which abolished slavery and introduced universal suffrage, she had voted against women getting the right to vote! Even ignorant and uneducated men got the vote, but French women were denied that right until 1946, long after almost all other civilized countries allowed women to vote.

I told Julia I'd been flummoxed by my two American roommates on the boat to France. They said they were perfectly content to perpetuate patriarchy. After their European sabbatical they would return to America, do their duty by marrying some bright young man with good prospects and live life exactly like their parents. "I'd quoted the poet T.S. Eliot to them: *If you accept the status quo, and the rules of conformity as the norm, you will always live a disgruntled life.* They'd looked at me with total incomprehension as if I was from another planet which no doubt I am."

"Probably never heard of T.S. Eliot," Julia commented with a grim smile. "Once apron a time, before women had been idealized into powerlessness, they had ruled the nest with men peripheral. We're still sort of powerful, but mostly we take the crap to avoid the rap. I suspect we lost out when the sneaks took over religion. Perhaps we didn't realize what was going on until it was too late. Probably glad to have men out of their hair. When they weren't out chasing animals, they were likely lying around waiting for dinner. The usual sort—sex and food types. Once men had their paws on religion, they grabbed the whole shebang and wham patriarchy was born. Then they had the chutzpa to claim their superiority was God given and used science to prove it."

"Did you make that up or is it was a known theory?"

> "Who knows? It's sort of an accepted theory."
>
> I ordered a couple of glasses of wine, and we drank to Simone de Beauvoir who had written: 'Man is defined as a human being and a woman as female—whenever she behaves as a human being, she is said to imitate the male.'

Below the notes on this conversation, I'd scribbled a few words from a poem by the sixteenth-century poet Anne Finch, Countess Winchelsea. She aptly describes how even in my lifetime my father wanted me *debarred from improvements of the mind, to be dulled and forced to bow to men's mistaken rules:*

> *Alas! a woman that attempts the pen,*
> *Such an intruder on the rights of men,*
> *Such a presumptuous creature, is esteemed,*
> *The fault can by no virtue be redeemed.*
> *To write, or read, or think, or to inquire*
> *Would cloud our beauty, and exhaust our time,*
> *And interrupt the conquests of our prime;*

xxx

I'd spent most of my young life dreaming of deserting that boring country town where my father had chosen to make his life. That town held more secrets than a politician's wife which gave it a minimum of significance but did not compensate for the lack of equality accorded women. Innocent and dumb-assed as I was, I mistakenly thought things were different in the big wide world. But they weren't, not until the end of the 1960s.

Fortunately for me, at a young age my father took me to visit his bourgeois family in Denmark. An earth-shaking experience, full of revelations and surprises that saved me, an optimistic child from dire mental troubles. My having grown up in ill-fated circumstances had turned me into a gloomy fearful recluse. In Denmark I discovered the art world. It altered me emotionally and transformed a demoralized, rebellious fifteen-year-old into a passionate art enthusiast. Sleeping Beauty was awakened not by the prince's kiss but by the fragrance of Van Gogh, Gauguin, and Cezanne in museums and oil paintings on the walls of my relatives. Like a starving cat getting his first real meal my art passion burst into bloom and filled me with an ardent desire to spend my life in those temples of artistic creation.

After a couple of months in Denmark, my father returned to Canada leaving me, an inexperienced, timid, and under-developed adolescent, (more a kid up shit creek with problems) to make my way back to Canada. Adventurous pioneers are inclined to say, *What doesn't kill you teaches you to cope with adversity.* Was his attitude 'fend for yourself' due to his having carelessly forgotten to purchase me a ticket? If I give my father the benefit of doubt, although he may not deserve it, he did have an unquestioning belief that nothing bad could happen to his children? People were amazingly trusting in those halcyon days. Now they worry about going to Walmart, a movie, a concert, a synagogue for fear of being mowed down like fish in a barrel by some crazed guy with an automatic rifle. Where have all the flowers gone?

Do we choose our obsessions, or do they choose us? A more daunting question was, can a person from an unartistic and unintellectual family be creative and truly contribute to the world of the arts? No one today would ask such dumb questions after John Lennon's success, who hailed from equally unpromising circumstances. He made more than a splash with his talents and inventive poetic song. So could have Arthur with his love of literature and poetic writings, had he not self-sabotaged himself by devoting his time to making a buck to finance Ciguapa worldly comforts. Let's just say the golden boy had it all until the kiss of the wicked Queen.

After my return to Canada, I applied to Art College on the advice of my art professor. His encouragement was all I needed. Once my application had been accepted, I'd giggled and danced around with Woody before announcing to my parents I intended to study art and live in Paris. "But you have no talent," my mother stated. I was dumbfounded. For at least thirty seconds her words wiped out my euphoria. My mother had no art education, nevertheless considered herself capable of judging talent because she copied old paintings, rather inexpertly in my opinion. There was no point in stating copying wasn't in the same bread pan with being creative. She would simply have dismissed me with, "What do you know?"

My father laughed as if it was a hilarious joke. As a chicken farmer he obviously thought women were hens only good to lay eggs. He said there were no female artists and women were incapable of doing more than obeying men's commands. They didn't need an education to wash dishes and scrub floors. Bitterness and anger washed over me. I was too incensed to point out that there were few women artists precisely because macho men like my father wouldn't put out a few of the same green backs he'd happily given for my brother's education.

My mother stayed quiet as a mouse. Not a peep! She'd spent much of her life seething with rage for a screwed-up world that had deprived her of an education. How could she and other women blame men for perpetuating inequality when they continued to treat their sons as privileged little gods while denying equal treatment to his sisters?

"I'll get a job!" I shouted gathering up my dignity. "Don't worry about me; I can look after myself." I'd turned, tripped, and had almost fallen down the stairs. No one laughed, although they might have, under the circumstance. "I'm never going to marry, ever. Take that for God's truth." Of course, I had never expected to meet a man like Arthur. To be truthful, I always imagined meeting a talented, sexy, cultivated artist like Arthur, I'd just never expected to meet him.

Chapter 8

The scars of your love remind me of us
keep me thinking that we almost had it all.
The scars of your love leave me breathless,
I can't help feeling, we could have had it all.
Adele

Why is childhood so upsetting for so many people? You might well ask. Certainly, mine was upsetting enough to make me decide to leave home at the age of six. Perhaps I was looking for a new home the way a cat leaves when she senses she is no longer wanted. Perhaps it was simply wishful escape? I can't say I was exactly unwanted, it was more I was unacceptable because I wasn't malleable. Being malleable seems a necessary trait for the sad fact of being born female.

"Off to join the Gypsies, were you?" my mother had asked after my father dragged me back, her eyes glistening with moisture, and on her face a look of despair – *why isn't she like other girls?*

The idea of joining the Gypsies was so captivating I almost forgot I'd wanted to join the cowboys. "Cowboys?" My mother shook her head. "Girls can't be cowboys! That's not your lot. You are heading for trouble. The world won't let you get away with it!"

Get away with what, I wanted to know? Whatever it was, I wanted it!

Reading Victor Hugo's novel *Notre Dame de Paris* years later, I'd jumped for joy at the idea I was a changeling, exchanged by the Gypsies and I had ended up in the wrong place with the wrong parents. My grandmother suggested another version. "The stork must have accidentally dropped you on our doorstep one miserable raining day." I knew she wished it had never happened. So, did I.

One of my favorite fairytales is the one about the fox who cannot reach the grapes so he decides he would rather live in a world without grapes. Or at least to be able to ignore the grapes to prevent exposing my vulnerability. While Arthur claimed he was the devoted son to his mother, I was begging the Gypsies to exchange mine for a pretty mom. One who would be inconspicuous, and blend like other moms. If I happened to see her in the street before she saw me, I would hide, mortified by her big feet, her too-loud voice, her inelegance and overpowering presence. Yeah, I know, Gypsies don't exchange parents, I was stuck with her. I mean who would want her? Surprisingly, my brother did. Hudson truly loved our mother with a passion. That seemed a sort of reassuring miracle especially when I discovered later that Arthur was born the same day and year as my brother. It made me hoped he was also capable of truly loving.

July 20, 2020.

> *Dear Katherine,*
>
> *Whatever you think, I do care and have always cared deeply for you. Ours was not a one-sided relationship; our marriage was an ongoing conversation of love. I feel foolish trying to claim some positive points for myself as an anxious child might claim it is not necessary to pull down and destroy everything. We get carried away by sorrow and bitterness and perhaps you don't mean all you say quite as cruelly as you have put it. Being with another woman does not mean breaking away from you, it just means we have a different relationship. In any case, we are two persons of intelligence, imagination, and kindness.*
>
> *I have experienced being left by Paula—it was very painful, but I did not consider it betrayal. I did not even reproach her. It is betrayal to take a lover or a mistress behind your companion or spouse's back, while keeping the comfortable married state. It is neither criminal nor monstrous to leave, and live with another person, however hurtful; it is not betrayal. Love Arthur*

xxx

July 28, 2020.

Dear Arthur.

I assume you have been reading the 'wicked bible' which was misprinted. It left out one vital word—the *not* in *thou shalt not commit adultery*—of course later corrected. To call you unfaithful sounds like a word made up by people who want to soften the blow of

84

their own treacherous, lying behavior. Lies attack the dignity of the person being lied to because they cause genuine harm. The difference between cat's lives and your lies is a cat has only nine lives while your lies are endless. The therapist said your brain may have malfunctioned because your childhood experiences had wired you to walk away when wrestling with chaos, rather than face up to your actions. Wake up, you fool. Stop being a manipulated puppet and regain some sense of decency. What did all this crap about recovering your Christian identity resolve? You remain as deceitful as ever.

Affairs may be exuberant acts of defiance but dumping your partner even if you claim you were bewitched, *is betrayal.* To hump this floozy in my studio and make elaborate plans behind my back to dump me is *cold hearted betrayal.* You insult my intelligence by asking, in all innocence, if sex matters all that much? This may sound like bitterness, but it does matter because it destroyed our partnership.

You again insult me by comparing our twenty years together with your brief affair with Paula, an affair you admit was not that serious. Honesty is the first chapter in the book of wisdom. Some acts are not examples of too much, too little, or just thoughtless; some acts are truly shameful. Aristotle the ancient Greek philosopher wrote that *justified anger is midpoint between being irascible and being a doormat. Anger is what prevents us from accepting rationalizations for wrongdoings. It helps restore balance.* Therefore, my reaction is a legitimate reaction to injustice. I am angry at the right person to the right extent.

Katherine

xxx

July 29, 2020.
Dear Katherine,
I apologize, I should never have written you any

reproaches. I have been wrong to put any blame on you, you have none, you have been a wonderful and loving companion, I am entirely to blame. You are a good and loving person. Please consider my foolish reproaches as unsaid. I ask forgiveness from you and from God every day for the pain I have caused. I've loved you all these years and still love you. I didn't leave out of resentment for you. You have been enormously important in my life, not only as a sweet companion and fellow spirit in the literary and artistic world, but also in your help and support for my work. I have wanted as much as possible and still do—to reciprocate.

I don't think my brain malfunctioned but certainly my emotions are confused. It is true this affair isn't just about sex. I was bewitched by the fusion of intense religious spirituality and amatory wildness that exploded in my brain and twisted my being. Confession is at the end of the process after a long and painful look at myself: the recognition of the wrongs, deceptions, and lies I have been guilty of throughout my life and my resolve to no longer do them.

I have difficulty in answering your questions, as I don't know the answers myself. I feel totally inadequate to respond to everything you said, including my bringing her into the house and being with her there. You are fully justified in your anger. I was torn away by this passion—that's what I meant earlier when I spoke of Paula, not that my couple of years with her can be compared to the mutual erotic passion that pulled us together and kept us together for twenty years.

Love Arthur

Curious to know more about Arthurs '*wrongs, deceptions, and lies I have been guilty of throughout my life*' I searched through my bookcase until I found his first journals marked 1954, six years after his mother's death.

May 3, 1954.

My earliest memory at the age of three, was playing near the restaurant where my mother worked as a waitress. I learned about God's wrath the day I found a watering can near the gasoline pumps. I filled it with gas and spent the next hour happily watering plants until someone, alerted by the strong smell, stopped me. Apparently, I'd sinned. How I'd sinned, my mother never explained, merely insisted I'd brought down God's wrath. From then on, I'd been locked in the restaurant basement, a cellar full of old crates and bottles of wine, but little else of interest except for a small window where I watched the world through the steam of my breath.

One dreary afternoon during the summer, the door opened and another boy, the nine-year-old son of one of the waitresses joined me in the cellar. "Hello, I'm Bob!" he'd said, giving me a friendly smile. I didn't feel friendly. I resented this older boy sniffing around my dark cellar in what I took to be a patronizing attitude. However, Bob's alighting in my place of confinement turned out to be a reprieve from solitude. He taught me many things: like how the sun came up and what made rocks. "Nothing comes from nowhere," Bob had explained. "And even stones have stories." When bored, we took turns pissing into the pot left for our needs. "Hey kid! Lem'me show you sumpin'," Bob exclaimed, jerking his hand up and down his penis. I liked the feel but nothing much changed for me.

After a thorough search of the cellar, we discovered a stack of dusty comic books bound with aging string. "Gosh, Tintin!" Bob had said flipping through the pages filled with images of a young boy with an odd haircut, strange knee length pants and a little white dog. Bob read and reread the Tintin stories until I knew them all by heart. At some point I suppose I crossed the line from memorizing the stories to being able to read them.

After Bob's return to school that autumn, I would lie for hours stroking my new toy while rereading Tintin. One afternoon a waitress who worked with my mother upstairs came into the storeroom which froze me in my favorite pastime. With a laugh she tickled my balls and gave me a kiss. Thrilled, I waited for her return, growing anxious with anticipation whenever I heard someone enter the storeroom. The next time she just laughed and shook her head.

At the age of six I was released from this dingy cellar and sent to school. Fear was my first reaction as I was hardly aware of the outdoors, except for being hurried home or through the streets on Sunday, a sinner on my way to confession. That left me ill-prepared for the troops of boisterous boys that poured across the school courtyard, hurrying right, and left, doors opening in all directions, spilling out children in what seemed a disorderly fashion. The teachers were astonished I could read. Even more astonished when I said comic books had taught me.

xxx

May 14, 1954,

I was pleased to wear white, to carry incense and be the Holy of Holies on my path is to become a priest. Flashes of divine light summon up my tears and made me curiosity and got me into trouble—it was considered misbehaving. As punishment I was forced to get up at an unholy hour and hustle along wintry streets to perform rituals on God's earth-bound altar. As if that wasn't enough, the school's authorities stuffed me into a trash can where they said I belonged. When I complained to my mother, she'd dismissed me with, "You likely provoked them. No one can put up with the things you do. Something's wrong with you. You're a troublemaker."

My own passivity and inability to protest about the punishments embarrassed me. One kind monk took pity on me, or so I thought until I felt his hand where it should not have been. My first reaction was disgust, but the electric charge which surged through me produced a spiritual and erotic short circuit.

xxx

Memories floated back of various conversations I'd had with Arthur. He'd said his mother spoiled him by giving him more freedom than he should have been allowed. She let him stay up until the early hours and eat whatever and whenever he wanted. When she became worried about his chaotic habits, she'd sent him to a rigorous Catholic school; a school which sounded more like a detention center where he fell somewhere in between different groups. One lot sniffed glue, stole for cigarettes, never did their schoolwork, and dogged off as much as possible. The other group had diverse problems, mostly they lacked fathers and had difficult circumstances at home.

His mother never mentioned his father except as a threat. "If you don't buck up, kid, I'll get your father to come and punish you, then you will know what punishment is!" When his father had shown up at the funeral, Arthur said he assumed he'd come to demand an account of his sins, sins that lay heavy on his conscience. He believed it was his fault that his mother was walloped by a bus. Yeah, he'd said *walloped*. Had he been watching too many mafia films? He admitted his inept attempts to be a good son were exactly what he was incapable of being. Punishments for not obeying his mother's rules became deeply rooted in his psyche. Once having admitted his sins he would be forgiven and swept up in his mother's arms. A sort of ritual which he came to relished, like rituals of the Catholic church.

His relationship with his mother did seem rather perverse when he said he occasionally gotten into his mother's bed and snuggled up to her. She didn't seem to mind, which confirmed to him she still thought him a child. However, when he'd reached out and accidently touched her breast, she'd struck him hard across the mouth as if he was an offending adult.

On the day his mother died he'd brought her coffee in bed. She'd been in one of her complaining moods saying no one cared for her, no one loved her, everyone was so selfish. When he'd reached out to give her a hug she'd reared back as if he was about to assault her sexually. He admitted he was kind of grown up at twelve, and boys did fancy their mothers. However, he had no intention of sinning, no intention other than to give her comfort.

With a sigh, I returned to reading Arthur's journal.

April 25,1954.

Six years have now passed since my mother's death crippled me with remorse and a terrible tiredness. Not the kind of tiredness that could be fixed with a good night's sleep, but a tiredness I have never been able to shake off. At the funeral my mother's sour chemical smell had been sickened me, as bent over to kiss her. I'd loved her smell; honey soap and under it a tangy body smell. Before she went out in the evenings, she would bend over to kiss me, all rustling and perfumed, her loving face held out to me like the Host as in the act of communion. I'd trembled with religious awe intoxicated by an erotic intensity.

xxx

April 28,1954.

The Vancouver social services handed me over to a father I'd never met, happy to rid themselves of a wild boy already expelled from school and likely to end up badly. The first morning on the isolated heights where my father's house was located, I'd traveled to school on the back of my stepbrother's bike. We'd headed down the sloping hills, avoiding the gullies until we reached the open highway. A few miles on, Michael had parked in front of a group of derelict-looking buildings, squat and ugly with brown walls, a tarred roof, and concrete steps.

"Looks awful, don't it?" Michael said. "An abandoned warehouse. Too many kids so they gonna build a new school but this here is all we got now." Inside it was just as stark: a long corridor with rows of clothes hooks, the wall opposite covered with maps and diagrams. Nothing superfluous, no pictures or lockers. The bell rang and a nearby door snapped open; the principal emerged; his well-fed but not happy face stared absentmindedly, suspiciously, at the clustered students. "What have we got here?" he said addressing Michael informally, almost tenderly.

"My brother. Can he join our class?"

The principal looked me over, his eyes narrowed as if taking aim. Then, brushing back, the thin wisps of hair that fell over his damp forehead, he ran his hands over his ill matched pants and coat, rumpled and put together blindly or so it seemed. He placed a hand on my shoulder and propelled me towards the hunched-back head-teacher following in his wake. "Give him a test," he announced with an impatience that bit off further words.

xxx

April 29, 1954

Having passed the exam, I relaxed into the role of younger sibling, bright, bookish, and clever beyond my years. That was an auspicious beginning, but the

91

school held another wonder. A row of bookcases lined two walls, their shelves literally sagging with books stacked carelessly, higgledy-piggledy one on top of another. This heterogeneous overflow donated by an early English pioneer made me shiver with excitement. I ran my index finger along each printed title, *Hamlet, A Midsummer Night's Dream, The Idiot, Oliver Twist*. This change of my environment feels like a chance to change my destiny. A book with portrait on the cover caught my eye. That book of poetry by Arthur Rimbaud became my guide, it is helping me make sense of who I am.

Chapter 9

You saw her bathing on the roof
Her beauty and the moonlight overthrew ya
She tied you to a kitchen chair
She broke your throne, and she cut your hair
And from your lips she drew the Hallelujah
Leonard Cohen

I returned to the bookcase in search of another journal to help fill in the blanks and understand Arthur's compulsive behavior vis a vis of womankind. I picked out one dated two years later when he was at university.

Sept. 23, 1956.

When the hour of my usual meeting with friends at the Hungarian bistro had long passed, I decided there was no point in waiting. Instead of leaving I ordered another coffee, a double espresso for the pleasure of watching the waitress weave her way to my table. Momentarily I was transfixed by the image of the waitress sprawled across my bed. I was both intimidated by my lack of experience and resentful for the fact that I was old enough to want it but too young to get it. However, it was not just sex my romantic nature wanted, I wanted a great love affair, a living romance to outstrip all fables and inspire a poetic passion.

When a couple of girls from one of my classes passed my table, I'd smiled encouragingly; with a slight nod they'd continued on their way probably intimidated by my interested look. With nothing particular to study that evening, I'd taken a stroll along the tree-lined avenue that bordered the university. The sweet smell of honeysuckle reminded me of dead summer afternoons spent behind the schoolhouse reading books. I reached down and trailed my fingertips in the stubble of fresh cut grass and listened to a bird calling above my head, an early evening call, sweet and clear. Glancing upward I searched the branches to catch a glimpse of the tiny creature, but no luck.

Nevertheless, it inspired me to scribble a short poem about the larks flying in a defensive front, over the distant pond where autumn leaves were beginning to fall.

About to return to my room my eye caught sight of a woman sitting cross-legged, reading a book on a bench nearby. She wore a white sweater, fluffy like an angora cat, which opened in a wide V at the front. Her hands encased in white gloves cause an erotic jolt to shoot through me. I whispered to myself in what I thought was bookish elegance: *this well-turned-out enigma, this seemingly chaste beauty has cast her light among the shadows and caught my eye. Why look for visions, when in the nature of things, they come to me!* Perhaps aware that I was staring, she glanced in my direction, a look that quickly dismissed me.

xxx

Sept 29, 1956.

This morning on my stroll, I caught sight of this same woman walking ahead of me, both graceful and seductive. A seductiveness that has little to do with breasts, hips, and legs, more the contrast of the Madonna dressed in flattering high heels. Flushed and nervous I followed in the wake of the light fabric of her skirt as it flicked back and forth in the wind. My mind raced with possible scenarios of how we might meet. At the cashier counter she turned to me and asked for help to bag her shopping. With a shock I realized although there was a resemblance, she was not the woman that captivated me the previous day.

"Oh, goodness. Thank you," she'd said, her soft sweltering voice almost that of a young starlet. "I'm Ciguapa."

How poetically apt to find a damsel in

distress called *how beautiful*. Her Cuban name played on my mind and became part of the riddle of my fascination. Many South American names are chosen from magical myths. Ciguapa is the name of mythical creature supposedly a wild and deceitful woman who was far from innocent. Had she chosen her own name? My curiosity intensified till my mind had room for only one thought, I must see her again.

xxx

Oct 6, 1956.

On Sunday the air was clear, the sky as blue as the sea as I hovered near Ciguapa's gate. As this Renaissance beauty emerged, I thought she could have stepped out of a sixteenth century painting or the pages of Dante. She was dressed in a thin flowery outfit that clung about her body the way I'd seen only in films. She was almost beside me before she lifted her head with an inquisitive look. I bowed politely, my heart thudded with desire to be a man yet discomforted by being an inexperienced boy. I managed a gesture of feigned astonishment. "Ah, we meet again. Quite by accident, n'est-pas?"

"A coincidence more likely," she corrected, her green eyes the perfect balance between indifference and appraisal. "Because, you see, an accident just happens, whereas a coincidence is going to happen and does." She took my arm with gentle authority, a gesture that put me in my place and ruled out further introductory chitchat. We walked, arm in arm, mother, and son like film stars in an old movie.

She suggested a drink. "Here, okay?" she asked slipping gracefully into the wicker-backed chair under a colorful maple. Her eyes on me as if I was a most intriguing and desirable man, we

97

lingered through the chilled bottle of white wine she suggested, talking quietly as if we were a longstanding couple. I glanced at the book she'd placed on the table, a textbook on the conflicting theories of Jung and Freud. My curiosity pricked, I asked if she was studying psychology? Just personal interest, she replied, adding she had been married and divorced several times and was curious to know what made people tick. Especially sexually.

I could not believe a woman saying something so trivial could produce an erection. Yet there it was irrefutably and showed little sign of resolution. For an instant it wasn't just her body I wanted to climb into, I wanted to climb inside her mind and know all there was to know about her.

xxx

Oct 7, 1956.

My earliest sexual imagining had always been about an older woman. Someone resourceful and responsible; a powerful, grown-up woman, who would not tell me sex was naughty, but lead me into it, step by step. I am captivated by Tennyson's poem: The Lady of Shalott and the romantic poetry of the Troubadours who worshipped the dual nature of the Virgin Mary and the fierce Mother Goddess of antiquity. Their poems at times refuted human love in preference for the unattainable feminine ideal.

I reproached myself for my foolishness. This older woman was far too worldly. Instinctively she sensed my susceptibility like a shark sensing blood before it attacks. She would eat me for lunch.

That thought did little to calm my desire for a grand amour even after I wrote a poem about the impossibility of a bird and a fish falling in love.

xxx

Oct 23,1956.

After several nights of tormented sleep, I tossed away all restraint and wrote to Ciguapa, to declare my love and ask permission to see her. A few days later in trepidation I received her brief reply:

Dear Arthur, I believe there is no point in continuing our acquaintance. Your interest in me is understandable; but your infatuation is simply the transient passion of a young man much my junior. Ciguapa

xxx

Oct 24,1956.

My feelings, which had not until that moment been fully anchored, took on a force that made the attainment of a name in literature an easy victory compared to success with this witty and gracious woman. I threw caution to the wind and trudged wearily back to her neighborhood, willing to face all obstacles just to speak to her.

She seemed shaken to find me installed on her doorstep and admonished me provocatively, reprimanding me like a child. "You make me feel like someone whose clothes have been stolen while I was out taking a swim. My decision is unshakable." The tone of her voice did little to dissuade me my attentions were misplaced. With a sigh of resignation, she suggested a walk. I reached out to kiss her, but she pulled away disdainfully. "Would you mind telling me how I can avoid this tiresome circle of your interest?"

She explained she was the kept woman of a corpulent, heavyset lawyer, a wealthy man who had set her up royally in an apartment and gave her a monthly allowance. No way would she jeopardize her comfort for a youth without resources. The full implication of this arrangement only dawned on me when on our return she made me duck into the bushes. She'd heard her protector's car coming up the drive. In broken phrases, she'd whispered the man was impotent, the relationship platonic. What else could she say? And I wanted to believe her.

xxx

Nov 18,1956.

Despite my misgivings the rush and blur of my fascination continues. I race through the days, pace, and organize my studies to spend moments with Ciguapa. I had no idea where this might lead until I arrived at her apartment soaked and shivering from the rain that poured down in torrents. She took my hand and led me to her enormous tub where I lay relaxing, the warm water caressing my body. Holding up a large bath towel, her arms outstretched, she whispered that this had nothing to do with anything. It will remain strictly between us. I looked at her with incomprehension. "What I am saying is don't read into this more than this moment. What happens next is our secret. You must agree to whatever I deem fit and pleasurable." She let the towel fall and pressed herself against me, her naked breasts and belly molded into the contours and hollows of my body. Touching her was as intimate as touching the pages of a beloved book, her skin the silky-smooth texture of her youth.

She knelt before me and began a careful stroking as she devoured my sex. Until that moment I had never imagined the pleasure of being passively done to. The girls I dated were too young and inexperienced to attempt oral sex. Despite my delirium I recalled reading somewhere that if a woman sucks that part of a man's body which most defines him as a man, he risks her gaining control

100

over his maleness. In my delirium my maleness meant next to nothing to me.

She carefully wiped her mouth and lay back on her bed, her eyes closed; her pale skin untouched by the sun seemed not quite real, more like that of an underwater creature that had been pulled up from the depth of the sea. She arched submissively beneath me as she welcomed me into her body, soft and yielding like touching flour dough. Tremors passed through me and left me almost breathless as I lost myself in this erotic oneness.

I remember nothing of the act, nothing except my subordinate role and being completely carried away by the physical delight of the flesh. Perhaps a less urgent and more experienced lover might have avoided coming so quickly, might have avoided collapsing on her chest after the longed-for relief. I did not spell it out to myself—her poised indifference freed me to pursue my own pleasure. No doubt it suited my sexual ignorance, a more demanding woman may well have inhibited me.

She'd wiggled away from under me and took a bath. With a sigh she retired to a chair and opened a book reminding me of women in medieval paintings chastely untouched. In my delirium, I struggled for words to express the oneness I felt through her and with her. "You are the fulfillment of my yearnings, of my deepest desire, you are my angel, my Beatrice, and my Virgin Mary. Was it as amazing for you as it was for me?"

She replied in an unemotional tone: "Sex is something that has never mattered to me. Your pleasure is my pleasure. It is receiving your love and knowing that you care for me is what I desire."

Her reply hit me like an icy blast, each word

filled me with crushing anxiety which I could not begin to fathom. And yet if in her offering me her body without pleasure was not what I'd hoped for, for the moment it was everything I thought I could ever want.

This is where his journal ended which was frustrating. The subsequent journal that should have followed had obviously been packed off to Belgium with his other possessions and that left a gap of more than two years.

Jan 20, 1958:

Ciguapa, this woman twice my age has changed red to green and has banished sexual frustrations. She intertwines Eros with our sacred spiritual union. Despite her assurance that she cares little for sex, I continued to be assailed by fears that my inexperience prevents her from having pleasure. Tormented by confused pride, I am fixated by the idea of arousing her, giving her pleasure, lighting up her body, zone by zone. She tries her best to be a good sport, and patiently humors me. She admonished me as if I am a child. "Although I may possess an active sense of humor it does not extend to my accepting your slobbering over my body. Take your pleasure and forget about me."

xxx

Feb 28, 1958.

This evening I stood gazing at her as she lay on the bed, one arm behind her head, a taffeta wrapper draped casually about her thighs, a pose I found almost indecent. As I ran my fingers along her thigh, she lashed out and struck me hard across the mouth. Stunned by her sudden brutality my mind reeled in confusion.

"I shall punish you for your persistence," she said. "I shall have you on your knees for your

102

audacity. In the future, you will submit to my will. The more you submit, the greater will be your joy and mine—it's a simple equation. Undress and lie on the bed."

When I hesitated, she struck me with a riding crop that had miraculously appeared in her hand. She lashed my arms and legs to the four-poster bed, checking my movements before she tightened the ropes. The smell of sandalwood and the carnal swish of her taffeta wrapper brushing against me awakened memories of a childhood erotic secret. I had seen a man jerking up and down over my mother. That illicit sight had not only confused me but detonated a grenade of tangled guilt in my brain. Excitement mixed with fear for having seen the forbidden created the irrational belief that I should be punished. Later the mystery unraveled but that did not end my fascination for a certain type of theatrical sadomasochism.

"I'm sorry I have to do this, but you need a lesson in discipline: you don't listen, you don't obey." She struck my naked body in rapid stinging blows; her mercilessness sent a frisson of trepidation through me, bewildering me with dizzy conflicting and disconnected emotions. She scrutinized my reaction; almost a sacrilegious examination of how I was taking this.

I tried to rise which seemed to enrage her, and she gave me a sharp kick with the pointed toe of her boot. "Are you saying stop to me? You'll suffer for your insolence." I bit back a cry of pain, even as my body yielded with the desire of a willing submissive. Flagellation stimulated my brain with ancient fantasies as did the idea of a powerful *femme fatal* vampirizing me. She followed those slaps with a few sensuous caresses which sent warm tingling sensations through my limbs and my insolent penis grew attentive. She struck my rigid member in a succession of quick sharp smacks almost bring me to orgasm. "I don't remember giving you permission for that. This is punishment, not pleasure. Are you going to stop all this nonsense and obey me?"

"Yes, yes." My tone may have sounded impertinent to her ears and perhaps a little too demanding for she flicked her hand across my sex, a light, admonitory smack, as if it were my penis, not me, being impudent. She poured oil on her latex gloves and grasped the tip of my penis which she stroked rhythmically while smacking my testicles sharply, making me jump and jerk as they emptied.

Once untied and tucked under the covers, Ciguapa surprised me with a smile; a smile one gives the afflicted. Afflicted I might well be. Certainly, my ecstatic pleasure in flagellation caused a tingling sensation to sweep through my groin. It made a mockery of my perverse desire for sainthood although the saints frequently indulged in physical punishment and self-flagellation. I reached down and touched myself surprised to find I had an erection. In panic I withdrew my hand as if my mother had smacked me.

Arthur said Ciguapa had at first seemed to enjoy treating him as one might a pet, a nuisance but useful in his way. Step by step she had taken him over, demanded that he give up his flawed self to her. She had forbidden him to look at other women as they walked down the street, and not to drink if she was absent. She controlled what he ate by making him packed lunches whenever he dined out with friends. Yeah, dear reader I hear you asking, why would a man, supposedly in his right mind, accept such manipulation, such dictatorship?

You might be thinking this is not simply passion gone wrong, but a repeat of his childhood when he'd had to tiptoe through a minefield of craziness. When life with Ciguapa became impossible, rather than leave he'd simply taken to hiding the larger kitchen knives and bolting his bedroom door at night.

xxx

My own parents had occasionally inflicted violence on me, but they were more inclined to use brutal honesty as an indispensable parenting tool to keep me undernourished in confidence and supposedly, ha-ha, controllable. Tactless remarks or passive aggression delivered in the face of innocent hopefulness, is a type of comedy that dates back to the ancient Greeks—amusing only in hindsight. My mother had a habit of saying: "Why don't you smarten yourself up, be normal, wear dresses? Be like other girls?" Yeah, like don't be that girl growing into a rebellious woman disappearing into the hills dressed in your brother's jeans. No way was I going to explain to a person who had never read Dostoevsky or Kafka, why I dressed the way I did. Nor why I called myself an Existentialist even though I hardly knew what that word meant. My mother would simply have called me a *Miss Know-it-All*. Yeah, I wanted to be a Miss Know-it-All, at least to be a big thinker to compensate for the fact that I was the smallest and youngest and most insignificant person in my school class.

When I did occasionally dress up in the hope, she would say I looked pretty, she would shake her head as if it was an effort without results. Even if I made a new outfit, she would raise her eyebrows, and shrug. "I don't happen to think it worth it, but I pray I'm wrong." As painful as these dismissals were, I persisted. Finally asked her point blank why she never said anything complimentary. "You are stuck up enough already." Stuck up? Good God, it was more the opposite.

My father had a habit of ridding himself of trauma by generously bequeathing it to his children. When he accidently ran over his dog, he said, "I cared more for that dog than I did for any of my children." Yeah, the sort of thing he might say to hit us in the face with a dead dog. And true to form the only remark he ever made about my success was a put down of Hudson. "Katherine makes more money than you." The perfect script to squash two toads in three easy lessons without the kiss. Quite a laugh to get praised for creatively filling my bank account, when what I wanted to do was stick it to my parents by my amazing talent.

A friend of mine, a famous writer, said he'd had a similar comedy lesson when he'd visited his father on his deathbed. Knowing his father was a jerk, he nevertheless hoped for some recognition of his own accomplishments: "So, Dad, I guess I surprised you by becoming a successful novelist." His father had answered, "Sure, but if you had become a doctor, I could have been proud of you." Wonders never cease.

I reread Arthur's autobiography, then searched through the discarded yellowing drafts which confirmed his fictionalized autobiography was only a more poetic, version of his brief happy years with Ciguapa before they curdled. As I picked through the papers one discarded sheet caught my eye.

Oct 4, 2002.

> This intense attraction I feel for Katherine is not the sort of *coup de foudre* I felt for Ciguapa; not the all-consuming violent, destructive passion that often made me feel suicidal. Having been seduced at a young age by stories founded in the great works of literature, my tender heart had been swallowed up by my beloved Ciguapa. With a voluptuous sense of abandonment, I'd given myself completely to this maternally indulgent woman who corresponded to my erotic fantasies. She was my goddess, my lethal angel, a character from the French poet François Villon who'd crept into a Chagall painting. Her endless repetitions, "You are my destiny—you are the love of my life," made me feel unique, invincible, and infinitely lovable. I had been both exultant and gratified by my passionate conquest, which combined not only the affinities of romance and incest but also the fierce opposites of the erotic and spiritual. For years I walked her path, wallowed

in her spiritual nature. She was my fate, and I was hers. I adored her as the troubadours adored perfect-yet-doomed love.

Ciguapa freed me from my belief sex was sinful when she stroked my sex and brought me to orgasm in a cathedral as I prayed. Eros and spiritual union as incarnated in God's cosmic love for man released me from guilt. I did not feel the perversity of the act only its holiness as pertaining to the mystical and the sensual. I had tremble with religious awe as I had trembled when taught to drink deeply the sense of God in my first communion.

Was it because I was not a Catholic that I found this perverse act in a cathedral incomprehensible. Why, with the heavenly father and angels hovering above, did he believe this perverse act released him from his guilt that sex was sinful? Mind-boggling to say the least as is Ciguapa, a Catholic developing a passion for Christian evangelist Billy Graham. No doubt that was a trial for Arthur but surely nothing compared to sleeping with the enemy as he does with Patasola. How can he tolerate her belief that it is Hitler will come back to save the world

xxx

My growing up in a small town with a mishmash of varying branches of Protestantism, Scientology, Seventh Day Adventist, Holly Rollers, and Catholics, had made me curious about all religions. It had more or less turn me into an Atheist which I classified as a non-*prophet* organization. My questions about religion often hit dry earth, like trying to find a proverbial needle in the entire field vacant of haystacks. No way would they let me get away with saying the Garden of Eden is a male fabrication little more than poetic hog wash. Instantly some religious fanatic wanted to strike me dead as doubting Thomas. Mark Twain got it right when he said: *Man is the only animal that loves his neighbor as himself and cuts his throat, if his theology isn't straight.* Canadians hicks can be as hypersensitive to questioning the bible, as rednecks from the American corn belt. The general reaction was: "Fifteen-year-old girls ain't got no right askin' them there questions and bein' all weird. No, sir, ain't right!"

When one ignorant fool told me women weren't mentioned in history because they had no souls, I asked, "Is that so? And why wouldn't we have souls as well as dicks with pricks?" That solicited peevish reproofs from my mother but mostly her objections were due to my language. Surprisingly, she more or less agreed when I said, "God somewhat overestimated his ability when he created man."

"Men made God in their own image and women don't get to choose in this unequal world. They become slaves of any man who manages to put a ring on our finger."

Nov. 20, 2020

Dear Arthur,

Rereading your autobiography would help you gain more insight into how you are blindly repeating your neurotic passion in another fantasy of sexual and spiritual insanity. Your autobiography is both dark, and erotic and it will surely live on as a brilliant demonstration of a muddled brain pursuing passion without reflection. The punch line in this recent adventure is not completely comparable to your love for Ciguapa, a woman with at least some intelligence and education. This present passion is more a last-minute gag likely to end badly.

When I first read your autobiography, many years ago I missed the phrase that would have alerted me to your deceptive nature: *The coincidence of this veneration of woman with the thrill of deception set the burlesque stage for my erotic adventures.* I'd simply thought it a cleverly fictionalized book, both self-aware, and revealing. Recently re-reading it I thought it was not only a cleverly written book, but a book written by a messed-up guy submerged in a neurotic passion. A demonstration of a mind driven by neurosis and uncontrolled confusion. On the third reading, I realized your protagonist could have stepped out of Robert Louis Stevenson, Dr Jekyll/Mr. Hyde. Dr Jekyll, the caring non-confrontational Petite Prince who represses his true nature in order to be loved and Mr. Hyde your out-of-control Billy Goat driven by sheer physical appetite and lust. You could now write a sequel, a follow-up autobiography dealing with your continual addictive behavior. It could be just as brilliant, tangled, and insane as your first autobiography.

Katherine

Chapter 10

*How does it feel/How does it feel
To be on your own/With no direction home
Like a complete unknown/Like a rolling stone?*
Bob Dylan

Karen Moller

Before the 1960s' and our incomplete female emancipation it was unusual for a young girl, with few savings and a small scholarship to takeoff for France. I mean who the hell would be so optimistic as to believe all would work out for the best when I wasn't even able to speak French? Needless to say, people were helpful. Jacob, an American student I'd met on the boat to France, mentioned the rat-infested Beat Hotel, a cheap rooming house full of eye-popping alternative culture, within walking distance of my college. Madame Rachou the owner had worked at an inn frequented by painters Claude Monet and Camille Pissarro and become fond of artists. She now acted as a sort of mother figure to poet Allen Ginsburg and writer William Burroughs, as well as to many poverty-stricken foreigners. Jacob thought it unlikely Madame Rachou would take a girl under her wing, but she might rent me a room. "Just keep your door locked at night; there are lots of weirdoes living there." Hayseed as I was, weirdoes weren't something I'd been worrying about until he mentioned it.

My first impression of the hotel was disturbing. The structure sagged over the street like an old woman's belly ready to collapse. There was no name on the glass door or any sign of a front desk, only a wooden bar in the large rectangular room where groups of people crowded around marble topped tables, talking in loud voices as if it was a club. The sharp-eyed, diminutive landlady hopped down from behind the bar. "Looking for a room? I rent by the month. Payable in advance." She said lifting a key from the board and beckoning me to follow. Humping my case up the stairs in her wake, my nostrils were assaulted by the smell of food cooking, leaking drains and Gauloise cigarettes while my ears took in the multiple conversations emanating from various rooms. The third floor was in darkness, the bulb long since died, according to Madam Rachou. "Been meaning to change it."

After the cash exchange, she'd said fix it up as you like and leave your passport. "For them police, they'll be checking." She'd sighed, "Always checking, always something. Can't leave a body in peace."

It seemed Paris was still suffering the deprivations of the war or that I had stepped back into the Middle Ages. The room was so grubby, and so unlike my dream of a romantic, cozy artist's attic, my spirits fell. It was sparsely furnished: a single bed with a sagging mattress set at an odd angle that prevented the door from opening completely, a solitary chair and a rickety table. The wardrobe in the corner gave the impression of a looming thief about to pounce. It stank of mothballs and vibrated a melancholy chime when I pulled it open. A small alcove with a cracked floor served as a kitchenette. No heating, no refrigerator or stove, only an alcohol burner, and cement sink with a cold-water faucet. Moldy patches covered the yellowing wallpaper. Damp air seeped through the cracks of a soot-flecked window that overlooked the tortured roof tops and chimney pots. I wondered how people managed without refrigerators until I discovered the vendors in open-air markets readily sliced off single portions of just about everything—for people like me with few comforts or mod-cons.

My spirits only lifted when I opened the door to Woody who was smiling shyly. He reassured me authors like Albert Camus and Welsh poet Dylan Thomas had imbued the world with amazing words while shut away in dwellings much like this. And painters Van Gogh and Modigliani had painted their masterpieces in places slightly worse.

However, nothing could be worse than the toilet, the only one on a floor for several rooms. The light went on when a slide bolted the door, an arrangement that might well have killed an unsuspecting person if they'd touched it with wet hands. Apparently, that problematic arrangement saved a few francs on electricity, which I soon learned was a priority for the French. Toilet paper readily available in other countries was virtually nonexistent, unless you had a friend who had access to stores provisioning American service families in France. I wasn't surprised to learn the rich had bidets, a special basin for washing their privates while the poor kept a stick with a cloth on the end in a pot of vinegar beside the toilet. People cut old newspaper into squares and attached them to a crude hook that protruded dangerously from the wall. These toilets were for some reason called Turkish toilets. They had two raised areas for feet above the hole where water from the cast-iron cistern cascaded down soaking one's feet if one wasn't quick to step out into the corridor after pulling the chain.

These toilets which populated almost all cheap hotels, cafés and restaurants were often frightful, smelly, damp holes in courtyards or off winding stairs. If they had lights, they were on timers that often shut off unexpectedly, leaving one stranded. The main character in Jean Genet's novel, *Our Lady of the Flowers,* a book he wrote while in prison after being condemned for being a homosexual and petty criminal, gives the most perfect description of his protagonist Darling endlessly searching through Paris for a decent sit-down toilet where he could have a comfortable shit.

My initial disappointment in the hotel dissipated as soon as I set off the next morning to enjoy my adventure. As I headed down rue Racine's narrow cobblestoned street to check out my college, I was thrilled to come across Hôtel des Étrangers where the poets Rimbaud and Verlaine, and the soon to be famous literary figures, known as the Circle of Poets Zutiques, had hung out. Once I'd decided my future was in France, I'd become a compulsive reader of France's great novelists. Particularly nineteenth century: Balzac, Stendhal, and Zola just to name a few.

The history of that period after France lost the Franco-Prussian war in 1871 fascinated me. The government had been voted out of office and the Commune, a sort of loosely united anarchist community, seized power and took over the organization of Paris and its workshops. As usual with French revolutions it failed dismally due to infighting, disunity, and incompetent leadership. The ex-government in Versailles tried to starve Parisians into submission before sending in the military months later to massacred more than ten thousand people in a day. Anyone with black hands was suspected of making bombs and immediately shot. When things settled down, the military realized they had killed every single chimney sweep in Paris. Not something to laugh about. Revolutions in France (the two

Napoleons excluded) have always left the country floundering in its wake with little benefit to anyone, and that includes the French Revolution of 1789.

After eight months my art studies were concluded I began my hunt for a job. I made a visit to the flea market in search of secondhand couture to create a special look – a break from my usual existential outfit – a black turtleneck, black skirt, and black tights. In that closely packed area of the flea market, on the outskirts of Paris the merchants had looked me up and down, surprised as to why anyone not poor would want to buy a second-hand outfit even if it was Chanel.

The next day full of confidence in my Bakst inspired creation, a colorful bias-cut, crepe-de-chine blouse, a tailored bolero jacket and high-waisted palazzo pants I'd set off to the couture house, of Emanuel Ungaro in Avenue Montagne, my portfolio under my arm. A stroll past that couture house had always been one of my favorite walks. I didn't ask myself if I liked Ungaro's designs; I thought the colorful flowing dresses, with their unique elegant touches were the ultimate in glamour. Emanuel's color sense was phenomenal, but more intriguing was how he rendered street vibrations to fit the elegant parameters of his couture house. I trembled with anxiety by the time I'd climbed the wide marble staircase to the first-floor showroom, all the while encouraging myself it was better to fail than not to try. In a hushed tone I asked the receptionist: "May I please show my portfolio to Mr. Ungaro?"

The dark-haired prima donna looked me up and down, not once but twice with an air of disdain. "We are not taking on anybody at the moment."

Just then a distinguished-looking man with a finely carved face and gentle air passed the desk. "You want to show me your portfolio?" With a wave of his hand, he ushered me into a showroom filled with racks of beautiful floating evening gowns in fabulous fabrics. The stylish decoration, gold chairs and white carpet thoroughly intimidated me and made me question how I had the audacity to come and ask for a job. René Ungaro introduced himself, glanced through my portfolio then disappeared to the adjoining room. A few minutes later he reappeared and introduced me to a dark Spanish-looking woman of indefinable age, Sonia Knot, the artistic director. She flipped through the portfolio, made a brief nod then bid me good day. René Ungaro said he could only offer me an apprenticeship. It didn't pay much but after six months perhaps a more permanent position. "When could you start?"

I trembled but managed to say anytime. I'd run back to the hotel, my heart pumping, frantic to tell someone my good news, but everyone was either asleep or out scratching for a bit of the ready. I'd gone from shop to shop collecting coins to call my parents till an icy knocking deep in my skull awaken an unpleasant memory which soon became a headache. I'd previously called my parents from Vancouver to tell them I was heading to Europe. My father had refused the 25-cent reversed charge call. His being more concerned about saving 25 cents than hearing from me had generated a palpable chill in my soul. Not unlike his reaction when I'd won the Alberta Arts Scholarship: "I'll need proof of that!" We forgive families endlessly but my father's refusal to pay 25 cents to hear from me and his lack of few words of congratulation for winning a scholarship could not easily be forgiven.

I took a seat in my favorite café and with my handful of cash I ordered a Pernod. It tasted better than I remembered so I ordered another. Soon I was quite drunk, the headache and heartache only a vague memory

I arrived Monday morning at Ungaro's workroom at seven, just as the sun began to light up the streets of Paris. A row of tables ran across the full length of the room from a wall lined with dress patterns cut in heavy brown paper and hooked on rods. They hung next to wooden racks of sample dresses in brightly colored fabrics. No one took any notice of me, until to my relief, I was given a job cutting swatches of different colored fabrics to attach to dress samples.

Everyone wanted to be Emanuel Ungaro's favorite, and we all scramble to please him. It was truly scary the way he could light up a person or destroyed them with a look. When he smiled, which he did occasionally, it was like turning your face to the sun on a balmy day. Emanuel pulled everyone into his personal vision. René put the collection together while running around smoothing ruffled feathers and apologizing for

Emanuel, who was kind of detached, self-absorbed, completely unaware that we are helping to create the collection.

It was a wonder I was not schizophrenic living on two different planets—both divorced from everyday normality. My days were spent in an industry where fortunes were made daily and lavish parties thrown on a grand scale, with muses, models, and designers all stars of this superficial world. My nights were spent in a flea bag hotel with poor artists and writers, misfits, and nonconformists. Few inhabitants in the Beat Hotel had a regular job so I was known as "madam normal" while the studio called me "our little mascot", teasing me that I'd been hired for my fancy duds, as much as for my portfolio because Rene had said, "We need a mad little bohemian like you hopping about the place and giving us ideas even if we can't always use them."

My first contact with the intense throng of uneasy, suppressed aggression characteristic of fashion shows was when Emanuel Ungaro presented the new collection. We were all in a state of hyperexcitation, egging each other on in a chaotic manner. The next day I'd collected the press cutting which quoted Ungaro as saying: "I live my life around women. They liberate me and trigger my imagination, it's for them I invent and create." *Figaro* said: "Ungaro has an unfailing ability to come up with a surprisingly innovative line, fresh and inspirational every season." The *New York Times'* critic had been even more favorable: "Ungaro's new collection is the purest, most coherent, expression of his style. It is colorful and assured; it synthesizes everything he holds dear: floating sensuality, ultra-femininity, all effortlessly wearable."

I had fallen for a dress on the reject rack; a silvery outfit that glows against my skin. Outfits that did not go into the line were sold off cheaply, well sort of cheaply. After paying a small amount of money weekly, the dress was mine. When on occasion, I joined my fellow worker on a special night out that dress made me feel I could pass for a worldly sophisticate.

Among my friends I often hung out with a painter who gave me the tingly feeling my common sense had deserted me. The French ban on contraceptives and my own ignorance of French contraceptive methods made it likely I would fall pregnant which is exactly what has happened. Good girls are bad girls who never get caught so they say. My being caught turned the planets, stars, and whatever upside down. Gloria Steinem's feminist formula: *A liberated woman is one who has sex before marriage and a job.* With French laws banning contraception she should have included *and only a child if she has an apartment.*

Just as autumn burst into Indian summer, I rented a small apartment near Place de la Contrescarpe, so named for its proximity to the exterior wall of Medieval Paris. It was still a cheap area where age and generations had worked its will on Medieval structures, transforming and disfiguring them, but they had endured in their patched and splendid state. In the 1930s, Ernest Hemingway, James Joyce and George Orwell had found cheap lodgings in la Contrescarpe area where various medieval buildings hung ominously over the curving streets around the church of Sainte-Geneviève and rue Mouffetard.

Baudelaire the nineteen-century poet had considered the Place de la Contrescarpe disreputable, yet he rented a room in the disreputable Beat Hotel, where he wrote his lyric poems *Les Fleurs du Mal.* The poems were banned for almost a hundred years because they criticized the town planner Haussmann for knocking down many of Paris's rougher areas and virtually rebuilding the Paris we now know and love.

Before my departure from the Beat Hotel, I invited some of the writers, painters and odd balls living there to have a last night drink with me in the bar. Despite the usual aggressive undercurrents floating around in the tobacco fumes and wine swilling, the party soon melted into pleasant confusion. When one of the blank-faced girls in existential black had asked if I would miss them, I realized I had a slight tinge of regret.

I pulled out my sketch book curious see what I had written about my being fired from Ungaro.

Dec 14, 1964.

> Today, two weeks before the probable birth date of my child, I was denounced and called to the administration office. I managed to disguise my pregnant state till then, partly due to unintentionally not gaining much weight and my

learning to walk as if I was not carrying a bundle on my belly. Perhaps people enjoy showing off their big bellies, but my aim was to keep my job for as long as possible.

Mister Baldy regarded me over his glasses perched on the end of his large nose. "You've put us in a difficult position. You should be ashamed of yourself being with child and unmarried," he said while furtively glancing at my belly, obviously trying to see my bump.

"Why a disgrace? It is how every human begins life. I am pregnant due to lack of contraceptives but still able to work."

"It's an unwritten rule, women do not continue to work when pregnant!"

"It's not a law." My disagreeing unsettled him, and he drew himself up and stated in a self-righteous tone. "I'd like to get through this as civilly as possible."

"Really?" I said without trying to hide my distain for this unworthy representative of male officiousness. 'I am being fired? On what grounds?"

"I think you know."

"Educate me." I leaned forward, eyeing him closely, deciding God must love stupid people since he made so many of them. "Being pregnant and unwed is no disgrace particularly in France. There are hundreds of thousands of couples with children who have never married. It is not as if I have a contagious disease, I don't have the flu. No one will catch having a baby from me." I like a laugh, but I was not trying to amuse. "I've yet to hear someone say a man can't combine children with a career. Do unmarried men get fired when they are about to become fathers?"

"Are you crazy? Mister Baldly suddenly

shrieked obviously at the end of his patience. "What? What are you talking about?"

"About equality. Equal treatment. It's hypothetical. If an unwed woman gets fired for being pregnant, so should the unwed man get fired if his partner becomes pregnant."

"Our code of conduct does not allow for this sort of thing. You need to sign this paper, then leave." He slapped down the termination notice in front of me.

Look here, I might say to you if we were sitting in a café having a glass of wine, I recognize the recklessness with which I approached both my own life and that of my young daughter. But is it not far better to embrace one's dreams, than to have a mother who blames her husband and children for depriving her of a more fulfilling life? Sure, at times I feel guilty for not giving Sarah a more normal life, *if there is such a thing as normal*, certainly mine wasn't. Let's just say I hoped my love would compensated for my being a single mother living an unconventional life.

I had enjoyed the companionship of my fellow workers and appreciated the kindness of René Ungaro. In no way did I blame anyone in particular for the administration's illegal treatment. Employment rules, which weren't rules, were about to change and become more humane, but we weren't there yet. France's liberalizing laws were far behind England. Then in the 1970s when they did a turnabout and surpassed all other countries by lifting bans on selling contraception pills and on abortion. More amazing they installed an amazing system of day care and nurseries for working women, married or unmarried and maternity schools for 3-6-year-olds.

I thought Sarah was born beautiful and grew more beautiful with each passing year—beautiful enough to stop a bull in its tracks. Her gracious face on her nervous, muscular body is still arresting enough to be considered surreal. When I first held her tiny body in my arms, my bottled-up love burst forth for that little creature which created powerful bond that will always be there. Amid tears of relief and joy, I made a vow to love her unconditionally and give her the kind of love I'd never been given. I am sure when she looked into the faces of her own babies, she didn't have to make all the radical promises I made, except perhaps not to let them be a wild child, running riot like her own mother.

Chapter 11

Like a bird on the wire
Like a drunk in a midnight choir
I have tried in my way to be free
Leonard Cohen

Arthur's memory is not only bad but selective. He has long forgotten his difficult childhood and tends to look back on his past with fondness. I am not so forgiving. Perhaps that is because of being virtually excluded from the family, in fact I'd even say abandoned. I had little contact with my mother until near my fortieth birthday, when I received a telegram saying she was unwell and wanted to see me. Like, really?

Matrophobia is the official word for the dread of becoming one's mother. I never wanted my mother's life; if anything, I actively unwanted it. I was more the ungrateful daughter trying to become me, while my mother mostly wanted me to be, not me. And yet I had not stopped hankering for some sort of reconciliation to ease the unrequited ache that lingered like a tooth that has never been looked after; difficult to pull out but painful to leave in place.

"It's not going to happen," Woody said. "Your mother is about to leave the wreckage of her life with you still fingering your scars. Only Disney movies have happy endings."

Yeah, real dumb. The past was not dead—it was still living with me.

Sarah accompanied me on that forty-two-hour trip back to that remote area in Canada. When the taxi dropped us off at the family farm, I was surprised the farmhouse looked much larger than I'd remembered—more imposing but showing its age and beginning to sag with neglect. My reflection in the glass-fronted door dumfounded me: the *Ugly Duckling* had acquired beauty, style, and wealth, and been transformed into a sophisticated Parisian glamourpuss. I'd found my family of swans and lived happily ever after until I didn't. But then I am getting ahead of myself—we will come to that later.

"Hello there!" someone said from the porch. A rather small, round woman sat in the shadows, her face screwed up half in concern, half in relief. "Been waiting for you. Weren't sure when you'd arrive. Wish I could say your mom was better."

We both stood there awkwardly, while I scrutinized the woman, unable to identify anything familiar.

"I was your teacher, fifth grade. I wouldn't have recognized you either."

"Been a while," I said, suddenly remembering the bully who had made that year of school unbearable. I wondered how she felt about her rebellious student, who she had tried to crush, having excelling in an international career while her own kids had completely screwed up.

I dropped my bag and pushed open my mother's bedroom door. The floor swayed, seemed about to come up to meet me as I took in the shrunken form of an old and harried woman, her pending death evident in her bewildered eyes.

"You better sit down before you drop. You look like something the cat dragged in." I slipped into a chair and rolled my eyes, unprepared for this reception, yet relieved she still had enough spirit to insult me. "I haven't finished with life," she continued with a bitter laugh looking down at her shapeless body. "I imagined better, perhaps even a miracle. At least something to lift me out of the ordinary. Now I am about to die."

I put out my hand in an automatic gesture of comfort, then caught myself, believing my mother shrank from my touch. The movement was so slight perhaps I only imagined it. I shoved my hands in my pockets not knowing what else to do with them, secretly wishing I was on a sunny beach under palm trees rather than in this pageant of a not happening reconciliation. And as true to life that no cats wear pajamas, there was no reconciliation.

After the funeral I roamed forlornly about the house with Sarah trying to comfort me. It was years since my father died yet the place remained encrusted with both their lives. The fridge was full of things that didn't belong, pens, papers, and last month's post. I picked up objects and put them down at random. I opened my mother's photograph album of long-dead ancestors, their roots on both sides of the ocean: my great grandfather having fled militarized Germany; my Scottish great grandmother having fled religious persecution. While my bourgeois Danish father had taken off for Canada on a whim.

I flipped through the photos from 1961 when my parents had stopped off in Paris, on their visit to Denmark. They had insisted, despite their numerous pieces of luggage, on taking the metro to the hotel. My mother's attempt to sit on one of the wooden pull-downs, metro seats, without holding it down meant she ended up on the floor. Everyone stared. Well, they always stare in Paris. But the smirk on their faces was not for the old lady I was helping off the floor, it was for the Balzacian comedy of a young girl trying to pass myself off as Parisian until her country parents came to town.

When I'd joined my parents for breakfast the next morning, I realized they had been discussing me. My father, with a critical look, said he had been very embarrassed in the metro because people saw him as an old guy with a young ... He didn't actually say whore but the comment that followed made it obvious. "Only whores wear eye make-up." A quick glance around Paris would have confirmed he was going blind or else convinced him all Parisian women were whores. Yeah, right. I couldn't help laughing.

Were my parents shocked by the state of my hotel? Of course, they were. My room and acquaintances hardly up to bourgeois standards even if they were hardly now up to bourgeois standards themselves. My father called the hotel a den of iniquity likely full of drug addicts. He got that about right. After they had climbed the rickety three floors of crooked and broken tiles, amid odd cooking odors mixed with the smell of marijuana and leaking drains, he could easily have called it something worse.

Let me ask you this: after seeing my living conditions, border line poverty with no mod coms or comfort, wouldn't any normal well-to-do parents offer a little financial help to their daughter who was working for a world-famous couture house on an apprentice's minimum wage? Not on your fanny they didn't. All my father said was, "I will pay your fare home to prevent you from doing something you will regret." Like what? Hanging out as a gangster moll to beardo, weirdo drug addicts, or a more likely scenario, selling my wares as a whore? I bit my tongue t rather than the bullet. With their low opinion of my talents, I should have said I was probably not cute enough or talented enough to even be a whore!

After the funeral I continued wandering around this house which had once been my home. My mother's diaries sat on the mantelpiece, a booby prize, a tempting dare to be read. Some had fabric covers with lined pages; others were scotched together with dates taped to the spine. I poured myself a large glass of wine and sat down on the sofa to read what she had written.

> *My mother's family wasn't eminent, they were ambitious frontiersmen who wore pelts and spent much of their time talking to God and trying to avoid being mauled by bears. Daddy often said, "America is a promise, an opportunity, a place where the earth belongs to the free-spirited, to those who refuse to be bound down by bigotry or bureaucracy." He never doubted that was the way things should have been, but they never were. He died a disillusioned man.*
>
> *The 1930s convinced me Communists were victims. Revolution was needed. I wanted drama, red flags waving, and big ideas with good people marching to mend the world. Communists were victims who suffer from injustice just as women suffer for being females in a man's world. I wanted to be a writer, at least to work with people who liked books. The depression killed all my hopes, left me only domestic jobs: scrubbing floors or serving meals. The boarding house where I worked brought me a husband with grand dreams which were never more than dreams. I wanted things nice, pictures on the wall, bookcases filled with books. Is it a crime to want to wear pearls and hats and to be married to a great man? Life must contain more than dreary sameness.*
>
> *The first few years and Hudson's birth, things settled - too settled for Dad perhaps. Children are a comfort, but they leave, and your life is gone with them! Hudson is clever, moving from one project to another. Katherine is besotted by books and wanting to know what is in them. A mischievous impossible*

*child who thinks "don't" means "I dare you". She
storms off in a huff, slamming doors when thwarted.
She gave me quite a surprise, becoming financially
successful despite her lack of talent.*

I'd rolled my eyes at my mother's arrogance. Why would an
artistically uneducated woman, whose smarts obviously fell
short of being smart, think she could judge talent? Foolish
people can sometimes be destructive and her telling me at a
young age that I had no talent was the sort of judgmental crap
that could have seared itself into my young mind and destroyed
all chance of artistic success. Only parents insensitive to a child's
fragility could be so irresponsible. I never reproached my father
for not paying for my education nor my mother for not
defending me. That would have been like trying to get an
apology out of an orangutan. Success in the fashion world is
often ephemeral yet despite my obvious success as a designer
year after year, getting my mother to change her opinion about
my talent would have been like hacking away at a freezer with a
screwdriver to unblock her gummed-up prejudice.

Many of my girlfriends have similar stories, and often
theirs beat mine. But none beat my selfish badass brother and
younger sister rushing in and dividing up the family trinkets
between themselves even before my mother's funeral was over.
I could well image such selfishness from my sister, but not my
brother. The Jerry Lewis laugh was my brother *suggesting I take
the broken bowl they had both fought over.*

As I plodded wearily through my mother's journal I came
to an unexpected sentence: *Girls will always live out the
unfulfilled dreams of the mother, even if they don't know what
those dreams are. Inevitably the daughter's accomplishments
will humiliate the mother for her own failure.* It seemed unlikely
my mother had come to that conclusion on her own! Yet having
copied the phrase made me question if she really believed I was
living her unfulfilled life. Secretly I hoped my success had
brought her some sort of secondhand sense of accomplishment
for having produced a daughter capable of flying to the moon.
Well not exactly, but at least capable of living her own dream.

Common sense is genius dressed in its working clothes

which means success is often just a matter of hard work, determination and passionately owning your own vision. Sarah commented that my belief in her potential—that she could accomplish anything she put her mind to had been a great boost to her confidence. However, she thought that didn't work out too well with other people. My belief in them was initially encouraging but they usually ended up resenting me when they couldn't accomplish what I thought they could.

The death of my mother was a wakeup call. It made me rethink my own career. Creating for others had meant compromising my intuition and initiatives to avoid stepping out of the image already established by various fashion companies I'd worked for. I decided to leave the seductive corporate realm since I now had the finances to create my own collection according to my own criteria no need to ask an uncaring father to be rental guarantor. Nor did I have a mother waiting to say "I told you so" if I failed.

It's a joke that the French have no word for entrepreneur, but I am convinced that they actually hate them. Their rules cripple start-ups with laws and taxes as unhelpful as a bucket without a mop. They just don't get that entrepreneurs are people with the courage to take off in a dinghy in the hope of ending up with a boat substantial enough to conquer new oceans.

Despite French endless complications, my boutique opened in September to flattering comments in the press: "The outfits are perfect for the newly emancipated working woman: The soft wrap around jersey dresses in swirling abstracts and optical prints have just the right touch of sensuality to get one through the afternoon, yet prefect for disco dancing later. The collection includes floor length coats and jumpsuits in whimsical prints in delicately spiced colors of dusty pinks and faded greens. They are bound to be hot sellers."

The department stores, alert to the potential of the youth market, began to send out wholesale buyers to raid boutiques and buy up stocks. It became hard to keep the sample clothes on the mannequins which meant frequent trips to Como to order more fabrics. I'd been a regular visitor to those various Italian print houses, but now as owner/designer, the male stylists looked me over in obvious puzzlement. Finally, one asked, "Where is your husband?"

I'd gazed at him a few seconds wondering the point of his question. "Do I look married?"

"You mean you don't work for your husband!" he exclaimed much to my astonishment. Italy, almost the last of the Mohicans in our changing world believed women's brains were too feeble to accomplish anything on their own.

Later when I bumped into my friends Bob and Arnold, I asked them if Italian print houses thought they worked for their wives. "I guess they assume one of us is the wife," Arnold said waving his hand in a delicate manner he winked at me. "What is most beautiful in virile men is feminine and what is most beautiful in women is masculine, so we've lucked out."

Bob chuckled. "We're off to a reception for Andy Warhol, the current sensation at the moment. This master manipulator of his own limitations is the shaman of kitsch. He is maybe what others think he is; but what that is, he probably doesn't know himself. Meet us later at the gallery, you will love how he outrages people."

I'd always been fascinated by Andy Warhol. An obvious trendsetter and deeply serious avant-garde artist who turned the world upside out and inside down by making himself into a caricature to attracted attention to his art. He didn't invent Pop Art, he simply framed it and by framing it he helped me see the actual crazy pop world we live in. He is unfairly criticized as the influencer of our present superficial world, but he merely predicted the superficiality. Nor is he to blame for the fame-obsessed people who create awful websites that follow the real-life activities of football stars, fashion models and actors as if they are all close friends.

When Andy Warhol wandered into the exhibition, he filled the air around us with the scent of sweet magnolia. He wore a checkered shirt and silver wig of a straw-like texture, adopted, so the myth ran, to create imitations of himself and give the impression he was appearing in many places at once. His 'Gee, that's cool', obviously meant to show shallowness was okay. He seemed uncomfortable with words and spoke as if he was sending short telegrams. With his voice barely above a whisper, it seemed as though the weather was making those telegraphic communications particularly difficult.

Arthur somehow skipped straight from adolescent to middle age never understanding what Andy Warhol represented to the artists of that period. He lived in the poetic past and was never part of youth culture, the Beat period, the hippie times. Being with Ciguapa a woman twice his age Arthur only became part of the avant-garde in Spain at the end of Franco's dictatorship in the late 60/70s when the cultural landscape of Spain shook itself into the modern world.

One of Warhol's hang outs in New York was Studio 54, designed by two well-known theatre set designers who had created a constantly changing environment in an abandoned TV theatre on West 54th Street. The idea was that DJs layered sounds and invented a mind-blowing ambiance for the dysfunctional regulars where they could forget the banalities of daily life and succumb to the disco rituals of dancing amid strobe lighting, and multimedia shows.

On one of my visits to New York, a client invited me to that total other worldly place. A hefty doorman looked us up and down before letting us into the inner sanctum. I am curious to know how doorman judged who they let in. Do they read the who's who gossip columns or go on intuition? No doubt a much-desired job for any man out to screw a lot of women. Apparently, the groupies lined up were ready to lay out to get into the inner sanctum.

At its zenith, Studio 54 was ideal for people-watching. The balcony overlooked the main disco and dance area. All sorts of fashion fantasies and trends were permanently on display, mostly in an exaggerated form: New Romantics celebrating glamour of long-gone eras, body pierced female warriors in mixtures of contrasting prints, combat boots, buttons, patches, and cultural memorabilia. Transvestites in torn trousers and peekaboo costumes exposed intimate body parts as they danced. All of ones most embarrassing fantasies had been rolled into to forgetfulness, collective inebriation, various drugs, and fast affairs. The place became an unbelievable success until the creators bragged on TV, they were making more money than the mafia. Bam, an investigation into their tax declarations, which closed the club. Wow, how to stab yourself in the foot by not paying your taxes when you've hit the jackpot of success.

Chapter 12

Covenant woman got a contract with the Lord
Way up yonder, great will be her reward.
Covenant woman, shining like a morning star,
I know I can trust you to stay where you are
Bob Dylan

R ather than stare at the walls and cry I picked my way through Arthur's remaining journals until I came to 2018, the year, he met this groupie in Madrid.

Sept 6, 2017.

I am pleased with my new album cover, a photo of a solemn man in a dark jacket and white shirt, the background in funereal grey tones, my scowling face almost a sneer. This photo was taken in a cheap photo booth. I would have tossed it except I looked like the Spanish poet Lorca, or how he might have looked, had he lived to my ripe old age.

My harmonious life with Katherine flourishes. Each day rushes by in complicity of work with the felicitous routine of breakfasts and dinners and endless conversations, which always seems too short. Katherine is full of suggestions and constantly provides an objective view of my work and helps bring my projects to fruition. While male colleagues bemoan the passing of fun, romance, and sexual relations with their wives I rejoice that life with Katherine runs as smoothly as a well-oiled clock.

xxx

Sept 10, 2018.

My most memorable performance this year was at an open-air festival near Paris. A half a million people were fired up by passionate expectations. Forgetting the usual, hackneyed nature of the opening skits I was pleased when the speaker introduced me with the words: "We have with us tonight a singular talent, a poet and writer popular here and across the Atlantic from where he hails."

Over the years I have developed a droll, self-depreciating manner of a stand-up comic ready to proclaim myself their arch-villain. What you might call ham acting. At this venue I sensed the musical elite was with me and I went out to prove I was as good as I never was. The organizer had sent early clips to all the press and many important producers and journalists were there. The early buzz was impressive. They claim I am just what is needed to counter act the current climate of stereotypes and kooky singers. For years I have remained on the margin of success, struggling for recognition and respect. While other singers received praise for their antagonistic song, nicely packaged and sung at high volume. It is not unusual to hear people say about me: *if he is really so talented why isn't he famous?* Now I secretly rejoice in the exaggerated accolades and being called an original, distinctive poet/singer, the voice of my generation.

xxx

Nov 21, 2018.

Alicious de Grande, one of the producers of the concert, suggested she should be my agent in Spain. "I can make you a star, bigger than Cohen," she insisted. After a couple of false starts this podgy cheeked prompter did propose a few concerts in various areas, but nothing came of it. Her agency obviously a work-in-progress. She has assured me once she finished the groundwork, she will stop demanding up-front payments from me for every effort she makes and will only take a percentage of earnings, which is normal procedure.

xxx

Dec 22, 2018.

The concert in Madrid was an invigorating success. Everything went like clockwork until Alicious, projecting instant devotion of an unrepentant seal

138

culler, gave me only the minimum amount of money to pay the expenses. Without a blink for her unscrupulousness, she claimed she had negotiated the rest for herself in payment for future concerts. I was lost without Katherine there to fight for my fair share. There had been some mix up over event dates and she was to join me the following day. Even if I was hero of the evening, star of the show, surrounded by admiring fans, being defrauded by Alicious deflated my self-esteem.

The drinks party after the concert did little to lift my spirits until I noticed a young woman eyeing me; her open invitation bluntly offered awakened my male ego. Groupies often played up to me but at my age of 84 I hadn't been looked at in quite that way for a while. I felt no immediate interest but gave her a smile. I had been quite a seducer in my younger years, not because of my romantic rhetoric, more because I created some sort of provocation that women found irresistible. Occasionally I had fantasies about seducing women, but I was unwilling to throw myself into a sexual adventure with the risk of disturbing my marital bliss and perfect work environment, where everything is taken care of by the person I love.

"I'm Patasola," she said as she leaned in towards me with puckered lips and batting eyes like a fisherman temping a fish with a choice worm. I smiled at the idea of a choice worm entangling me. Patasola was surely aware I spoke Spanish, but she insisted on speaking English in the mistaken belief she spoke it perfectly. Without being beautiful, this Patasola was sexy in an easy sluttish way as she labored on high heels as if she was not used to wearing shoes. Her allure, that of a young animal appealed to me, as did her spin on how she had, as a barefoot nymph, inched her way up from the swamps of Columbia into the polyglot artistic community of Madrid. Normally I am suspicious of fans overtly making a play for me. Her claim that I bore the sexy resemblance to her favorite saint was original. She said she wanted to be photographed with me because she'd made a bit of a reputation by photographing herself with famous men.

I noticed everyone had disappeared and feeling friendless, I suggested dinner to this intriguing half-Indian creature. Desire doesn't stop, doesn't go away and throughout the dinner I wrestled with the opposite poles of attraction and keeping faith with Katherine. Perhaps it was the candlelight, or I drank too much but when her bewitching eyes, began to draw me in, I stated quite flatly that I was in a serious partnership, married for almost twenty years to a wonderful woman.

Patasola snickered. "Yea. Why den we here?" She put out her hand and stroked my leg, creating a sensation that a million ants had been let loose to run wild over my body. Life was good but I suddenly I thought it could be amazing. My next thought was why not have her? Who would know? And who could blame me for wanting this exotic dish? After all, there was nothing-unusual about two people desiring each other and having it off as long as the fisherwoman didn't go about bragging about the choice worm she bagged.

Patasola must have sensed my resistance weakening because she reached over and took a sip of wine out of my glass as if I was now hers. She pressed herself against me like a hound in hot pursuit and said she was ready to follow me back to my hotel. A woman so wanton thrilled me, a woman so demanding lit sparks I thought long extinguished.

At the hotel she climbed over my body and took me with her mouth and tongue. She was incredibly direct and perverse, as was my preference with my favorite whores. Nothing wrong with being a whore if she had learned to service older men. Humbly grateful I asked myself, how had I survived before this woman in all her tacky earthiness was delivered to me?

xxx

Dec 23, 2019.

The next morning on opening my suitcase the faint smell of Katherine's perfume caused my brain to hit a wreck on critical issues. No way could I excuse my lapse as having been overcome by a drunken moment or that Patasola's sexual pheromones had enveloped me by forces not exactly benevolent. My fault or not, bedlam was sure to arrive, especially as I had foolishly given Patasola the money for a train ticket and hotel room to attend my concert in the north of Spain. A gesture that obviously confirmed I was a man willing to pay.

xxx

Dec 29, 2019.

When I saw Patasola coming down the steps slowly, undulating her body, moistening her lips, her hand gliding along the railing, I froze. Katherine was likely nearby and making two and twenty. Her ominous smile filled me with fear that my foolhardy actions were about to wreak havoc on my domestic bliss. At the reception, that night I made a special effort to thank my muse, my helpmate and loving companion Katherine for her love and support.

xxx

Dec 30, 2019.

For want of acceptance of myself, and the reality of this disturbing link, I set out this morning in search of the splendid Oviedo Cathedral. Searching for mystical forgiveness in a place of worship filled with curious tourists normally made my spirits deflate like a balloon with a slow leak. It made me question if I am entering a dangerous period of religious skepticism. For the most part churches, like Jewish synagogues of Jesus's time, have become unabashedly unspiritual, little more than museums, religious money markets and theme parks. Thankfully, the magnificent Oviedo Cathedral was virtually empty. I knelt and offered up my prayers.

Near the exit I froze in astonishment. Patasola lay prostrated on the floor, her body framed by the grey pattern of the marble, a pattern I hardly saw, so entirely was my gaze concentrated on this exquisite vignette that ignited my religious nerve center. In that instant I was filled with a longing to prostrate myself before this Patasola, to be struck dumb in poetic adoration for this angelic creature, this pure and rare soul giving herself up to the Lord's protection. Her eyes glazed heavenward, her cheap bracelets rattling on her outstretched arms as if to wake God from his trance. "Madonna," she muttered like a voice during a séance predicting imminent doom. "Sé que estás para mí. Sé que me amas y quieres expulsar a todos esos perros y malhechores que me miran y me desprecian. Confío en el Señor Jesús para darme todo lo que merezco."

It wasn't the length of her calves, or the way the colored fabric of the dress fell against her skin, it was her religious passion that touched and sexualized my desire to be vampirized by intense emotions and found loveable. It sent electric shocks through me, which burst in my groin like an echo of the erotic feelings produced by Joan of Arc being led to the flames. No doubt God had a variety of tricks up his heavenly white sleeves when he let Eros invade my deepest religious sentiments. I sank down nearby and prayed with a solemnity and duration that had long disappeared from my daily habits.

At the door I invited Patasola to sit with me. Her primitive speech and manner of speaking was music to my ears. She told me her name was inspired by the myth of a young girl who would climb to the top of a tree and sing the song: "*I'm more than a siren, I live alone in the world where no one can resist me. I am the Patasola. On the road, at home, on the mountains and the rivers, in the air and in the clouds all that exists can be mine*."

I hummed the words of this old folk tale almost involuntarily injecting a noble configuration into the words, until the words became mine.

xxx

Dec 31, 2019.

Before the concert Patasola prostrated herself on the sidewalk and abandoned herself to me with wild screams. "Arthur, I love you." An electrifying sexual shock engulfed me like a tsunami of awakening, similar to the shock in my groin that had overtaken me as she lay on the cathedral floor. With a shrug I tried to ignore the discomfort of assembled friends who stared, horrified by her behavior, and whispered amongst themselves about the danger of drugs. Predictably the guards refused her entrance to the concert for fear of possible consequence.

xxx

Jan 12, 2020

Patasola addresses me as Mister Arthur, which is not unusual for people from the working class. But for South Americans, a superstitious lot, addressing

143

another as Mister is often an attempt to bewitch and take control. Experience taught me magic does exist when a powerful South American witch banished my headaches, not temporarily, but permanently. Another said I had the mark of duality on me, it was inscribed in my life blood. This duality created deceptive patterns that have all my life driven me unthinkingly, in opposite directions.

My tryst with this mystical creature has little to do with wistfulness for my lost youth, nor a desire to caress different breasts and lips. This Narcissus in love with her own reflection is as endearing as a child. Her throaty voice enhances the charm of her often-repeated banalities and incorrect words which in another I would dismiss as coarse.

xxx

Jan 20, 2020.

Katherine my nurturing, sweet woman is my muse, and sister spirit who has been with me physically and mentally in my happiest and most difficult moments. My affection for her is undiminished. Nothing has changed in my feelings which calms my growing sense of unease.

Patasola continues to follow me, to stalk me, dogging my steps, and provoking me. I look for her at concerts and events and await her texts and phone calls to the detriment of everything else. I am filled with sadness if I do not hear her endless: "Te quiero, te quiero, te quiero. This intriguing child born in the wastelands of South America, who slept on an earth floor and ran barefoot through the wild grass of the pampas has bewitched me. I am compelled to question if am I falling in love or simply intrigued by this Latino, this mystical woman who communes with saints and the dead?

144

Dreams plague me night after night. Memories flare like grainy, distorted notes from the past, a shade too manic, a shade too frantic. I am slowly being drawn away from Katherine not by Patasola but by flashbacks of Ciguapa, where we embraced in tears, more emotional than arousing. This revives feelings which have lain dormant since our separation more than fifty years ago. The word separation is too neutral a term, it was a bloody tearing apart after bitter incompatibility, sexual deprivation, infidelities, and endless bickering.

The manner of my leaving Ciguapa—I had been unable to do it any other way—was unforgivably abrupt, cowardly a more accurate description. Yet I continued to cling to her in the infantile illusion that our erotic and spiritual love was unique. As terrible as the later years were, I now find myself hungering to relive another overwhelming passion. To run the full gamut of spiritual mania, from erotic obsession to being "possessed and vampirized" by a perfect fit to my neurotic self.

xxx

Feb 02, 2020:

I fear I have crossed a line in my Walter Mitty–ish dreams, as much Thurber as Fellini. They bump against each other, the gulf so thin the slightest whisper carries an awful echo. I now live for my nights where I am irresistibly mesmerized. My parched night-soul unties dark knots as Ciguapa's fleshless embrace mutates to Patasola as in those ancient cinematic books, where if one quickly flips the pages, it creates the illusion of one figure becoming another. Ciguapa, the clearly discernible temptress of Tennyson's poem: *The Lady of Shallot*, is slowly transforming into the deeply provoking

Patasola, the Lady Fatima of the sonnets. I hear her fearful words—*my heart pierce thro' with fierce delight. I/will possess him or will die/I will grow round him and take his place*. In these words, I am the sacrificial lamb being led to slaughter by an irresistible force.

xxx

Feb 19, 2020.

I have rarely been outrageously false to women; more polite inaccuracies, and small falsehoods that oiled the machinery and promotes harmony, almost merciful in character. Now I am wrapped in a Freudian coat of denial where it is increasingly difficult to conceal my obsessive preoccupation from Katherine. I hadn't spent time with her, haven't whispered sweet nothings in her ear or kissed her or talked to her about anything personal. The other day, when she bent to kiss me, I shuddered. It is not that I have ceased to care for her, my mind is too crowded with confused thoughts. To ease my guilt, and justify my straying, I've begun to justify my actions by blaming it on her occasional snapping at my careless habits and absentmindedness.

xxx

Feb 23, 2020.

This foolish dreamer is now immersed in an avalanche of contrary emotions that invite disaster. I am on the brink of embarking on the folly. Like the fox with one paw in the chicken coop, I anxiously awaiting the rifle shot for my unforgivable crime. I have sent Patasola an airplane ticket to come for four days in Katherine's absence. I half expected Katherine to accuse me of treachery when unintentionally I turned my face from her kiss. Her questioning look transformed my duplicity into a barbed shaft which doomed me to suffer remorse for betraying a woman who loves me.

xxx

Feb 24, 2020.

The sky, a riot of color on an unpredictably beautiful winter's day, soon became as dark as my own duplicity when I brought Patasola into Katherine's domain. Perhaps unused to such luxury Patasola became a little frenzied, sneaking around touching everything as if she had found her pot of gold. Like a naughty child she slipped into the bedroom and lay on the bed with proprietorial glee as if she was the promised mistress of all that surrounded her.

The idea of using our marriage bed was too crass. I grabbed a few sheets and headed for the sofa in Katherine's atelier. To avoid displaying our romping to the neighbors' eager eyes, I lit a few candles. Patasola in a wild dance began dripping candle wax over the cushions, bed, and studio floor, calling them love trails. I am not one to panic even if a bull is bouncing about in a china shop, but in fear she would set the place on fire, I called a stop.

I don't remember what I expected but it was relief when her vampiric fangs did not appear. She merely grabbed the back of my neck and thrust her nipples in my face. "Grab them, suck them," she demanded. I tend to be claustrophobic, and although she was half suffocating me, my heart began to race. Not from lack of breath, more because she awakened my infantile obsession to sink my head into my mother's breast where the milk had once flowed beneath its softness. However, there was nothing motherly about this wild creature from the swamps of Columbia. More a crazed animal ready to whoop it up in the back barn.

"Say ya love mee. Don't stop. Don't stop saying it. Tell mee ya love mee. You'll love mee forever."

I thought it best to obey than be reproached, better still to get naked before everything didn't go my way. She shed her frippery in a hurricane of wild exultation and changed her tune to: "Go on hit me, hit me, crush me like God love me."

I'm not into hitting women even if they are asking for it, nor was I into that God crushing thing. A slap and tickle is more my inclination, but I was not against being bated about a bit while she ravished me with her vampire trick of sucking my vitals dry.

xxx

Feb 25, 2020.

This flirtation, this heady lure in pursuit of euphoric confrontation with my own mortality has given this illicit meeting an uninhibited violent intensity that thrills me. I admit I slept badly, my dreams troubled by the words of John Donne. That great lover-poet and anatomist of the soul who had intimately entwined the polarities of opposites: the amorous and the ascetic, the profane and the sacred, Eros the God of love and Thanatos the God of death.

My thoughts on Donne, I took his book of poems from the shelf to read his Holy Sonnet 14 where he addresses God with a wish for violent love: *Take me to you, imprison me, for I, /Except you enthrall me, never shall be free, /Nor ever chaste, except you ravish me.*

xxx

Jan 26, 2020.

This flirtation with this bipolar, premillennial bloomer half my age would have been superficial had it not been for the glorious mass we attended. In that place of worship, I trembled as she spread herself on the marble floor, trembled when she offered to be my intercessor with God to help me find my Christian identity.

Overcome by guilt I knelt and prayed with all my force asking God's forgiveness, for being a two-faced husband and a vacillating human who deliberately went against moral and holy teaching by denying sex its proper place of dignity with boundaries.

xxx

Feb 27, 2020.

The morning breezes stirred the drifts of air, which surprisingly were not cold for this time of year as we promenaded about the streets of Paris; me a new bridegroom with a flashy, noticeably stereotypical indigenous woman half my age masquerading as a virginal Catholic saint on my arm. In this plenitude of passion there are seeds of embarrassment for a man old enough to be Patasola's grandfather, when I bumped into my artist friend Emanuel. Like the wolf who believes he can fool the seven little goats by dipping himself into a bin of flour, I tried to pass Patasola off as a friend of the family. Emanuel's eyes clearly said, *He must be paying her.*

Had the devil sprung up from the ground there and then and offered me the restoration of my youth, I might have consented to sell my soul. I do not exactly pretend to a second youth. Nor desire to live forever, but I refuse the category of being old. Why, I asked in my delirium, be encumbered with a withering body, eighty odd years long passed when my mind is as spry and young as ever?

xxx

Feb 28, 2020:

I am convinced Job in heaven is toying with me; sadistically, rubbing his hands together in glee for my having gambled all in a four-day orgy of passion. Like Houdini I am caught in my own delirium and suffer a bad conscience. My habit of misjudging people is not born out of ignorance or stupidity, but more a naïve wish to see the best in others. I can ignore Patasola's trivial flaws and her inability to grasp ideas, but I realize she is as wily as a fox after a prized cockle. Fear swept away the temporary pleasure of our four-day orgy when she returned to the house and asked Hélène, Katherine's assistant, to help her look for her lost earring in the sofa, the site of our illicit romping. *Did she do it deliberately, to leave her footprint—to sow seeds for Katherine to discover in the hope to bring about our separation?*

xxx

Feb 29, 2020:

My love for Katherine may have lost some of its sparkle but it is deep; and having sex with another woman does not alter that. Despite everyman's wish for a harem, in my twenty years with Katherine I have been a decent monogamist. Until this encounter with Patasola, I had only been unfaithful in thought and with the occasional prostitute. Like a weasel trying to cover my tracks, my treachery destresses me. I want to be a decent man with a seamless narrative, not caught in a Johnny Depp marathon of tangled lies. But truth is as hard to hold on to as soap if not more difficult.

Chapter 13

When you're sad and when you're lonely,
And you haven't got a friend,
Just remember that death is not the end.
And all that you've held sacred,
Falls down and does not mend,
Just remember that death is not the end
Bob Dylan

S ecrets seldom stay in the dark. My friend Julia, a very perceptive woman, had years ago raised questions as to Arthur's ability to resist temptation. "Arthur defines the cliché that men are flawed and incomplete beings, incapable of sexual control. Women need a reason to have sex, men like Arthur just need the opportunity." That had shocked me at the time as did Arthur's recent hint that his new song create an odd type of dislocation, a sort of tripped-up sentence structure that danced back and forth between borders of the holy and the carnal, where sex and spirituality shared a bed. I had wanted to ask what kind of creepy-crawly poppycock was that? He might just as well have said don't pee on my leg and tell me it's raining for all the sense it made!

Even with the sky so blue, the temperature so perfect and the wisteria making beautiful trails of petals on the paving stones things were not popping up roses in my Land of Disenchantment. At that point it was not just intuition prickling the back of my neck, I suspected for obvious reasons, that Arthur had bedded a woman when I had been away. On my return the house was a mess: the sofa in my studio had been pulled out and candle wax dripped everywhere. My assistant said a woman had come back looking for her earring. Nauseous sensations cramped my stomach with doubts about his fidelity. When I'd asked him if he was having an affair, he said no, but Alicious had spent a night in the house (he made a point of reminding me she was a lesbian). Despite his rather evil smirk and evidence to the contrary I wanted to believe him. But a small fissure of doubt played over and over becoming a scab, I couldn't resist picking at. Like a plaster crack it had widen and spread. Much as I tried to blot out the thought, to crush it, squash it, it rolled inexorably back like a dead carcass hidden in Christie's woodwork.

The thought of Arthur embracing another woman in our home, in my studio, had sent me on a roller coaster ride to hell like walking across a minefield where any moment I might step on a bomb. Nothing hurt more than when I searched his eyes, and he looked away. Arthur who had kissed me in a way that made me feel alive, now gave me closed-lipped kisses as if his passion has gone missing. Of our five senses—touch is the one I missed. I was dying from lack of affection. No hugs, no kisses, not that he was ever that affectionate, but now in those months, before he dumped, it was as if I did not exist. Occasionally a fleeting micro-expression of distress clouded his face when a lightning-fast glimpse leaked out that all was not well. We were no longer on the same page, not even in the same library. For brief moments Arthur was present, when we'd have dinners and talk as chums, friends, and lovers. Then, like a cartoon horse chasing a carrot, puff he was mentally absent, and I was on my own again fearfully waiting for the next shoe to drop, always another shoe it seems, always another goddamn shoe.

His claim he was going through a religious crisis had not stop doubts filling Jill's bucket with muddy water. It was as if the love that once held us together was disappeared down the drain—well down the internet drain or the bathroom drain where Arthur now spent hours with a bottle of liquor and phone. When he finally came to bed, there was only a kind of Woody Allen half-naked, rough and tumble grapple—only a brief, "Goodnight, sleep well, darling." As much fun as trying to make out with a turtle.

Woody suggestion that I stop burying my head in the sand and confront him had forced me to go into his workroom. I remember wanting to be firm and had said, "I don't know what you want from me, Arthur. I don't know what's wrong. I'm trying to give you all the space you need but I have no idea what's going on." His Cheshire Cat's smile twisted as he'd paled. "Where are you? Where are we? Do you even like me?"

"Of course, I do. I love you," he had replied. "We are timeless souls, and you are mine."

When I think about this now, I am shocked that I could so naïvely have believed in those healing words. "Is something on your mind? You seem... I don't know... distant. I'm not used to you cutting yourself off from me." A new wave of doubt tore through me, but I shoved it under a cushion of faith and sobbed. "Will you come back to me."

His eyes had turned sorrowful as if he was a small boy watching a clown die in a grotesque circus accident. "Hey, come on. Don't be silly. Don't cry," he had babbled incoherently, tears trickling from the corners of his eyes. "I hardly know what's going on in my head. It's chaotic in there. Anybody who looked inside would conclude I rush around in a kind of interior urgency and generally respond in exactly the wrong way."

He'd buried his face in my hair, his breath warm as he'd softly uttered, "Katherine." His voice caused a ripple of desire to reverberate through me and lace its way along my skin. My heart had fluttered as our bodies met, his lips promise laden as he whispered that he loved me and vowed not to let me down. A pulse had flamed through me, a flashing, throbbing wave of desire filled my chest as his cuddles had escalated into an exquisite assault of loving caresses. Later we had lain peaceful in our old way—curled up together, half knotted, sweet and salty and familiar in each other's arms with me the innocent fool.

xxx

Arthur sat gazing at Katherine sleeping peacefully next to him; the innocent flush on her cheeks touched him. She did not deserve his coldness. He wondered if she would have seen his deceit had he been looking into her big, blue eyes when he'd held her in his arms and said he loved her. Guilt rose in him at the thought of how unavailable he had been as he stumbled along auditioning for all the different parts in this unwritten script. Everything within him now raced to keep control of his tangled emotions, to disguise the kangaroo bag he had filled with lies. Crazy stuff ran through his head like why penises were so ragingly predisposed to being suckled and why brains were so naively susceptible to promises of love. *Passions were madness. We don't reason, where we feel; we just feel.*

His favorite poet Aragon had written: *Light is meaningful only in relation to darkness, and truth presupposes error.* These opposites made his life pungently intoxicating. They intrigue him because he was the sort of fellow who often ignored what he had and desired what he had not. On a beautiful Sunday he might be walking about with Patasola and laughing at her silliest traits, her exaggerated behavior and thinking it was lovely. Yet he was also thinking, wouldn't it be great to be with Katherine, having a drink and watching the sunset while sharing our deepest thoughts.

A dozen times a day he declared this twist with Patasola was over, only to be conflicted instantly by the notion to stay and enjoy this half-Indian savage warming his balls with exhibitionistic porno exchanges of her sexual parts so obscenely displayed so gut wrenchingly vulgar, they suited his desire to pass the boundaries of the acceptable. His early fascination with internet porno had been purely voyeuristic. Occasionally he'd noted the telephone numbers of the women, telling himself he just wanted to hear their voices. When he'd accidentally left his computer open, Katherine had seen his intimate praise for the performances of various prostitutes who had occasionally beaten him. She had not objected, merely said she would accompany him to protect him. Despite this openness he now lived in fear of what her reaction would be if she discovered his new deception. Women's rage terrified him. Obsessive memory fragments still haunted him from the day he'd left Ciguapa for Paula, another South American. Her rage and threats against him had truly frightened him.

He knew the risk, not only the risk of losing Katherine but that this affair could poison his life. And as true as fish can fly the poison hit him like a blow in the solar plexus when Patasola, bitterly accused him of a crime he did not know he had committed.

April 9, 2020.

> *Dear Mister Arthur*
> *You give me dem herpes and I sick. You done this to*
> *me and you gotta be lookin after me now. I cannot be*
> *havin sex with other misters now. Nobody want marry*
> *me now.*
> *Patasola.*

Arthur was stunned, shocked to the core. Eros tainted by love of the illicit had ignited his impulsive nature and caused this unpredictable consequence. Shame ripped through him at the possibility he had polluted this celestial being, this creature who sent both spiritual and erotic thrills through his groin. *What have I done? What have I done?* His stomach contracted under the weight of his irresponsible behavior; not just to Patasola, but for his irresponsible behavior throughout his life.

He knew about herpes; people could have herpes for years with no manifestation. His doctor told him everybody has herpes—even his mother, his sister, and the president. Even his sofa cushions had been exposed to herpes. "Don't get caught in that trap," the doctor had said. "Women frequently accuse men of such crimes to gain their predefined goals or to blackmail for money.

That night his dreams were no longer slumbers of desire, more a rude awakening. Patasola sat by the fountain near the Plaza, bent over as if praying, her hands clenched in her lap, staring straight into the evening grayness as if waiting for Armageddon. The vailed sky, like a cloud of guilt hung over her as a wicked grin stole across Patasola's face, almost a leer. She murmured she liked exposing her privates as it got her what she wanted. "You not be so rich as I thinks but you got enough to be givin' me some, everybody like money."

April 10, 2020.
> Dear Patasola.
> Why do you want me? I'm not a sex mad forty-years-old anymore. I am twice your age, and I don't need sex. I am a poet who wants to spend his days working on his poetic legacy. My legacy is my words. I have the enormous pretension that my poetic vision is important. I do not want to waste a minute of my time left on earth on anything but my work.
> Love Arthur
> xxx

April 11, 2020.
> *Dear Mister Arthur:*
> *No person be caring for me till you comes along and loves me. I don't want be fighting you, but you done this. You have gone and ripped up me life. I got this*

*here dagger splitting me inside cause nobody gonna
be marryin me now. My life ruined.
Patasola.*

To be cynical, it was not his coming along but her offering her
wares as a plate of *hors-d'œuvre* that titillated and tempted him
to spice up his life, which had perhaps become too comfortable
for his quirky taste. Patasola had bewitched him and made him
believe he could dance over decades and turn back insidious
clocks as if they were simply white spaces between paragraphs.

Six months earlier he had been a contented husband in a
Patasola-less world. Foolhardiness had made quick work of that!
Katherine was an essential part of his life, the person he had
shared with, dreamed with, and grown with? How could he
willfully hurt the little girl inside her that just wanted to be loved.

Sane enough to recognize not deciding what to do was his
worst-case scenario, likely to generate more frightening
consequences. He was desperate enough to accept any scheme
even the most outlandish if proposed to him. Many times, he
was seized by the impulse to give himself relief, to tell Katherine
all, and end this association with Patasola. His illogical lapses
prevented his brain from focusing and indecision lodged like a
spiky boulder in his chest. The cannon ball that drove him was
suspended in mid-air, caught between his love for Katherine and
the path of least resistance—a desire to sacrifice himself to atone
for his sins. George Bernard Shaw, a man with an immense
sense of humor filled his thoughts: *A man doing something
stupid, something he is ashamed of, always declares he is
sacrificing himself because it is his duty.*

That night he dreamt of a nymph from the pampas
dancing towards him out of the darkness of the forest, her eyes
of fire sent him captivating glances of lust. This scantily clad
enchantress with long hair, slithered with promise and filled his
thoughts with passionate poetry. She reached out her hand and
whispered: "Come." Enthralled he took her hand, his heart
tattooing an orectic rhythm in his chest. The massive waves of
black hair tumbling about her shoulders caught the wind and
entangled his body in tingling lustful surges as she drew him into
the dark woods. When the amber glow of her skin turned blue,

her eyes glowed red like a creature possessed of primordial evil.

He turned to run, but he no longer had custody of his limbs. He was doomed, doomed by Satan who had dropped him in a bottomless well with no garlic or cross as protection. He awoke from this grip of horror in a bath of perspiration and began to pray. Not for the arms of either woman, but for God and God's love to somehow sort out this mess without hurting anyone.

April 12, 2020

> Dear Patasola:
> Please bear with me. You are deep in my spirit. I love you, admire you and honor you. You inhabit me like the light of my life. It's not that I don't want to answer you more fully, it's that this little boat called me is in very high seas.
> > Love Arthur
>
> > xxx

April 13, 2020

> *Mister Arthur:*
> *You be saying you be looking after me, but it's all lies and circumstances. You be knowin what happen when you and me cross up? Me soul browned and me body shaked and me submit to them illusion. I suffer every night. I masturbate, I cry. I not talk to no one, only me sister who live in Columbia but never play topic with her. Things slave me as live meat. You guilty of everything. I think you lie, you be juggler by illusion. If I sees you one more time and you still tied to her I drop me dead at your feet.*
> > *Patasola*
>
> > xxx

April 14, 2020

> Dear Patasola:
> You wrote the most beautiful, truest, most profound letter I have ever received in my life. I am writing you now after masturbating with love for you. You are my perfect fit. I will write more tomorrow.

159

Love Arthur

He thought Patasola as a pathetic creature, an injured animal who deserved his pity. Her email was as lamentable as his answer. With hindsight he realized his impetuous course among womankind contained the essence of foolishness and wrong decisions. A friend who knew him well had once asked: "Now Arthur, are you sure you are making the wrong decision?"

His mind wandered like lost kid chased by a security guard in a department store. Never for a moment had he contemplated making a life with Patasola. Now there seemed he had no choice. Driven by a sudden rush of impulsivity that Dostoevsky would have imputed to his being a gambler he wrote just one line to Patasola. One line that condemned him to a fragile future. In that instance he leapt into an abyss and blurted out, "Don't worry, I'll marry you."

Chapter 14

Come writers and critics
Who prophesize with your pen
And keep your eyes wide
The chance won't come again
Bob Dylan

Given how much of Arthur's thoughts were flooded with confusion it was not easy for him to turn his attention to the earlier decades of his life, let alone attempt to uncover the root of his addictive actions. Many times, in spontaneous bursts of emotions he had asked women to marry him. What else was there, amid all the glorious follies, urges, weaknesses, but the glorious idea of marriage. After his initial euphoria yielded to reality, he sensed this fatal weakness in his character would again prove his undoing.

He mulled over how trusting he had been in the early phase of his grand passion for Ciguapa. He was now ready to acknowledge this older experienced woman, had literally led him like a lamb to the bridal bed. Had he slept a few years more, he might have learned to play another tune and been saved from many years of torment. His proposal of marriage, made in the flush of passion, had been the result of the elephant in the room—Ciguapa's intention to spend Christmas holidays with her protector. It had shaken him to his toenails, and he'd blurted out in a sudden rush of emotion: Marry me?

He scoffed softly to himself now at how similar both Ciguapa's and Patasola's response to his marriage proposal had been. In other words, the serpent in his obsessive passions was a pig in an empty backpack, unless he could provide the goodies, they both desired. Ciguapa and Patasola fused the qualities of nun and whore: Ciguapa the kept woman of a man twenty-one years her senior, had been eager to become the kept woman of a man twenty-one years her junior. Now it was the reverse: forty-two-year-old Patasola was eager to be the kept woman of the eighty-four, a man twice her age.

Arthur flipped back through a few of the journals Katherine had sent to him until he found the 1957 journal where he had asked Ciguapa to marry him.

Dec 19, 1957.

Neither of my parents imagined a less likely fiancée than Ciguapa. My father, who I could swear was asexual except for the fact I exist, believed marriage was for procreation. Something unlikely at Ciguapa's age. So, it had to be the animal thing. "Now son, are you sure? An older woman with a doubtful past? At least wait until you've graduated. I cannot support you both."

My stepmother warned me that my would-be bride, a woman almost the same age as herself was an ageing demi-mondaine, who craved power, and status. "Ciguapa is a narcissistic woman with a huge ego who feels through her brain. A domineering sort of person whose happiness lies entirely in the comfort you can provide. She is a master manipulator at pulling the strings on her prey." Despite the shock her words created I'd hugged my stepmother tightly and assured her she was wrong. No way was I ready to admit I was as impulsive as a jack rabbit who rarely thought before I leapt and that I was now filled with doubt.

Arthur could not bear to continue to read more. He search for a later journal in the unpacked boxes and suitcases the movers had dumped in heaps in the storeroom. He pulled out one from 1966 almost ten years later, the time of his first separation from Ciguapa after a long discussion with Walter, one of his gambling pals. As he glanced through his journals, he laughed to himself wondering what historians might make of his foolish illusions if he became famous enough to have someone interested in reading them after his death. Would they see this love story with Ciguapa as a great romance—or a badly thought-out horror movie?

Walter had said they were both vulnerable to narcissists because they tended to submit to the will of others in order to avoid acknowledging their own justified anger. Walter admitted this flaw in his own character had encouraged him to become a therapist. During his training, and years of listening to thousands of people talk about their troubled love affairs, he had come to the conclusion that pathological narcissists didn't have normal emotions, but they certainly understood them. These neurotics formed quick and intense romantic attachments, as romantic as one could wish, in the beginning. After that—unless the co-dependent did exactly as these narcissists demand—disaster.

Arthur admitted he usually ended up apologizing to Ciguapa even though he didn't think he had anything to apologize for. Walter had snapped back, "Don't ever apologize. Just as there is no point in arguing with a drunk, it's pointless to apologize to a pathological narcissist. It's the worst thing you can do. They consider apologies weakness, a flaw in character. Take my advice, you can either accept a narcissist, suffer her, or turn her into literature.

On returning home, Arthur had fallen on his knees before Ciguapa and asked her to forget the past and to just love him. The light falling unflatteringly across her aging features seemed to reveal the gratification she took in slaughtering him with her cool indifference. With a grimace she again insisted he sit at her bedside to be reprimanded for his sins and shallow behavior. His worse sin, which she harped on endlessly, had been committed many years earlier. when, as a student he had deserted her for a university party. He became so stressed by this rehashing of his past sins he contemplated throwing myself through our plate glass window.

The next morning still distressed he packed a few things, his guitar and notebooks and walked out, literally vanished like a cat. But a cat with regret because he hesitated, listening for Ciguapa's footsteps, aware of how badly he wanted to hear her say, "Come back, I love you."

As the morning thickened, he'd wandered through the indigo shadows and patches of snow that hinted winter was not yet over. Later he found himself outside the apartment block where Ciguapa had lived before they married. He'd leaned on the gate; let it swing gently back and forth until the landlady stepped out on the landing, nodded in answer to his impulsive question. "Yes, there is an apartment vacant, if you want it." He dragged his case up the stairs and sat down bewildered before undressing and getting into bed. The wind and the creaking of the tree in the front of the house and the occasional banging of a shutter kept him in a state of panic throughout the night.

The next morning, after a strong coffee Arthur had rubbed the sleep from his eyes, and for someone who sensed he had no home he was incredibly homesick. After apologizing to the landlady, he threw his things in a bag, and boarded the long-haul bus. Many hours later, the driver woke him with a nudge to his shoulder. The pale light that crowded the hills and trees brought little comfort as he walked up the driveway to my father's house. In a distracted state he kept asking myself over and over, *What am I doing here? Why don't I just keep going? Why not wade into the American vastness, start over, shape a new destiny? Come up with a new beginning?*

His father and stepmother greeted him with caution aware of his fragile state. After dinner he retired to the porch for a smoke. For health reasons his father has given up cigarettes and now smoked cigars. Are cigar so different, Arthur I asked, trusting his father knew about such practical matters. His father hummed and hawed before admitting it was all comparative. What Arthur really wanted to ask but dare not was why he was so disappointed with life. Instead, he blurted out: "Are you disappointed with me?"

Nah, he'd said I never worry on other people's behalf. Best to let people get on with their lives. Guess I'm just wondering if you are gonna make the right decisions now. Don't mess up your life unthinkingly like I did."

All Arthur knew was that if he wasn't here with his father, he'd probably be in a roadside ditch.

The next morning his stepmother had mentioned his similarity to my father when she first met him. "Handsome Dad was then, but older than you, getting on, over thirty. Looked so lost, he did. Said his date had forsaken him for another fellow. I thought he was being witty and laughed. But it was true. We all get ditched sometimes or do the ditching."

She'd straightened herself restively and took a sip of her weak coffee. Then added, more to herself than to Arthur, "I know about being ditched, I was ditched by your father. But he returned. We don't talk about such things. I know he's worried, not just about you. The trouble is he simply can't face up to things; never faced anything, ever. He just sits there hoping it will all work out in the end. You are both like that."

Arthur's sense of belonging continued to evade him. He prowl around the way a cat does, looking for the spot that was his. Some hidden corner where he could fold his wings and watch protected. Without work and largely friendless, his friends all off in university, he passed his days picking books off the shelf, one after another, working his way progressively through the vast selection, most of which he'd already read. Or sitting unthinking in front of the television, switching back and forth between Canadian and the nearby American TV stations. Sometimes a film was halfway through before he realized he'd already seen it. The American stations removed all sex scenes, while the Canadians removed all violence scenes, which made the film almost unrecognizable.

His stepmother sat at the kitchen table working on what she called her scribbling. She said if Arthur returned to his writing, she'd be a happy listener, a helpful critic. Her encouragement filled him with a near-hopeless optimism that someone, somewhere, would want to hear his poetry. He'd returned to his room where his notebooks lay in heaps on the desk, their contents beckoning to be taken up again. His ancient typewriter on the shelf, its antiquated ribbons alongside dried-out ink bottles, encrusted nibs, cartridges for pens, and pencils empty of lead. He re-read a few of his old poems that had been rejected by every major magazine, journal, agent, and publisher. Later under the influence of Charles Olson, his university professor, several poems had been accepted in important literary magazines, but he'd never been paid a penny from any of them. Taking up his pen he felt he was taking himself as sneaky witness on his own anarchistic life. With a sigh Arthur admitted that only a person who had no choice in the matter would spend the better part of his day locked in a room struggling to put words on paper.

Arthur had doubts about his stepmother's capacity to appreciate his projective verse, but he continued to read his work to her. One evening just as he was about to hit he full poetic stride, his stepmother made a throaty cough. "No," she'd said forcefully, her pale eyes revealing inflexibility. "I don't like the way you are going about this. I know you've had moments when you've been down. Don't get me wrong, I'm sympathetic, but why this endless self-reproach, this guilt? I could be wrong but if you wrote something more like *The Rime of the Ancient Mariner,* you'd leave everything transfigured in your wake."

He explained writing a poem like Coleridge's *The Rime of the Ancient Mariner* was equivalent to a painter painting like Rembrandt. A small, crooked smile crossed her mouth. A smile of pity or embarrassment? He couldn't tell, it looked like both, if such a thing were possible.

"Only trying to help." She said with awkward determination, "I'm thinking a poem should leave something beautiful behind, not just get inside your head with upsetting words. I don't bring this up lightly, poetry should be more than a mere whimper!"

That left him a bit speechless. He crossed the hall to the room that he had shared with Michael and closed the door. It was a traditional room, sunny and small and squashed with books. He picked up Michael's pen and wrote: *Who do you think you are? The only thing you have in common with Keats or Shelley is your ability to annoy the hell out of everyone.* He tossed his notebook aside and flipped the pen shut. Few people read poetry and now he had lost my audience of one.

The next morning he'd whistled for the dog and moved off into the Canadian wilderness. The path lay under the feathery shadows of rust-colored maples and led across a stream and up a steep, rocky hill to bluffs overlooking the valley. Autumn had come early and snows, already thick on the high mountains, reflected the sunlight with a violence that hurt his eyes. He glanced around out of habit to check for lurking hazards and sat down to pray. Words began to weave together a poem about being stranded on a dry, waterless plain where he struggled, the way a fish might struggle in a pond fast drying in the heat. It was then he'd decided to go to Montreal. It had been a wise decision. Montreal had changed his life and his direction due to his meeting Leonard Cohen. He again rummaged through the suitcases and boxed until he found the 1966 journal about his months in Montreal.

Sept. 9, 1966.

This morning I hugged my stepmother and thanked my father when he slipped a handful of cash into my pocket. Then hopped on the long-haul bus which connected to the Trans-Canada train heading for Montreal. The train sped through various towns, occasionally lights jerked across the windows, lightening up the dim almost empty carriage. I'd rested my forehead on the cold, smooth windowpane, a cigarette in my mouth, the puffs of smoke hanging in bunched blue balls in the air. The sensation of being carried forward through black nothingness, to the sound of pounding wheels was like a heartbeat of contentment. Trains feel familiar. The sound of their passing in the night had often lulled me to sleep.

xxx

Sept. 12, 1966.

After a coffee in the Montreal station, I wandered off from the central square and came to McGill university, a sort of city within a city. That area, with its solid stony structures, reminded me of photos I'd seen of English universities especially the grander buildings: the Arts Building and library. Many streets of Montreal were named after prominent Scottish men like Stanley, Peel and McTavish.

I was pleased to discover the middle-class Hungarians fleeing the 1956 Russian repression of their country, had imported their European traditions and avant-garde culture to Canada. In Stanley Street, in the St. Katherine area dozens of Hungarian literary coffee houses had sprung up. They were frequented by a very anti-establishment artistic community and interesting mix of unemployed locals reading newspapers, playing chess, and they lingered over an espresso to argue politics with the college-skipping McGill students.

The local custom of this floating population was to adopt a café as a mailing address and use the payphones for messages. The owners were an easy-going lot and scribbled our messages on the wall. Love affairs began and ended with the owner's teasing: "She called." Or "She didn't call."

xxx

Oct 21, 1966.

With the few hundred dollars in my backpack, the misunderstood genius starving in a garret appeared an acceptable alternative to Marcuse's theory of how people are programmed to do certain jobs, who they marry, what they bought, even what they were supposed to think. In sympathy with Bartleby, Melville's rebellious scribe in his book *Bartleby*, I prefer not to succumb to modern, commercial life, but to expose myself to influences that might strengthen and fortify my poetry.

xxx

Oct 29, 1966.

This evening, after a jazz session in a club, I noticed a young girl flashing me a smile. "Gonna sit a minute if you don't mind," she said. "There's a whole bunch of guys coming on to me, aggressive like. Kind of boring they are, letting everyone know how exciting it is to be a Beatnik instead of just getting on with being a Beatnik."

After my years of trauma with Ciguapa I was not exactly comfortable with women coming on to me. Especially as I was a little awed by her, she was so hip in her black turtleneck and jeans, so carelessly in; the kind of woman I thought could have anything she wanted. Was she asking my protection or trying to pick me up? In this polyglot environment it seemed people were having sex as casually as mountain climbing or sailing but with less preparation. When this intriguing woman offered me a handful of pills, I refused. I wanted a different story, not one about living a short life ingesting chemicals and wasting my talents.

xxx

Dec. 24, 1966.

I am curiously adrift in these dreary months of northern squalls and freezing weather, where people leave these deserted streets to beggars and cats. I can't settle, can't engage. While others deck the halls and make merry, I have no friends with whom to share holiday feelings. My room in a rundown area has few signs of approaching Christmas, just some stray tinsel decorations here and there on various door fronts. To capture some Christmas Eve comfort, I drifted into a movie theater with a score of other lonely idlers. Spending the evening with my bag of popcorn in the back of a cinema was the least cheery thing imaginable.

xxx

Jan 10, 1967.

Spring creeps forward with blasts of sunlight one minute, fits of freezing rain the next, all mixed with angry gusts of wind. Today amid a moment of sun, I strolled idly about the rougher areas of the city and came across Brian, a brilliant college friend, if one of the laziest. He was sweeping up in front of a bar. Her offered me his job and I accepted the broom. Galvanized by this event I signed up at McGill University for evening classes in comparative literature, modern poetry, and language courses.

A few evenings later Arthur met Leonard Cohen at the Le Vieux Moulin, a club that played jazz into the early hours. Listening to

Cohen sing gave Arthur a glimpse of John Keats, his own guiding star. Cohen poems were courtly, biblical, and timeless. They expressed his inner despair for the irreparably brokenness of the world. He told Cohen one in particularly touched him. "Let's not talk of love and chains and things we can't untie. Your eyes are soft with sorrow. Hey, that's no way to say goodbye."

"Poets often disappoint," Cohen admitted. "There is a significant part in all of us capable of great carelessness. Poetically, I would describe myself as a travelling body of pain, a poetic wanderer living inside my own head and that's not really living anywhere." Cohen shook his head and added. "Music makes me feel a feeling and a song makes me feel a thought. The rhythms of poetry and music are exactly the same, so it mattered not if they are sung or written on a page and yet the literary community claims singing poetry is anti-intellectual and low culture concerned with sensual, bodily effects."

Apparently at a party of various editors of influential Canadian literary magazines editors, Cohen had insulted the guardians of traditional poetry by saying nobody cared about poetry written in the old traditional way. As he mentioned this he gave a chuckle, a rich, deep sound. He'd told these Canadian philistines they were too scared of being labeled hicks to be truly inventive like Bob Dylan' whose poetry was as valid as the Troubadours. Or as valid as the poets of the golden age of Shelley and Byron. None of those various editors had ever heard of Dylan. And to Arthur's embarrassment neither had he! Except for his having read in the *Village Voice* what John Lennon had written about Dylan: *Who is there among us who has not had his consciousness shaped by the poetic words and music of Bob Dylan?*. When he met up the next day with Cohen at Le Vieux Moulin Arthur admitted he had been so curious to find out more about Dylan he'd spent the whole day listening to Dylan's cryptic, haunting, lyrics.

Cohen said poetry had been his passion since at the age of fifteen, but it was in a used bookshop that he had stumbled upon *Autumn Song* by Federico García Lorca, a Spanish poet with a bruised, and noble soul. He had immediately responded to Lorca's crystalline, electrical imagery. It had mirrored his own state of mind and had marked him as no other poet ever had.

Arthur managed to acquire a copy of Lorca's *Autumn Song,* in the hope of discussing it with Cohen, but Cohen was no longer in Montreal. His loneliness increased and during one of his frantic searches for his notebooks, which he often lost, Arthur heard Rimbaud's cry, *change life.* That decided him to go to Spain in search of Lorca's influences.

With boats to Spain being cheaper from New York he decided to splurge on a stopover at the Chelsea Hotel, a haunt frequented by outsider artists, and writers, a type of bohemian fraternity house with many long-term residents. Cheap but more expensive than the average run-down hotels in that New York area. He remember being surprised to see a large canvas by Larry Rivers that jostled with other paintings over the front desk. Perhaps it had been given in lieu of rent, or hocked to Stanley Bard, the hotel manager. A slow elevator had transported him to the twelfth floor which opened out on a corridor painted yellow. Among a warren of rooms of various shapes, sizes, and comfort, his thought his must be one of the smallest, and lit only by an overhead bulb. The furnishings were minimal with a black and white television, a hotplate, and a washbasin where cold rust-brown water gushed out in a wild spray often soaking him unexpectedly.

He returned to his journals to read what he'd written about that trip.

March 31, 1968.

> I shared the elevator today with the silver-haired Andy Warhol who invited me to The Factory, where The Velvet Underground is performing their *Exploding Plastic Inevitable.* To my surprise and pleasure, the first person I saw on my arrival was Cohen. A corner of his mouth crinkled into a mischievous grin. "I'm here even though I don't join groups, whether they want me or not. I'm a bit embarrassed to be one of the multitude of men trailing after Nico the tall, blonde singer of The Velvet Underground. She just told me to forget it, she likes younger men."

I smiled unsure if Cohen was being sincere. Women seemed to love him. I told him I had been staring into dead ends until I 'd read *Autumn Song* and for the moment I was walking in Lorca's shoes and on my way to Barcelona.

Cohen nodded thoughtfully. "To be inspired literally means someone has breathed life into the pathways of your soul. My guides are the verses of Lorca which resonate closely with my emotional sorrow. The philosophy of Camus, and the wisdom of Zen masters have helped me immeasurably." He laughed before and admitting he'd spent nearly a decade learning to be a poet, and half a decade recording his poems, but here in New York, he was in the position of a beginner showing his work to traditional publishers. "They tell me at thirty-three I'm a bit old to be a singer and a bit too sad to be popular. I'm more hopeful since meeting Mary Martin, the assistant to Albert Grossman. She's Bob Dylan's manager and has a track record for helping Canadians."

At that moment Lou Reed the jittery, skinny singer and songwriter of The Velvet Underground headed our way. "Hey man, are you Leonard Cohen, who wrote *Beautiful Losers*?"

Cohen became visibly excited. "I thought nobody read it! It only sold a few copies."

Lou's smile is infectious. "Well, I read it! A great book. Let's move on to Max's Kansas City."

Lou's crowd is very in and. I was amazed to find myself sitting in New York's *in place,* Max's Kansas City, at a table full of New York's art luminaries.

xxx

April 6, 1968.

As I prepared for my boat trip to Spain and Barcelona, I made a last visit to hear Cohen in a

Birdland club where he supported himself by giving midnight poetic readings, accompanied by a six-piece band. We drank champagne to celebrate that he had now secured Grossman as manager. All thanks to Mary Martin who had recommended him to Grossman and introduced him to Judy Collins who had chosen two of his songs, "Suzanne" and "Dress Rehearsal Rag", for her next record.

Chapter 15

When your rooster crows at the break of dawn
Look out your window and I'll be gone
You're the reason I'm a-traveling on
But don't think twice, it's all right
Bob Dylan

Karen Moller

On Arthur's arrival in Barcelona on April 15, 1968, he had been horrified by the news of the assassination of the civil rights leader, Martin Luther King Jr. He took refuge in a café and ordered a cognac to alleviate the sensation of not only being trapped in a world of lunatics but in city where Spaniards had more or less given up caring about events happening in America or anywhere else. Fear permeated much of Spanish life. Franco aimed to create a uniform, nationalist country, and readily imprisoned anyone stepping out of line. He had banned everything pertaining to regional culture, arts, music, and poetry. Not only had Franco have Lorca killed, but he'd also burnt all his poetic works.

Arthur began to suspect he would have fared better searching for Lorca's roots in Paris where he had collaborated with the writer/poet Pablo Neruda and with the painter Salvador Dalí. They had formed magnetic poles, with Dalí the apex of the triangle. Dalí and Buñuel had made a notorious surrealist film, *Un Chien Andalou*. Arthur noted that their aim had been to avoid ideas or images that might lend themselves to any form of reason, morality, aesthetic, or rational explanation. With the film's unexpected success, Buñuel had raged: *What can I do about the people who adore all that is new, even when it goes against their deepest convictions. The insincere, corrupt press, and inane herd see beauty and poetry in our film which is basically no more than a desperate impassioned call for murder!* That made Arthur love the man.

Apparently, Lorca was the only one offended by the film for a totally different reason. A huge trauma, which he described as a short circuit from Hell. The three friends had a habit of calling themselves dogs, with Lorca the Andalusian dog. When Dalí and Buñuel called the film *Un Chien Andalou*, Lorca assumed the character in the film was modeled on him.

Arthur made a visit to the University of Granada where Lorca had studied law before becoming known for his poetry recitals. Despite years of Franco's repression Arthur discovered of the ballads of the Occitan Troubadours, and folkloric medieval Andalusian flamenco had not disappeared, they have merely gone underground. In his enthusiasm for Lorca's love of a flamenco Arthur had learned to play the rapid six chord flamenco progression that had influenced Lorca's poetry.

He pull out another journal to see what he had written about his return to Barcelona.

June 1, 1968.

> I rented a room in a shoddy Barcelona neighborhood, which I would not have considered, had not a local barman specified the area as perfectly safe. He had indicated a three-story jumble of fragile looking structures as a likely place to find a room. Taking the barman's word for it, I knocked on the door several times with no result. About to turn away, the door was wrenched open by an old woman in a worn dressing gown and cheap brown wig. She looked me up and down, eyed me mistrustfully as some sort of unfamiliar species. "Whaddaya want?"

> In answer to my enquiry, she handed me a key and pointed to the staircase. "Third floor, on the left, number six. See for yourself." With that her door closed with a snap. The dark stairwell was imbued with a musty odor of accumulated dirt, domestic cooking smells and tobacco. Two women in the hall were immediately suspicious of my presence but eventually helped me find door number six. After a difficult fiddle with the key, it opened onto a tidy, spartan room large enough for a man who intended to live alone. It contained the barest essentials: a single bed, an old and battered chest of drawers, a table with a hot plate, and bookcase desk. Had someone offered me a more luxurious place I would have perversely chosen this one. My nature being rather masochistic, I'm the

sort of fellow who loves a cold shower, but instead takes a hot one. Or having found the perfect pair of shoes, I buy something not nearly as suitable for the same money, knowing all the while it makes no sense.

I tossed my small bag and guitar in the corner and paid the rent. After eating a hearty soup with heavy country bread at the now busy café, I ordered a brandy, and leaned back in my chair. A blaring TV showed the smiling, triumphant Robert Kennedy after the returns of the California primary. A minute later in a rigorous test of the speaker's prose ability to contain alarm, the screen filled with chaos and the horror of Kennedy's assassination.

My enthusiasm sank like a balloon slowly deflating, not only for Kennedy's assassination but for Martin Luther King Jr's murder, the turbulent riots in the ghettoes and for all the young Americans coming home from Vietnam in caskets. These horrifying events make me question why I bother to write. What good was poetry? It goes into a void, like a message in a bottle being flung out to sea which might, with luck, one day be read. Cohen was right, rather than singing love songs we should be singing protest songs.

xxx

Sept 30, 1969.

The Beatles concert in Madrid, Plaza de Toros de Las Ventas in July 1965 has been the de facto catalyst for the cultural and youth revolution to begin in Spain. Not exactly welcomed by the Franco regime, there had been some rough moments with the Guardia Civil. Until that moment, Spain had been playing coward to the cross-tensions of the 1950s clashes and the cultural changes happening in other countries. The group Chicago, a jazz-infused rock band followed in the Beatles' wake, then other great rock stars like Jimi Hendrix and Joni Mitchel. The concerts are a great encouragement for Spanish beat groups and the young are beginning to dance to the social upheavals of the post-beatnik and hippie era. There is little Franco could do now to prevent Spain from opening to outside influences and following in the footprints of Europe.

xxx

Dec. 3, 1969.

I have achieved a measure of success in cafés and smoky coffeehouses which support fringe artists and Underground progressive rock groups. It is near impossible to be taken up by a producer or to arouse interest in having a record produced. Not only are the Francoists opposed to Pop music, but many on the left condemn it as bourgeois deviationism and cultural imperialism.

People sip their cappuccinos, which we have suddenly discovered, while listening to my songs that come to me easily but fade if I am not quick to turn them into songs. The public response is heartening and occasionally I manage to sweep the legs out from under the people sitting cross-legged on dusty faded carpets. They come up to me after the concerts and say they are telling their friends.

xxx

Dec. 13, 1970.

Despite being formally separated from Ciguapa I continue to supply her with funds I earn as I also work as a translator. Her grateful letters and declarations of undying love nourish my nostalgia for our once great romance.

I have invited her to Barcelona after I received God's message: *embrace the cracks of human brokenness; forgive your dear and*

182

possessive other with the humility of a penitent,
When she arrived, she fell into my arms, tore off my shirt and pulled down my trousers. I liken those orgasms to the statues of saints falling when Samson pulled down the temple. This renewal of love brings an unbearable lightness to my being, which Saint John of the Cross called the *nada*, the loss of self in encompassing love. Ciguapa is again my obsession, my spouse, my mother and spirit woman.

xxx

Jan 23, 1972.

My poetic evolution has now begun to fail due to Ciguapa's jealous interference with the organizers. Her endless accusations of disloyalty at any departures from her wishes has caused me to be pushed aside in preference to other performers at various festivals, performers who have no more talent, or charisma than me. In this final smash-up of my romantic fantasy Ciguapa does nothing but complain about the planets, stars, black holes or whatever else she has decided annoys her. It was Aragon's poems that triggered my decision in university to become a poet. Now Aragon's poetry has helped me face the reality that Ciguapa presence in Barcelona is a failed experiment.

After this second separation from Ciguapa and the end of my brief affair with Paula, who helped me find the courage to separate, I pass my days working my dark thoughts into painful poetry; spiritually uplifting but too sad to be commercial.

June 28, 1972

I participated in the cutting-edge international Encuentros Festival in Pamplona on 26th of June which I believe will help to revive my poetic evolution to regain some of its earlier momentum. This festival has opened its doors to the international community and brought Spanish art movements together with the outside world of John Cage David Tudor and many other well-known avant-garde figures. It was coordinated by my friend Professor Ignacio Gómez de Liaño who managed to avoid the limits institutions were trying to impose on it. More than three hundred and fifty artists participated from various countries and groups: Fluxus, Situationism, Action artists, Poetic performances, and happenings. Surprisingly it was somewhat tolerated by the authorities.

xxx

Sept 11, 1976.

Now as I have become rather famous as a poet/singer I have been invited to perform at a concert in Vancouver. An invitation I welcome as a chance to escape Spain's autumn heat for the cooler days of Canada. I decided to stop off on my way to Vancouver to celebrate my fortieth birthday with my father and stepmother. As the long-haul bus made its way through the Rocky Mountains, I was overwhelmed by the beauty of the landscape and physical immensity of Canada's untamed nature. I watched the splendor on all sides until only the North Star was left flaring in the darkness.

My father waiting at the station in his pick-up truck appeared genuinely glad to see me. he said, "Well, son, making good, are you? Never thought you could make a living singing poetry and all. But then what do I know?"

My stepmother embraced me while coquettishly tucking stray wisps of grey hair into her

184

braided plaits. Completely absorbed in her community activities, she rambled on about helping the needy and saving the neighborhood's stray animals. "So, you are still adopting strays like me?"

She'd blushed like a young schoolgirl and admitted she wished there were more strays like me to keep her busy.

It being my birthday, my father suggested I join him in the beer parlor. "Remember him, my son, the little ragamuffin?" he said proudly introducing me to his friends, showing his satisfaction by frequent nods. "He's a famous singer/poet now though I doubt any of you ignorant folk have ever heard of him."

The local inhabitants regarded me with curiosity and one farmer asked if poetry paid good money. I smiled remembering the difficult years until Franco's death in 1975 when the young Spaniards had started freaking out as if they had finally been released from prison. Jim Morrison summed it up to the Spanish crowd: with "We want the world... and we want it now!"

xxx

Sept 21, 1976.

The next morning, I took the bus to Vancouver. As an untrained musician, I lack the skill to explain to producers that I want to control every aspect of my poem/songs, from conception to realization. I am grateful to my friend Herminio Molero. His remarkable sophistication in the use of synthesizers has influenced my own artistic development and has allowed me to develop a softer touch with more delicate fingering.

His avant-garde band, Ateneo de Madrid is not only ahead of its time, but his music perfectly suited to Spain's easing up on uncensored possibilities, not only ideologically but also aesthetically. Two of his compositions have remained top of the pop charts for over a year and rank among his most notable works.

xxx

Sept 22, 1978.

The crowd at the Vancouver concert was massive; just a whisper became a roar. My reputation for being somewhat of a madman has enhanced my notoriety and magnified my mystique. It also adds extra worry for the Canadian festival organizers already overwhelmed. The crowd nevertheless quietened as I began to sing which made me feel like Moses before the parting the Red Sea.

The concert was deemed a great success even if a few of the groups left me feeling I was holding my head out the window of a speeding car. Most of the concert could have been bundled into one big variety show. The inconsistencies and occasional incompetence of the performances seemed expected by all and challenged by none. My favorite moment in this unfavorite concert was so provocative it was strangely heart-warming. The singer who performed a version of *Night Fever* wandered so far off any conventional notion of the melody it single-handedly ushered in a new regime of dissonant noise that made it quite original.

xxx

Sept 25, 1978.

The poetry/song festival over, I took a walk around my old neighborhood. The area now seemed shaggier and more overgrown, the houses unpainted, with vacant lots between like missing teeth, were filled with junk. Everywhere was shabbiness: fast food trash and broken plastic toys moldering in the gutter. Unlike Europe, houses

186

weren't built to endure. They disintegrated and people disappeared into the Canada vastness rarely returning to where they were born.

The weather was surprisingly warm, and in a very short time my shirt was uncomfortably damp. I turned to the right then to the left looking for something I might recognize. Were these iron railings the ones I had run along, banging my stick against the posts? Perhaps I'd climbed the high brick wall to see what wonders lay beyond.

I took a rest on the steps of a plain, two-storied building much like the others with a steep roof, the edges in carved wood reaching down to the first floor, the upper windows similar to ones where I'd often waited for my mother's return from work. We'd moved about, staying in many different rooming houses, and rarely had separate bedrooms, often only a heavy curtain divided us. I'd once cut a hole in the curtain and had seen my mother's dark furry triangle which looked for all the world like a magical creature completely independent of her. My belief that she was complicit in my spying thrilled me and that set the burlesque stage for my future exotic adventures. In particular, the lascivious pleasure I found in peepholes in houses of ill repute.

For a moment, I expected my mother to emerge from the front door in her pale blue dress and take me to task for my laziness. That thought caused an onslaught of depression to hit me with a blow that sent a shiver of regret through me. To ward off my stricken state I watched two young girls as they passed. They reminded me of girls I'd followed as a boy, my hands deep in my bottomless pockets. Confident of my now elegant form and the effect it always had on women, I decided to follow their firm round bottoms bouncing under their light skirts. The dark-haired girl glanced in my direction, turned to her friend, and giggled. It dawned on me, not only did she not recognize me as the visiting poet/singer, she'd said something like: "See that dirty old man following us." My face flushed crimson, certain she'd seen my self-satisfied grin. At the age of twelve I'd been invisible to young girls, now at forty I was a dirty old man. How quickly the years had passed!

xxx

Sept 26, 1978.

In my imagination, Vancouver had remained the capital of debaucheries; now it appears a sleepy provincial town. I took the treeless stretch to the port. The once famous brothel area was now drab, stained grey from harsh winters of rain and snow. It lacked the excitement of my youthful desire to be pampered and disciplined for my uncontrollable sexual cravings.

Now as I strolled slowly through this area, I watched each woman as she wandered aimlessly from bar to bar, waiting for the next trick. Each woman brought back memories of some long-forgotten fling, a one-night stand or simply someone I'd desired, like the pretty blonde with steely blue eyes I'd first kissed; an open invitation to bathe in vanilla cream.

I noticed a blowsy blonde, her plump posterior reminded me of the sexual kick I'd got as a young boy envisaging kneeling down, pulling up the cleaning woman's skirt and sinking between her plump cheeks as she scumbled the school floor. For a moment, I was tempted to live out my ancient fantasy on her wide haunches; however, the idea that I could pay and avoid an angry rebuke lost much of the intense thrill of the forbidden.

My interested stare attracted a coal black girl, perhaps Ethiopian. She waved me towards her, almost winning me over with her blend of brazenness. I shook my head and she turned away, her ass moving rhythmically towards another potential client. I smiled to myself. Some women look best from behind but what good was that, since they were taking their leave. I would have liked to see a woman animally approaching me ass-first, compliant and submissive as monkeys do when mating.

A slender brunette with bright red lipstick streaked across her mouth reminded me of a girl I'd known briefly, who painted both her upper and lower sets of lips. After sex with her, I would watch the water turn red as it ran down my legs in the shower. I next spied a strutting creature, whose grin showed her missing front teeth. The tingling sensation in my groin tempted me to let her unleash her toothless skill on me until I caught sight of a voluptuous Turk. Her fat, warm body, and spicy smell reminded me of a prostitute I'd once lain with. Surprisingly, she had proved rather indolent, her efforts falling short of my expectations. Somehow, it hadn't mattered, and I'd left her grubby couch feeling warmed and soothed.

As I passed from one bar to the next, I decided I wasn't ready to make a choice. Retracing my steps, I caught sight of a woman slowly descending a stair, a breeze lifted her dark hair that curled gently down her back. Something stirred and I froze. She gave me a quick look, direct as a knifepoint. My hesitation and the way I shivered made her solicitous. "Come along, dear," her voice the tone of my mother's. "The first time, is it, my little man?

Don't be frightened. Come to Mommy."

In her rather sordid room reminiscent of the rooms of much of my childhood, I felt the steel cuffs of my mother's all demanding love tighten round me. When she slipped her dress over her head and began to remove her black stockings. I shouted, "Don't. Stay dressed." Fierce with lust I'd grabbed her and drew her forcibly to me, sinking my face into breasts that smelt musky with sweat and stale perfume. Ripping her floating cami-knickers aside with a rough gesture I tore into her, furious to enter the murky depths of my birthplace. Her cry, perhaps in pain, but more likely in fear, satisfied my insane desire to feel I was forcing myself on her. As I came, I saw the wasted face of my mother, her withered body in loose clothes smelt of the grave. Her hands a grayish hue clutched at me. Suddenly, horribly, my mouth filled with ashes. I began to choke, my breath coming in short gasps.

The woman's face, full of apprehension peered at me as I zipped up my trousers, glanced about the room barely registering my surroundings. I pushed a few bills into the woman's hand and fled. Once outside, I began to run. The hotel lobby, when I reached it, had the depressing look common to cheap hotels. Thankfully it was empty. I hurried to my room, the ash still sharp in my mouth I tried to spit in the sink, but only managed a few dry coughs. Suddenly I remembered my mother had been cremated, rare for a Catholic. Her will had stated: Cremate me, I don't want to be buried alive.

I poured myself a whiskey from the fridge, then another until I'd emptied the supply. *Why did you have to die? Why did you abandon me?* I said in my half-drunken state. Instead of my mother's voice Ciguapa plaintively replied. "it was you who abandoned me. You forsook me in that moment of our full blossoming love. You tore yourself away cruelly. You violated your nature!"

My romantic smash up with Ciguapa had not been a total smash-up, it had dragged on for years, as grueling and painful as any passionate love story gone wrong could be. She claimed she had given herself *entire*; in the end she had taken me *entirely*—for everything, even a small inheritance. And I'd given it to her willingly out of guilt for not living up to my promises.

I dabbed at my eyes with a towel as the tears continued down my cheeks, dribbling around my chin. At length I blew my nose and fell into a deep sleep only to awake a short time later. The curtains were open, the moon perfectly ringed with clouds, shifted the light in the room and gradually filled it. On a sheet of paper, I scribbled: "I am condemned to wander blindly. My only wish is to end it all."

When I reached the street, I was dizzy as if I were falling off the roof of a very tall building. I began to pray as I continued doggedly onward, down one street, then another. By the time I reached the secluded end of the waterfront, I sagged with exhaustion. The beach area was deserted, the sky gaudy with crimson clouds, the color evaporating as the mist rose. I walked across a wooden dock to where the estuary opened out to the sea with no need to wade through the sucking mud. I stripped off my clothes, flicked away a halo of insects that hovered about me and leapt into the dark depths, then came crashing up for air a few seconds later. The slimy wetness clutched my legs. I'd forgotten to remove my shoes. Why bother I decided as I struck out towards the open water, swimming in long even strokes, my breath coming easily.

I rolled over on my back, looked at the distant shore and marveled at how the urge to live kept people going, how animals died while people, even those starving, went on struggling until they lost all hope. My fascination with death suddenly seemed idiotic. With all my strength I began to resist the current, zigzagging across it as I inched towards the shore. After what seemed a lifespan, the current calmed and I was in the inner waters. Exhausted I dragged myself ashore and shook first one leg and then the other, to free the greasy seaweed clinging to my sodden shoes.

The cold puckered my flesh and salt stung my eyes as I sprawled carelessly on the sand. A pair of birds were busy building their nest, my proximity no more disturbing to them than if I were a piece of timber. After recovering my clothes, I headed into the city. A couple of rough-looking youths moving in the shadows near the dock area alerted me to my danger. A moment later they sprang out of an alley. The dark-haired boy grabbed me from behind, the other, a tall, Nordic type held a pistol to my head. "One move and you die," he growled menacingly.

Joy flooded through me at the idea that my suffering was about to end. "Go ahead, shoot; you'll be doing me a favor," I jeered. My mouth spewing furious taunts seemed to confuse the two youths. "Hurry up and get it over with, you pig-head bastards. Shoot, for Christ's sake."

Unpredictably I began to feel foolish for not being frightened and a surge of adrenaline kicked in. I struck the dark pimply youth who reached into my pocket for my wallet and lunged at the other, twisting the gun out of his hand. Before I could aim the gun, they disappeared down the alley with my few bills and passport. After several gulps of fishy air, I began to laugh. *I could be dead instead of half dead.* Pocketing the gun, I made for the police station to report the attack and hand in the gun.

xxx

Oct 15, 1976.

After my frightening experience in Vancouver, Barcelona felt calmer even if it shrieked and clattered and roared around me. To quiet my mind, I spent today day following a winding path on the outskirts of the city. It unwound like a scroll and led me through wooded pines into a strange landscape, stripped of habitual distractions. The silence was not silence, more a hum of wind as it moved through the upper branches where woodpeckers pecked, and birds sang. Groups of small animals scuttled away, while larger animals stood frozen in mid-graze, staring at me.

Not exactly wanting to meet anyone, I was half hopeful I might. As twilight descended, I came apron a white chapel with a tall stone tower. In that barren and sacrificial place an existential angst embed itself in my bones and I flung myself to the ground to pray. What I heard was not God's words, but John Donne's. *Never send to know for whom the bell tolls; it tolls for thee.* Those words spread an exhilaration through my body like butterflies seeking to flee.

My return along the secluded trail, attractive in daylight, was now filled with sinister shadows, each a hiding place for evils about to attack. When the wind picked up, the shadows came alive with the furious rustling of lemon trees above my head and cries of hungry cats. I ran, knowing full well there was nothing to fear, yet full of fear. Back in my lodgings, soaked and dripping sweat, I didn't bother to change, I sank down at my desk to write. As long as my hand kept moving from left to right the words continued, one poem after the next, waiting to come out of my pen. The words came quickly, smoothly, transforming and reshaping themselves, always running ahead of me, stunning me each time I emerged from my trance to discover what I had written. A wake of happiness washed over me, filling me with a sense that I had, after a long and difficult journey, conquered my demons, slain the dragon and claimed my poetic place.

Chapter 16

Sometimes I wake up crying at night
And sometimes I scream out your name
What right does she have to take you away
When for so long you were mine
Dixie Chicks

Arthur sighed. It didn't take a whizz-kid to dupe it out, this tryst with Patasola was no free lunch. When she said she depended on the kindness of others he knew the gig was up. He was on shaky ground unless he came up with, as Woody Allen would say, genuine coin of the realm. She expected him to pay while she expected to spend—not on food or coffee but expensive Colombian brews and meals from the local café. In his innocence he had thought himself poor enough to avoid attracting a self-interested woman looking to be kept.

Any clever man would have twigged to Patasola's unspoken but clear stipulation: *If you have a ton of free time and would like to take care of a self-absorbed, needy, demanding child only interested in her own neurotic problems, I doubt you will find a better fit than me.* She was not a companion; there was no reciprocity or respect for his need to devote himself to his work. She often complained, "Oh, Arthur, life wit you soo borin. You annoyin. Never thought eet be like dees. It all work and spaghetti." With a twist of her eyebrows, her nostril would crinkle as if hit by a nasty smell.

Arthur bemoaned the fact he had once had an understanding wife sensitive to his needs, a knowledgeable, competent wife who let him get on with his work. Why had he been such an unfathomable imbecile to indiscriminately tear up everything—his marriage, his home, and his deepest self?

Alexia, with whom he often spoke, said, "Patasola is not a good match for a poet. She is neither sensitive, nor capable of higher thought. A hook without bait. Her doubtful past makes your claim to her saintliness questionable. She is not only foxy, but a cold, calculating woman with just enough of a brain to get what she wants. In crude words, she pimps off men. One porky plutocrat set her and her son up in an apartment and sent 8,000 smackers to her family every month. This arriviste now past her youth and getting a bit long in the tooth has reduced her expectations of capturing a millionaire, you are her latest victim.

When he told Patasola it was Katherine who had the

goodies, she had merely instructed him, "Get divorce, get cash." Her next suggestion that she be included in his will brought reality to the surface: *this is not love, this is payment for services rendered and hope for future riches in the event of my demise.*

Arthur sent out emails to friends hoping to correct the allegations circulating that Patasola was a predator who cozied up to rich old men. It didn't bother him that Patasola had been a kept woman or that she had paying protectors or whether they were, as she claimed, non-sexual. What he disliked was people seeing him as the old fool being taken for a squelching.

He could not bring himself to be entirely honest with Katherine or himself. I reality he was not ready to totally relinquish the present circumstance. Even if this ménage-a-trois caused him fretful, sleepless nights at the end of the day, he found equal and opposite pleasure in bringing home a special cheese to eat with Patasola and sending a reassuring email to his weeping wife.

Arthur could not now recall who had written the text that ran through his brain, a text that aptly describing his state of confusion. *A guy stacked like a deck of cards for things set to unfold entirely differently was in no way prepared for impossible tragedy. But who is set up for what is going to hit him? Who is set up for the tragedy of implausible suffering? Nobody. The tragedy of man it that he is not set up for either— that is every man's tragedy.*

Aug. 15, 2020:

> *Dear Katherine.*
>
> *One thing I can say I will be honest with you. I have habitually said things because I wanted the person— whom I cared about—to be happy, pleased. No more. I have nothing to hide. Neither am I obliged to disclose everything. No, I will not tell any more lies. Nor do I owe my entire life and conscience to anyone. Whereas I have aways thought this was the case. My feelings towards you, however clumsy, have not changed; I have always loved you and miss not being with you. I did not leave because of any resentment or loss of love for you! I do not blame you*

for anything. I failed, not you. Life changes but love is never lost. I am sure of that if of nothing else. And I admit I am not sure of anything!

Those years I spent with you were happy years. I desired you and grew to love you even if, at first, I feared your strength and determination. Our love of knowledge and contemplation of ideas and philosophy were the highest expression of Eros. Please let your mind and heart rest. I do love you and care about you deeply. I do understand you feel a bit spooked by my asking to come to see you for a couple of days in Venice after what you have been through. I do desperately want to see you.

Love Arthur

His philosopher friend had urged him to come to his senses and set things right with Katherine. In truth he cherished the hope of re-awakening her past tenderness and reconciling her to the present state, a state unlikely to endure. Katherine had not taken his departure quite the way he expected. Not that he had given much thought of how she would take it nor the depth of the scars his selfish act would open. He had just imagined she would be a bit more accepting. Physically she was absent, but never absent from his thoughts.

Despite his screw-ups and unkept promises having sliced away tiny pieces of their togetherness, he had for two decades treasured the safety and security of his marriage. With their linking and Katherine's supportive impetus his creativity had doubled. Their partnership flowered effortlessly in exuberance and communication of their interests and ideas.

Patasola's tantrums were as immutably difficult to avoid as finding the Holy Grail. Her lack of compassion and her flagrant disrespect for his desire to be correct in his dealings with Katherine made him question her religious saintliness, which had originally sparked his passion. Both Ciguapa, and even more so Patasola wanted total control and possession of their bedfellow for their personal use. The words of his friend Walter hit him full force: With a pathological neurotic, emotional abuse is borderline sadistic, their vampiric ways will destroy you if you don't do exactly as they want.

When he refused Patasola's request to accompany him on his visit to Katherine in the last days of August, her words echoed the words of Ciguapa. *If you loved me as much as I love you, you will give in to my wishes.* Well, not exactly Ciguapa's words, because Patasola was not capable of precise language whether Spanish or English. It was, "You a bee goin half a way. Either you bee lettin mee wit you or I not bee wit you never."

"Sorry, my brain didn't get that. There must be a hitch in my hearing, or my batteries need recharging. Are you saying I can't do anything without your consent?"

"Ya gotta stop," she would scream. "I donna want you writin her, talkin to her or seein her. Shee nothing. Dat's what you signed for. Dat's the contract." In an attempt to wrench his hand away from the computer she sent his computer crashing to the floor. It happened so fast he hadn't seen it coming, nor did he see Patasola grab a large kitchen knife and shred one of their cushions to ribbons before threatening to kill herself.

A leopard doesn't change its spots nor does a Columbian. It was no surprise when coked-up she began again to demand she accompany him to Venice. For peace of mind, he gave in, regretting he didn't ever do things his way, he always did them her way.

xxx

When Arthur met with Katherine in Venice the trepidation so evident on her face, and her emaciated form caused feelings of regret to flood his veins. Her expression, that of a weary traveler, and her attempt to hide her shaking brought his guilt to the surface. She crowded his mind with memories of their life together so full of mutual respect and creativity. He put an arm around her shoulder, pulling her close enough to drop a kiss on the top of her head. He wished this affair had never happened as it did or simply hadn't happened at all.

Their lunch on the Venetian Zattere was at times stressful but loving. "It's so good so see you," he murmured, as he reached out and tenderly wiped a tear off Katherine's cheek with his thumb. The vexing question was where they went from here? Perhaps Katherine was asking the same question as they headed back to the apartment because she began hyperventilating and sank to the ground gasping for breath. For an unbearable moment he panicked. Eventually, she recovered and as he helped her up and held in his arms she whisper, "We aren't on the same wavelength, we are pushing in different directions."

"No, not true," he said. "I'll be back after I've been to the bank."

She wanted him to say come with me and she almost believed he would. But he smiled and nodded and scurried away, his shadow disappearing in the shade.

xxx

Before he returned to Katherine, he called Patasola. The first indication that crazy had come a-knocking in his absence was the tone of her voice. It sounded like she'd been cornered by a menacing madman. It shook the ground and whatever part of him held to reason was swept away as he rushed back to the hotel. Patasola greeted him with an onslaught that made him feel the biblical Salome was not dancing on the head of John the Baptist, but on his own head. Ciguapa's kitchen knives were nothing compared to his fright as Patasola's fangs snapped as viciously as a piranha fish.

He responded with all the charm and poise of an angry gorilla, but it did not calm her hysteria. She accused him of every type of cruelty and disloyalty, while her eyes piercing him as if she was scanning the horizon through the sights of a high-velocity sniper rifle. "You is dirty shitty. You makin up to her after she writ dem things on Facebook about mee sendin you dirty photos? I gonna sue her."

"You can't sue for something that is true."

"You donna see mee face. I dinna show mee face."

He was astonished. The situation hit him like a kick to his vulnerability. Hard to identify a vagina mug shot while his face was on the porno photos for all the ghouls to see. Suddenly he felt vulnerable, should Patasola want to blackmail him, he was caught in a booby trap, his vitals cooked.

He locked himself in the bathroom. Shakily he took out his telephone to call Katherine and accidently dropped it in the toilet. He sighed. As least that settled one conflict. The uncontrollable woman screaming her lungs out in the next room could not so easily be dealt with. However, having accomplished her purpose of wrenching him away from Katherine her fiery temper began to subside. He heard her call room service for food and drink. No doubt she was now lounging about in her expensive silk underwear which she was so fond of having him buy.

He took off his glasses, rubbed his eyes and knelt to pray. Just as the Venetian bells struck midnight, God spoke to him, soft at first then louder, "Renounce!" He'd heard—or felt—the voice of the Creator only once before in answer to his prayers. He did not want to hear it now, but he heard the word "Renounce!" clear and precise. It was undeniable.

When he picked up the Bible it fell open, like a wet rag, at Romans 8:5-6 NIV: *Those who live according to the flesh have their minds set on what the flesh desires; but those that live in accordance with the true spirit of God have their mind set on what the spirit desires. The mind governed by the flesh is death; the mind governed by the spirit is light and peace.*

The next day, overwrought by feelings of guilt, Arthur sent a lame email to Katherine. His nose grew longer with his excuse he'd dropped his phone in the toilet and had gone in search for a shop to fix it. To his suggestion they meet for a coffee, Katherine replied with a simple, *No.*

Chapter 17

What good am I then to others and me
If I had every chance and yet still fail to see
If my hands are tied must I not wonder within
Who tied them and why and where must I have been
Bob Dylan

This trauma of being dumped again in Venice which caused the memory loss made it hard for me to understand what exactly had transpired. Arthur's emails supplied part of that answer.

Sept 30, 2020.

> *Dear Katherine.*
>
> *The fact that I could not refuse Patasola accompanying me to Venice exposes my fickle and feckless nature. I have decided after conversations with friends and a tough spiritual struggle, I could only resolve what has become an agony, by living alone. I have been living alone since mid-September when I refused to allow Patasola to return to Belgium. It is not a temporary thing; it is the way I want to live.*
>
> *I had a vision—or a symbolic perception in Venice, which shook me. Subsequently my view of things turned like a page, and I saw everything differently. I had been praying with all my soul when the voice of the Creator spoke—the words were clear and precise: "Renounce!" This REVELATION is the acknowledgement that I am the Creator of my own life and that I must remove these chains of passions and obey other chains. It is up to me to take responsibility for the way I need to live. I want no more lies or deceptions. I want to act and decide in accordance with my own deep feelings.*
>
> *Things will be all right between us. I am sure of it. I loved you and still love you. I know you think these are empty words, but they aren't. Voluntary changes are healthier than imposed or neurotic changes. I have just realized a new sculpture-poem, which is dedicated to you. I'll send you a photo.*
>
> *Love Arthur*

Arthur's decisions and actions were as changeable as a hurricane in the tropics. There was no way of knowing where the wind might blow him next. His second dumping did nothing to heal my digestive system. With my health in such a delicate state, I should never have agreed to meet with him. I'd only accepted after receiving an email from a good friend in Spain who said he'd spoken twice to Arthur about the importance of relinquishing his inappropriate relationship with Patasola and renewing our partnership. The penny dropped that my friend's real concern was centered on Arthur and the undesirable consequences of his continuing his association with, as my friend said, this peculiar woman.

As I'd waited for Arthur on the bridge in the pale Venetian sun a tsunami of emotions hit me, something between sorrow, and more sorrow mixed with grief, and anticipation. It cause my limbs to shake as if I was a toy whose batteries were making a last effort before they died.

During lunch, I tried to put Arthur at his ease hoping he might open up to me and explain his intentions. I was not too fond of his clownish shredded Weetabix type moustache and shaggy goatee which now spread across his chin as some kind of disguise. Later as we walked along the sea front, I was hit by the suspicion he was playing me. That he had he come to Venice, not as he'd said, to rebuild our relationship, but in the faint hope of convincing me to be the loving wife on the side while he paid the groupie for services rendered. The shock of this thought left grief in its wake and caused me to collapse.

Arthur saw me home, promising to return shortly, but as the lonely hours passed and no Arthur, I began to suspect he had tucked his groupie away in a hotel room, and she had prevented his returning. My exhaustion increased as each panicky minute ticked by underlining the utterly dismal appraisal of my lonely future. I looked at the sleeping pills on my bedside table. I took a couple of them, then thought why not take the whole bottle? *Why suffer the slings and arrows of my outrageous future?* Why go on with this misery, why not be free from absence. What stopped me was imaging myself choking to death, my hands clawing desperately at my throat, as I wheezed my way purple-faced into the afterlife. Just as revolting was the image of Patasola doing the can-can with her arthritic priest in joy at the news of my death.

In that bleak moment of hesitation, I heard the church bells ring out midnight. Suddenly I felt Arthur's presence, I heard his voice in my ear, I smelt him. The sensation was so overwhelming I jumped out of bed and began to search the apartment. It wasn't Arthur, it was Woody, my fairytale hero and fairy godmother. He smiled wistfully. "Hang in there. Anything worth dying for is certainly worth living for. Arthur can play you, but he can't destroy you. You are what you are, and you have plenty to live for." I wept in his arms cursing myself for having let Arthur upset the life I was trying to recreate.

Alexia, one of Arthur's closest friends in Madrid sent me an email to say she was completely disgusted by Arthur's behavior. "I know the whole story and I sincerely believe Arthur never meant to hurt you. He can't help his lies as he believes what he says when he says them. I've told him many times Patasola is an 'interested' woman who wants to piggyback off whatever he can offer her. It's about greed and opportunity. He is a cowardly person, full of fears, always wanting to be the protector of women who do not need his protection. He idealizes this Columbian, despite her being a kept woman of little intellect, he thinks she is quite splendid. With his enormous ego he has actually convinced himself she is in love with him."

Oct 15, 2020.

> Dear Arthur,
>
> I am only now recovering my memory which I lost after your second dumping. Somehow, I made it back to Paris although I have no idea how. Apparently, according to the therapist, the brain goes on automatic pilot in a case of memory loss. I am still working through a marathon of bits and pieces as memories return. I am racked by the question of why you asked to see me then brought your sordid garbage with you? Are you completely off your rocker or what? Until you unleashed this second dumping, I'd been holding on to the irrational hope we might find each other again. Who had I been kidding?

Certainly myself.

It is time to end this scandalous penny dreadful novel stuffed to bursting with handwringing torturous emotions. Not since Schlock has there been such a shoddy end to a loving partnership. If some crap-eyed producer slung this tale together into an awkward TV soap, no one would ever deem it good enough to watch, much less embody it.

You go about in a fog, never seeing the whole picture. Invariably you self-sabotage rather like Nixon in fear you might not be up to scratch. You are nothing more to me now than a one-dimensional cartoon, a mere chapter in my life—the itch that remains after the limb has been amputated. If you lie down with dogs, you get up with fleas. Fleas are all you deserve.

Katherine

You might well ask, why did I need a therapist? Certainly, I would not have bothered except for the insistence of my doctor who hoped it would help keep what I ate down rather than each mouthful filling the toilet. I had doubts about therapists but the lift in my spirits I routinely experience after each session made me believe was doing me good. My appointments were now in her office and to pass the waiting time, I picked up one of the pamphlets left out on a side table.

It was entitled: *Emotional vampires are toxic, they drain us of our energy and leave us feeling emotionally exhausted and often unable to engage in self-care. Emotional vampires are parasitic pathological neurotics who 'feed off' the emotions and resources of empathetic and highly sensitive people who have poor boundaries. They cater to the victim's ego, distracting them with manipulative tactics in order to gain control over them. They drain people emotionally, mentally, physically, and financially, in the belief these resources will make them superior and more powerful. There is no such thing as reciprocity with emotional vampires. Often, they make their victims feel guilty for their lack of total loyalty to them while never owning up to their abusive behavior.*

Emotional vampires cause victims to feel depressed, anxious, frightened, and confused. They cause them to question their own reality, including their overall mental, physical, and emotional well-being. Often the victim's work and productivity and ability to focus is affected. The key to recovery, for co-dependents, is to acknowledge their own vulnerability and weaknesses to malignant predators. Above all they must avoid self-blame and turn their energy towards getting out of the relationship.

A chill crept up the back of my neck as I stared blankly about the consulting office. These weren't woo-woo phrases one might hear from a palm reader at the fair. They described Patasola exactly and confirm Arthur's claim that he had been emotionally vampirized. As I read on, an unexpected rush of emotions suddenly clogged my throat. The following text not only applied to the groupie but to Arthur's actions. Which made me question if he was also a pathological narcissist?

Any relationships with a narcissist is an illusion. Narcissists lie and believe their own lies. Their claim to love is illusionary. They can't be honest about their feelings because they lack empathy. Like an alcoholic hiding a bottle, a narcissist wants to know where their victim is even after separation. They will keep track of them because they want their victim's emotion and attention to be focused on them.

xxx

The therapist greeted me warmly, folded her hands together and asked me how I was doing? I said my reading the pamphlet entitled: *Emotional vampires are toxic,* had disorientated me.

She weighed my words as her eyes gave me a slow once-over. "Are you asking me, do vampires exist? Of course, they do. Not as blood suckers, but emotional vampires take possession of the vulnerable in an attempt to acquire their talents and financial resources. Kipling's interpretation of the word 'vampire' was a woman who takes demonic possession of vulnerable men to suck out their life force. Let's face it, we are all fascinated by vampires because they epitomized the *femme fatale.* In the film *The Vampire,* Theda Bara, one of the first sex symbol of the film industry, seduces and bleeds men not of their blood but of their free will. Emotional vampires are certainly dangerous to their victims, but just remember Patasola can't hurt you except with Arthur's assistance."

"Exactly. I am afraid he is vulnerable to her manipulating tactics."

She waved her hand as if brushing aside that possibility. "All forms of trauma share the character of disempowerment which shatters our worldview. It attacks our confidence and floods us with morbid images, emotions, and fears. The best protection against temptation is cowardice. I would assume Arthur is more frightened of you than he is of disobeying the demands of this pathological neurotic." She cleared her throat, as one might clear away thoughts that were no longer relevant. "My function here is to form a narrative with my patient, but no productive therapeutic work can be done until the patient has recouped some sense of their own agency."

"Arthur confuses me by saying his feelings have not changed. That and he still loves me."

The therapist looked bemused. "Nothing is more confusing than the betrayer saying to the betrayed 'I've never stopped loving you'. Believe it or not, it's a rather standard phrase. And the heartbroken spouse wants to believe it! Betrayers cheat then rationalize with trite narratives that have little basis in reality. One should not put up with disordered people. They want engagement if only to throw others off the scent of their misdeeds. I imagine Arthur feels love for you and lust for this new person, but neither meet the criteria for being in love. Fidelity allows you to believe in love. Fidelity allows you to sustain love. Fidelity is the one thing promised in virtually every religious tradition. If you cheat on someone, you deny their reality, bit by bit, lie by lie. Infidelity is the theft of reality. Breaking faith breaks the marriage."

She paused and looked at me questioningly through her finger-stained glasses as my eyes filled with tears for the old Arthur—the one who I thought loved me, the one who asked me to marry him on an ordinary Saturday afternoon. Not for the new Arthur the hypocrite who had now given me his mother's role, or more likely Ciguapa's role, as the dumped woman he pretended to still love. "Please God, bin this guy, he's defective and not who I thought he was. It's not my wasted years I want back it is my dignity."

"Your story is not unique, it happens every day. Women discover the person they love is nothing more than a mediocre man with mediocre morals. In this youth-oriented society, midlife crisis is just as likely to hit at the age of eighty-four as any other time. His sex addiction is as real as any other addiction. But Arthur's problem may well be more complicated; his ventromedial prefrontal cortex, the gland behind the nose, a small, but critical part of the brain may be damaged. People with a damaged cortex can be highly intelligent and functional but they lack judgment. They literally trust every whim and invariably make wrong decisions. Something Kierkegaard suffered from. He loved a woman, she loved him, but he broke off his engagement for all the wrong reasons and suffered excruciating regret when reality dawned."

It was just as likely Arthur was still the greedy egocentric child. Certainly, he reminded me of the guys in Fellini's early Italian film *I Vitelloni* (the young bulls). I'd found Fellini's films endlessly fascinating and certainly *I Vitelloni* is an unforgettable masterpiece of four sharply drawn Italian male character sketches. Each man embodies characteristics not only similar to Arthur's, but characteristics that are evident in all men to varying degrees. The film was a great success and secured Fellini's reputation. It is set in Fellini's hometown of Rimini. Four young overgrown layabouts stumble into various misadventures as they seek to spice up their lives. Faust is the skirt chasing leader of the pack. He is married to his pregnant sweetheart but that does not prevent him from carrying on as if single. The clownish Alberto, the perpetual child and hopeless dreamer, is partly supported financially by his sister and yet he insists he has a male right to watch over her morals. Leopoldo, the would-be playwright thirsts for fame and dreams he can be a great writer and will one day stage a play. Moraldo plays the conscience of the group as they trek their way through various scenes never at any moment taking responsibility for their actions. Like Arthur they are ready to grab the pastry in the window and gobble it down while taking pleasure in having got away with it.

I was recently invited to a Venetian dinner party for the

director of Fellini's least successful film *City of Women*. A hilarious but serious film that not only totally captured my attention but amused me far more than any of his other films. In *City of Women,* Fellini reveals, in a self-mocking, poetic way, the male gaze: how men desire, view and objectify women. I assumed this film was Fellini's confession of his amused impotence when faced with the new woman of today. Male critics thought it too near the knuckle and most said they left the cinema nostalgic for the compliant women of the past.

Marcello Mastroianni plays the main character in this film, *City of Women*. He is perfect as the classy but lecherous older man who never fully matured. He sees women as sexual objects he must conquer, a classic theme that populates so many European sex farces. He encounters Donatella, a beautiful temptress, on a train, and instantly decides he must have her. Impulsively he follows her like a dog in heat when she disembarks from the train in the middle of nowhere. After stumbling through some fields, he finds himself at a convention of militant feminists. To flee this nightmare, he is helped by a heavy-set female motorcyclist, who, in a reversal of roles, gives him a ride, then threatens to abandon him in the middle of an agricultural field if he refuses her desperate advances. He escapes but is picked up and terrorized by a group of hell-raising nymphets in a jeep, acting exactly as macho young males would act towards a woman they had bailed out of a predicament.

Later, we see Mastroianni on the estate of Dr. Xavier Katzone, a caricature of the ultimate womanizer. In his perverse mausoleum, a lavish shrine of floor to ceiling portraits of women Katzone has seduced, he is hosting a party to commemorate his 10,000th female conquest. Mastroianni dances with the scantily clad Donatella and her friend but fails to seduce either. An encounter with his wife Elena causes his guilt to surface and makes him reconsider his frivolous lusts. In a dream sequence he glides down a birth-like chute while re-living pivotal scenes of his childhood crushes: his mother, a babysitter, a nurse, and a prostitute. He is thrilled when he pops out into a room filled with all his past conquests. This lecherous old man expects to be pardoned and adored by all these past loves instead they turn on him and condemn him for his lies and betrayals. In the last scene, he is in the basket of a hot air balloon which has the form of naked Donatella. From below Donatella with a machine-gun fire at the balloon, bursting it and sending Mastroianni plummeting to the earth. I doubt many women cinema goers felt sorry for him.

Chapter 18

I've looked at love from both sides now
From give and take and still somehow
It's love's illusions that I recall
I really don't know love
Really don't know love at all
Joni Mitchell

Acquaintances and friends were as much astonished as I was when Arthur dumped me. Some were embarrassed into silence but most burst into laughter at the idea that an intelligent 84-year-old man could have such ridiculous illusions. Everything is funny if it is happening to somebody else, not you.

Friends went on inviting me to dinner—to dinners I couldn't eat. They listened without judging or telling me to pull myself together as I poured out my heart to just about everyone including the mover as he loaded Arthur's possessions into the van. He merely nodded and said he'd heard worse stories, mine wasn't so bad.

Thankfully, Sarah stayed grounded. "Sparks that fly don't come back," she insisted. Stop believing Arthur has your best interests at heart, he doesn't. Cheaters cheat because they can, they lie because they can, they never change their spots because they can't."

Those isolating Covid-19 days forbid socializing, so I was doubly pleased when my friend Cassandra, an old friend of Arthur's as well from his New York days, dropped by bearing gifts and a bottle of wine. Her blonde hair tied back in a neat bun revealed a face that had hardly altered in the years I'd known her. I smiled as she plunked her elegant self-down among the cushions and cocked her head with frank alertness, "How are you?"

"Strange you should ask. I'd set my heart on waking up today forgetting I ever knew Arthur. Other than that, everything's peachy."

Cassandra poured out a couple glasses of wine. "In his younger years, Arthur was a major-league flirt and world-class adulterer, but an absolute novice in love. no doubt this groupie inflates his ego and makes him act like a dog in heat chasing his tail or what he thinks is his tail."

I sighed. "I'm convinced his background had a detrimental effect on him as did the strict Catholic school.

Instead of becoming aware of girls in the playground, he hung about the Vancouver dock area, ogling prostitutes in minimum attire. He had often amused friends with his stories of being lost in the dock labyrinth. Retracing his steps in panic, the prostitutes would recognize his having passed many times and would call out to him. In quiet moments they talked to him, even touched his penis through his trousers and asked if he had the money. One of the girls had said he was so cute they should give it free, the others objected, *don't corrupt him, he's only a boy*. One teased and ask him to show his what not and he'd run away fainting with desire."

She smiled and shook her head. "Not exactly the best environment for a sensitive boy. A few months ago, I bumped into Arthur in the street. Over a drink he told me that he loved you, then added something about his not being a good partner. I remember thinking: why is he telling me this? The two of you seem a perfect match, so I asked point blank: 'Is there another woman?' He'd nodded and said he had no plan to carry on with this Columbian, but she had a hold over him. He felt guilty about something he had done to her. At first, he wouldn't tell me, then broke down and admitted he may have given her herpes. 'Did you?' I asked. He said he didn't know but felt responsible." She lifted her eyebrows. "Hardly responsible for him to go whole hog and brutally dump you because he'd carelessly infected a hot Colombian with herpes."

I looked at her in shock.

"You didn't know?"

I shook my head.

"When I asked if she managed to bring back some of his youthful vigor, he said it wasn't like that. She'd made herself available and he'd become entangled because of her deep religious dedication. I had a bit of a laugh when you told me about her sending him porno photos. A truly religious person is unlikely to send porno photos of her sexual organs to a man she hardly knows!"

I grimaced. "She sent them to a gullible idiot."

"From what Arthur told me about this woman, I suspected straight off she was a professional tracker with vampiric tendencies. A new type of witch turned courtesan lurking on the dark side collecting wealthy males by using pussy power. Latinos are particularly agile at attracting male attention. Can't blame them! Almost the only way they have to get what they want. Some are capable of mesmerizing men with theatrical promises of eternal love and a fairytale relationship. They act like devoted guardian angels, full of care and attentiveness but as Arthur will find out, as he did with Ciguapa, it is an exercise in futility unless he does exactly as this Latino wants."

"Many of his friends warned Arthur that Patasola survives by collecting old guy willing to pay. I doubt it ever troubled him that Ciguapa was kept by an old guy or that it's the same with Patasola. I imagine what he cannot admit is that it is not love she is simply after a meal ticket."

Cassandra nodded. "In a way Arthur thinks all women are whores. No disrespect intended because he doesn't think there is anything wrong with being a whore. It's a stigma that applies to any woman who steps outside the bounds of 'appropriate' sexuality. It is likely Arthur does not distinguish between prostitutes who are there for his sexual pleasure and nonprofessionals, except that nonprofessionals are often less amenable to his sexual predilections than indulgent prostitutes. He treats prostitutes with respect and wants to know them. For that reason, we have always been friends."

She gave me her Mona Lisa smile, but I couldn't smile. Her words reminded me of all the extra-curricular vulgar stuff Arthur wanted to indulge in. *If it had been elegant or refined okay, but peepholes in Pigalle, dinners feeling other people up and swingers' parties—all sordid and sleazy.* "Arthur often hinted he would not mind my gently beating him, but no way could I associate beatings with affection. It was nevertheless quite a shock when I discovered Arthur writing love letters to a prostitute who beat him."

She pulled a philosophical face, as if she'd picked up a puppy and it had peed all over her. "Wow! It's one thing to provide a veneer of civility to being beaten, but to write her love letters is more than just tipping your hat to a prostitute."

I rolled my eyes with a distinct feeling Arthur was a complete loser. "Condemning him for indulging in this perversity would only have made him more determined to hide it. As a discouragement, I went with him to make sure nothing bad happened to him."

She lifted her chin a little and met my eyes with something not far from amusement. "Arthur is not quite normal. You must have recognized that. Artists often crave experience that is gross but stimulating, they live in a rarefied atmosphere in which art is born. Ugliness is part of their animalistic excitement. Throughout history, artists have claimed they need to *s'encanailler un peu*, you know, sink into debauchery, an impulse conveniently entitled, *nostalgie de la boue*. It's like the sensual pleasure a pig gets from rolling around in his own shit, getting down in the muck. But it's not just artists; many men are attracted by sodomy and want to be peed on. A return to the first treasure they produced—their own shit and pee. Vulgarity turns some men on, but they don't like to live with it. I think Arthur, for the moment, is living with it, but it won't last."

The idea seemed to amuse her, and a flush passed over her pale countenance. "You say Arthur claims this groupie's religious fanaticism captured him, but it's more likely he was mesmerized by this sexual vamp masquerading as a nun. Our psychosexual stages are oral, anal, phallic, and genital. By this logic, men like Arthur are stuck in the oral stage, babies searching for their next comforting feed. A vamp gives oral men the illusion they are getting what *they think they want*."

She gave me a close look laced with a soupçon of ennui. "It isn't just that Arthur is a codependent neurotic, he also has a desire for divine love inherent between the Goddess and lesser creatures. He was the lover/son of Ciguapa. Now it's the reverse, he is the father/lover of his granddaughter."

I pressed my hand to my forehead, which had begun to ache. Arthur mostly hadn't followed up on any flirts except one, a woman who could have been his daughter. He claimed nothing happened but that did not mean he hadn't been up for it. He'd call Suzie eighteen times in one day attempting to meet up with her. Obviously, since I paid the bills, I saw his calls. With his bad memory he'd likely forgotten I was not Mommy back home—but his lover and helpmate who at that moment was doing his tax declaration. He would have been humiliated to hear how young Suzie mocked his ridiculous fantasy to friends.

Calling him a silly old man to imagine she could be interested in a man the age of her father!

Cassandra stared out at the fading afternoon, her face slightly flushed, shadows deepening in the corner of her eyes. "I'm sure you are aware I'm what people call demi-mondaine. Like Patasola, I want to be kept. Things have changed but as a kid I thought my choice was marriage or a boring job. I soon gave up any idea of working. Well, my dear, who'd give me a job? Believe me I'm useless. When I failed to fill my New England role of perfect child and ideal adult, I left my family to my family. You leaving your family implied the possibility of success, but I never wanted success. I wanted comfort, money, and leisure. I refused to be a slave in an office or a domestic slave to a man. I prefer men slaving for me. Everything has its price and I saw no reason why it should upset moral sensibilities to capitalized on men's vulnerabilities. Since they regard women as sexual objects, I decided to be one." Her smug look had something graceless about it that slightly offended me.

"The world might look down on a mistress or courtesan, but she doesn't just offer her body; a man invests in what she might be willing to do for him sexually. Men pay one way or another; with whores they usually get their money's worth. Since I have an indifference to my physical self, men can do with me as they please." She laughed before adding, "within limits."

I shook my head. *Maybe it's true nothing is given without hope of return, and nothing is wholly unselfish. Foolishly I supposed I'd hoped, that in return for my love and financial support, Arthur would love me and be faithful.*

Cassandra picked up the bottle of wine and poured out the remains. "It's all about power, not men's power, but my power because of a man's acceptance of the unstated agreement. You might think I'm not a feminist because I exchange my sexual favors for material advantage, but I am a feminist precisely because I don't accept gender inequality. I love pro-sex feminists because they know their worth. They call the shots. In their exaggerated ultra-sexy way, they assert their right to be who they wish to be and to live as they please. An undeniable advance in women's empowerment in this semi-stalled feminist revolution."

I nodded. "One has to admire how pro-sex feminists openly confront the evil men who accused us of taking all the fun out of being a man because we oppose the commercial entertainment of the female body being stripped, bound, raped, tortured, mutilated, and murdered. And it's a definite change to have these men calling pro-sex feminists, whores rather than manhaters or lesbians as they called us." The 1960s had been amazing with all those publications like *Spare Rib* and the remarkable monthly, *Nova Magazine*. "Sixty years on, I still don't think men will ever catch up to us and become our equal."

"Not likely!" She laughed and smoothed back the strands of streaked blond hair that enhanced the purity of her porcelain perfection. "I like to believe God is rather illusive whereas Satan is a seagull waiting for inattention to sweep in and make off with the toast. Arthur is toast to Patasola's manipulations."

"Yeah, most men don't notice they are being manipulated, what they notice is a woman being decisive. They seems to think that upset the natural order of things. They think only men have the right to be decisive even if the woman is cleverer."

She sighed, "Hard not to laugh at the poetic justice of this herpes infested vampire now having to ask her old men protectors to wear condoms. A downer for those eighty-year-olds already having trouble keeping it up." She obviously couldn't help from sniggering.

"Arthur will wake up one day and feel humiliated for his being a gargoyle wrapped in a bathrobe of ridicule."

"True. Arthur's saying—just the music of chance, just the way I am is ridiculous. We are not unalterable; we are not caricatures. Eventually, Arthur will have to lie down in his uncomfortable bed he has so carelessly made. Whether he sleeps depends on his ability to live with how destructive he has been to himself as well as you."

"Well, he does have a bad memory, so who knows?"

Chapter 19

Honey, just allow me one more chance
To get along with you
Honey, just allow me one more chance
Ah'll do anything with you
Bob Dylan

WE'RE
ALL
MAD
HERE

His adventure with Patasola which had held a certain perverse appeal to Arthur, now swung into ham-fisted remorse like left over porridge. He felt like a circus clown pirouetting across a tight rope when he suggest to Patasola she remain in Spain after her return ticket expired mid-September. "I need to recover," he said lamely.

"Recover? You bee goin' off cliff or somein'? You crazee man, somein' bee fishy in you. I ask dee Lord to save mee from devil work."

Dec 4, 2020.

> *Dear Katherine,*
>
> *I read you carefully, agree generally, where you are understandably mistaken is when you say you doubt this passion is over, because it is over. My illusions about Patasola as the perfect fit dissipated long time ago. Her lack of compassion for your health and my need to talk to you caused fierce, outbursts that showed me a side of her I did not like—a total contradiction of religious teachings.*
>
> *I am so sorry for everything. I have been especially marked by your sadness and suffering. I know you doubt this, but I do love you. You're not weak, you reacted to my departure like a neglected tigress! Nonetheless, I see that this has weakened you. To say I was torn up from my roots by this passion is not just a ridiculous excuse. To say I lost control in my ravings is not an attempt to avoid censure for my behavior. I'm careless, unthinking, irresponsible and selfish. Yes, I am deeply guilty.*
>
> *I've used up energy and time in many wasteful ways during my life, and a good share of it I wasted on women. This has to end. I need to put my total energy and total time into work. I want to act and*

decide in accordance with my own deep feelings and needs. This is the step I have decided to take with respect to my life. I want no more lies or deceptions. I say with certainty that I will be honest and transparent from now on. I'm going to Madrid next week to return Patasola's possessions and explain how things stand between us—that we can only be friends. I will be at the Las Murallas hotel for a week.

Just one more thought before going to sleep—it happened, yes, and it was a misery, but it is in the past. My question to you is why weigh anchor instead of heisting up and taking the wind of life in your sails? A huge breath of air! We can be friends, we can be close, we can recover much—it depends on your feelings and wishes. Please let's be simple. We are broken but the broken pieces can fit together and create something workable, even wonderful.

Love Arthur

xxx

Dec 6, 2020.

Dear Arthur,

Vladimir Nabokov didn't just write the novel Lolita, he wrote the lesser known, *Laughter in the Dark* which is rather close to our own story. The protagonist's young mistress plots to replace his wife and after a visit to his apartment she leaves her footprints for the wife to discover in the hope of upsetting their ménage. Patasola left her footprints, but instead of confronting you, I gave you space in the hope our partnership and love were strong enough to survive a fling.

You recently questioned me about our future as if you were waiting for me to decide it. With so much uncertainly on your side and your inability to stick to what you say you are going to do, I find it impossible to imagine what future you have in mind. I only know if I am not the woman of your life, I cannot be anything to you. I cannot be the woman you turn to in moments of need, while you pretend to live alone yet carry on exchanging endless declaration of love with this groupie. I know you do this because I know you. It took you thirty years to give up your fairytale fictions about Ciguapa. I suspect this is just a repeat scenario.

Renounce may be a **REVELATION** but only if you are ready to renounce. Breakthroughs don't happen spontaneously. They sit in the margins of our minds waiting for the micro-shift click, when finally, we pay attention to what our gut is telling us. Are you ready to admit your irrational decisions are famous for going wrong? Can you extricate yourself from this crazy obsession? Will you now follow the voice of the Creator? This **REVELATION** is meaningless unless you actually do *Renounce* and begin to be honest with me?

Katherine

xxx

Dec 8, 2020.

Dear Katherine,

I regret what I say still leaves you in doubt. Please understand I am not trying to convince you of anything. Poetry matters if it reveals something of the world beyond. Rilke was a fool in everyday but an angel of intuition. His advice was: "The work of the eyes is done. Go now and do the heart-work on the images imprisoned within you". Life does not get better by chance, it gets better by change. I am on a different path. Walking towards death but with a consciousness I never had before. I know my soul, this is a sea-change. From now on no more pretense, no more frivolous intent, or romantic fictions.

Look, Katherine, let's be peaceful and get this out of our heads; life does change and will continue to change—for the good if we let it. I believe that many couples have been able to reconcile, no doubt a minority—it takes creativity. Very good things can bloom here! Life is not closed or predetermined! There is no reason why it should be between us! For

> *my part, I believe we can make something beautiful,*
> *but it is up to you. I am happy you are better, and*
> *you're going to recover thoroughly. It is what I most*
> *ardently wish for. It is a good thing you tell me that if*
> *you are not the woman of my life, you cannot be*
> *anything to me. That is fresh and open. It will be as*
> *you wish. We'll talk again when I get back from*
> *Spain. If you wish, a real sit-down pleasant restaurant*
> *talk. You take care of yourself, be well.*
> *Love Arthur*

His passion for Patasola had lasted until the shower. The shower being her un-Christian lack of sympathy for Katherine's suffering. As he headed for Spain, that made him determined to obey the voice of the Creator. But even before the plane took off for the lustful Billy Goat/Mr. Hyde kicked in and he invited Patasola to the Canaries. He'd even joked that they could marry there. The trip to the Canaries fell by the wayside after her hysteria scene, her behavior had embarrassed him and his friends at his birthday lunch in Madrid.

He had not seen Patasola again until the evening before his departure from Madrid when he arranged to deliver her possessions to her home outside the city. One drink led to two drinks, then to kicking off their shoes, to peeling off their clothes and doing things he swore he would no longer indulge in. Intrigued as he was by sexual perversions, even perversions had their limits. It wasn't just his abhorrence for Patasola's perverse nature, he actually became ill; almost too ill to make it back to Belgium.

Dec 17, 2020.

Dear Arthur.

I may love to shop but I'm not buying your bullshit. You were beautiful in my dreams, but you are a nightmare in reality. Am I annoyed, or angry that you are unable to stick to your resolutions, but I have simply hit the ultimate degree of speechlessness caused by your unashamedly deceitful actions. I want to put duct tape across your mouth to stop your

'Trump like' lies that pile up like sour-smelling refuse sacks. Any normal right minded intelligent woman would have given up on this charade long ago. It is humiliating that I haven't.

You said: *I read you carefully, agree generally, where you are understandably mistaken is when you say you doubt this passion is over, because it is over. I want no more lies or deceptions. I can say with certainty I will be honest and transparent from now on.* Instead, of renouncing this carnal relationship and setting the story straight, you invited her to spend a week in the Canaries. You are so careless and slowwitted you don't even realize all purchases show up on the old iPad. You even provided queasy chuckles for boggle-eyed friends who told me you were so ill after your latest sex session you were not sure you could get on the airplane. Perhaps you expect sympathy as a victim of the inexcusable actions of your lustful Billy Goat betrayal.

The movie star Robin Williams was surely speaking about you when he said: *God gave man a penis and a brain but not enough blood to use both at the same time.* How do you live with your deceitful, spineless lies? Where is that Christian Identity you claim to have found? Lost again?

You claim you do not want to sin, yet you continue to submit to temptation. You sense the call to holiness, but you do not answer. You want to repent, but you don't. For your sake, I hope God has a sense of humor and forgives disobedient sinners.

Katherine.

Katherine's email turned the marrow of Arthur's bones cold. His thoughts drifted to a time when he believed worldly things were simpler, a time when the Petit Prince would have been true to himself. His actions were pitiful, and he had entered into them willingly. In disobeying God's command, he had set the seal against reconciliation with Katherine. That left him a lonely old man, gasping in pain on a starched white hospital bed. That thought plunged him into the depths of self-loathing.

Dec 20, 2020.

> *Dear Katherine,*
>
> *It is very hard to spit it all out. I have no defenses, no resistance. In a word, like Charles Dickens I was too cowardly to do what I knew to be right, and too cowardly to avoid doing what I knew to be wrong. You are a more honest human being. It's true there is no such thing as just sex, it all passes through the mind and the imagination. An enormous force that channels social and romantic constructs propelling all species heedlessly. It is a mistake to think desire is love, passions are much more related to hate, to illusions, to delusions, and fantasies than to love. In the mind alone, it undergoes innumerable appearances and forms. It catches one by surprise. Sex is a huge force. It can be good and fruitful, or it can be extraordinarily destructive as it was with her. A punch line to my foolishness. You cannot imagine what it was like because you have a healthy normal sexuality.*
>
> *With obsessions there are no satisfying answers. When you're mentally off on another planet, you may know something isn't right but at the time it just seemed like reality. Interacting with her I was out of control, swept up in her crazy chaos. I was drawn into a vortex of perversion, into dark humiliating and degrading sexual practices of a sadistic nature. It was foolish of me to think I could possibly enter that dangerous realm. It was totally perverse. Patasola is not a normal woman. She prays to avoid punishment for her evil acts. I realized that too late. No normal healthy woman would act as she did. This last session has destroyed any sexual need in me. I now risk losing my precious gift of health for having ignored God's words.*
>
> *Love Arthur*

Arthur wandered about his empty apartment, which appeared stripped of life. He had never bothered to furnish it completely. He liked it that way. What he did not like was coming home to eat from an empty fridge and sleep in an empty bed. Worse were the complicated machines he didn't know how to use: the washing machine, dishwasher, and stove. All required knowledge he did not have.

Any experience not shared—whether a meal, a show or music made him feel like his handful of monkey-nuts had been ripped from his grasp by a passing drunk. Arthur's only friend in the city was less friendly, repelled that Arthur could have participated in such a riotous absurdity. To ease his loneliness, he watched an extraordinary Cronenberg film about Freud and Jung called, *A Dangerous Method.* Jung claimed he was not a victim of his repressed psyche; but a victim of his choice to yield to an affair with Spielrein. A necessary kind of madness because creativity required such boundary violations. Jung tells Spielrein she is the most important love of his life, which at that point he believes. Jung's role could have been cast for him because his own adulterous affair had returned him to loving God and the spiritual meaning of prayer. His mistake had been falling victim to the superfluous pap of this unruly Medea in the belief she was his religious guide.

South American Christian beliefs are often mixed the previous primitive religions and witchcraft. Patasola claims she has vivid hallucinations and frenzied flights where she visits people, influences events, punishes offenders, and has long conversations with God. Arthur was skeptical and assumed her imaginary flights were due her applying 'witch's brew', a mixture similar to the ointments medieval witches had made and spread on the broomsticks they rode.

As the festive season approached, Christmas, hovering like a ghost made him feel like a boat loosed from its moorings, or Cinderella bereft of a fairy godmother. Unable to bear the idea of being alone, he attended church, participated in the sacraments, lived frugally, and loved God.

Sharing Christmas with Katherine's family had given him a pleasure he had missed by not having children. He had become an integral part of the family, adoring the grandchildren as if they were his own. Even if they did not know the full details of his deceit, they had been gravely wounded by his carelessly abandoning the family and they had now rejected him.

This pantomime with Patasola had injured him and drained him physically as well as causing a serious dimple in his finances. And yet he still grieved for her, for the pitiable barefoot child from the Pampas, abandoned in the street and made pregnant at a young age. In a moment of weakness his mind switched like the hands of a clock, reversing his resolutions. Anything seemed better than this intolerable loneliness.

Dec 25, 2020.

Dear Patasola,

Merry Christmas my love, my thoughts are with you this morning. It is almost a year since we spent those four magical days together. You ask me constantly if I really love you, the answer is simply yes. I have not wanted any woman as I have wanted you. You ask why we are not together? Why this has been so painful? Because when I met you, I was with a woman in a loving relationship that had lasted twenty years. Instead of being honest with her I wounded her dreadfully which caused my concern for her physical and mental health. I'm not proud of my behavior.

Her telling friends she opened her heart and purse to me mortified me as did her saying you sent me porno photos. Wounding yes, but nevertheless true. I am not saying this justified her letting people know about my betrayal and our treachery, but her reaction came out of her grief and anger.

Now for my own physical crisis. Once the plane landed, I went straight to the doctor who confirmed my physical health, which had been good into my eighties, is now fragile. The doctor is not going to do a radical operation. He has done a delicate and painful intervention, which is enough for now. A bit like a hysterectomy. I want to maintain my good health for another ten years if God gives me those years. The doctor warned me the crisis could reoccur. I have been foolishly living under the illusion of still being a young man and now I am neutered. The shared bed is doubtful. See how you feel about this imposition. As well there's little chance of my cashing in immediately on my 'celebrity status' or of being able to implement my finances in the near future. I want to preserve our relationship and do projects together, but to take it slowly.

I embrace you with tenderness. The love I feel for you, I will always feel. We will see what happens when I have my apartment in Madrid.

Love Arthur

Chapter 20

Life is sad/Life is a bust,
All ya can do is do what you must
Bob Dylan

Comedians offer the hope, however slim, that it's not us who are broken but the world. Yeah, like really! And who broke the world in the first place? Many physiological studies have established that being helpful financially to another person creates a troubled emotional state in both the receiver and the giver. Had I been a pessimist or what Sarah claims is a realist, I would have twigged to the peril that awaited me when Lina, my fashion forecasting partner in *The Magazine*, hinted early on in our working partnership: *people don't want to owe anybody anything.* Yeah, straight from the horse's horoscope. According to psychological studies, nobody wants to be reminded they had once been without resources.

What is for sure is, if you help a starving dog and make him prosper, he will not turn around and bite you. I admit I was drawn like a moth to a candle, by both Arthur, and Lina. In thanks for me financial help they both turned around and dumped me when they felt they no longer needed me. Of course, you don't just get dumped by people you love; you are just as likely to get dumped by anyone you lend money to. Yeah, just for being generous. Want to test that? Want to get rid of someone? Just lend them money and they are gone.

One freaky Friday twenty-five years ago, my friends Bob and Arnold suggested I help their Dutch friend Lina, an amazing person with great talents get off their floor. Apparently, she had the habit of indulging in all sorts of weird traits, like smoking in bed even when she was dead drunk and getting up in the middle of the night to watch TV or eating leftovers for breakfast. I'd smiled at the idea of helping them to get her off their floor. Had they warned me, as they did many years later that Lina was a shark in disguise, I would let sleeping dogs lie.

The film *All About Eve* mimics my relationship with Lina. Me, Bette Davis meets a penniless fan Eve/Lina, Bette befriends Eve, and Eve becomes her understudy. Unbeknown to Bette, Eve is ruthless. She is out for what she can get, and she is willing to use anyone and everybody in her ruthless ambition to takeover and fulfill her aim to succeed no matter the cost.

Twenty-five odd years earlier Lina had rung my doorbell, just as I was about to have a glass of wine. "Join me?" I'd said holding up a glass.

"Wouldn't be having whiskey by any chance?"

I dug in the back of the cupboard and pulled out an old malt whiskey that someone had given me as a present.

"When I heard about you," she gushed like a fountain about to overflow, "I got this here weird feeling we gotta meet. I mean unisex is avant-garde and all, but I didn't get it till I see your designs predictin' what we all wanta wear."

No doubt just sweet talk but I loved it; who doesn't?

Lina in those days was a pugnacious little spirit with sparkling eyes, not exactly pretty nor plain; her alabaster skin like a blank canvas waiting for the painter. Aware of my scrutiny, she took out her lipstick and with a swift movement covered her cupid bow mouth in red without so much as a glance in the mirror.

As time went on, I became more enamored by her and the unique bubble of intimacy we created due to our common interests in art and literature. I had yet to meet Arthur, so our evenings together were often alcohol fueled, with Lina living up to the Dutch mastery of being an empty vessel for alcohol. She admitted she had a habit of drinking with fifty-year-old dudes one-day, and twenty-odd-year-old dudes the next. She would pick up who she wanted to screw for a night, keep them or dump them for another the next night. With a lopsided smile she said, "If I be truly honest, the male body is better designed than the male mind. Mostly I be wanting men for only for one reason. Sex."

If love and affection is the answer to anything, I'd like the question rephrased because love blinded me to Lina egocentric nature. She proposed we create an avant-garde, elite magazine for the fashion industry and she wanted my fashion intuition and financial help. She stretched out an imploring hand like an enticing queen bee, while I buzzed under her spell like a drone, intrigued by the idea of sharing a project with a fellow spirit. Of course, it is foolish to give a hand to someone so egocentric.

Something I was slow to learn as they are likely to take the whole arm without the least prick of a bad faith.

My talents, my fashion intuition and business sense were the secrets of my success in the design world. They wrapped me in folds like a silver lining which gave me a great shot at the roll of the dice. You might think people make their luck, but it has a lot more to do with preparation seizing opportunity. The 1970/80s were exceptional years where opportunities abounded for ambitious designers with the kudos to create their Jack and the Beanstalk dreams. *The Magazine* became a success against all the narratives of the impossibility of foreigners, especially women, being fashion futurists in a market the French once controlled. I had to hand it to Lina, she was a supreme editor, a sort of one-off imprint of many disjointed parts including being an erratic entrepreneur with a genius for mismanagement. Lina simply got by on her amazing intuition and the ability to create out of chaos. Like a screwball pantomime, her business reference simply her confidence in her eccentric destiny. Working with her was like trying to hold up a bank with a water pistol in the hope I would never have to defend myself from her vampirizing ways.

Much as I like the cartoon character of an upper-class cat psychiatrist who smokes with a cigarette holder spouts theories about people becoming stronger at the broken places, I believe it is perfect crap. In truth when our life raft goes over the falls and bursts into a million fragments, no way are we ever going to completely heal. If I am not totally cynical it is because I do not believe either Arthur and Lina, had the original intention to use me and discard me. Certainly, it never occurred to me that they would take my love and help for twenty years then spit me out without the least prick of bad conscience.

In the last year with Arthur there was plenty of evidence to raise my doubts about his fidelity. But with Lina it was only after bumping into Arnold and Bob as I drifted about the flea market that my misgivings about Lina's dealings behind my back actually surface.

Arnold greeted me with, "So, here's the genius observing and assimilating."

"Searching for stimulation more like it. This fitness craze

has led to developments in fabric technology and suddenly everything is high shine fabrics in bright electric colors.

They both laughed. "And the kids strolling the streets in tight sport clothes and tank tops believe it makes them instantly athletic. Like wearing sport shoes makes them a marathon runner."

Arnold threw me a curious look. "How are things going with Lina and *The Magazine*?"

"Okay, I think. We're reviewing this year's finances tonight." I wasn't about to admit to that Lina's lack of business sense and her annoying spendthrift ways was a constant worry.

"Be careful! Scratch beneath the surface and things get murky." I'd gazed at Arnold in alarm. "I'm just guessing. But I noticed your name is no longer on the credits."

A chill passed over me. I hadn't notice my name had been removed, but then I wasn't interested in credits. "Is this a warning?"

"Lina's grateful for your input and financial help, but with her, ethics and honesty fall by the wayside in the game of power and ambition. It's all about ego. She wants to take over control to prove she's the only genius."

Later I was still feeling apprehensive as I took a seat in Lina's living room, a transformed Bedouin camp of rugs and cushions. Lina bounced into the room in a stained Yohji Yamamoto sculptured dress and collapsed on the cushions. "Can't talk about finances or anythin' today. Christ, too depressed! Me father died on me holiday." She opened a bottle of whiskey and poured two hefty glasses. "When I was a kid, I fancied me dad. Guess like a lotta of girls, he bein' the most important person around and all. I never thought about doin' anythin' with him, but the idea of incest dinna upset me. Anyway, as you know, in my way I'm sexually uninhibited. I mean I like doin' them reckless things."

She took an energetic drag on her cigarette, then stubbed it out in the ashtray. "Well, me and two sisters were takin' turns different nights with Dad. On the night he died he suddenly said: 'Help me. For God's sake, help me.' I was scared cause he had an erection!" She gave a feeble shrug. "People dying get erections or what? Who knows? It wasn't that I thought it wrong to help him, but his sex is me Mom's." She chucked with an impish grin. "To be honest, I kept wantin' to know as I jerked him off, if he knew it was me."

I blanched, almost choked on my whiskey, horrified by her conversational tone. "Put him in a peaceful sleep so I thought, till the nurse come around and say, prepare yourself, dear. He passed."

A couple of weeks later at our video presentation of *The Magazine* I overheard a client say: "Lina is beginning to sound like the egocentric Vivienne Westwood. You know, thinking she's an intellectual, giving out all that blah, blah. It's so pretentious. Why doesn't she just present the essentials without all that guff?" The client was about to say something further before she noticed I was nearby and had overheard her. "Can't you bring her down to earth?"

I was not about to tell her or anybody I feared Lina was being eaten up by too many late nights of alcohol, drugs, and promiscuity, as she flitted around the globe gathering soundbites and trends. I simply said I found it difficult to talk to her as she only wanted praise.

She screwed up her eyes and looked heavenward. "Ah, the Mussolini complex. An exaggerated sense of her own self-glorifying illusions. It happens when people surround themselves with mediocre yes men."

I was flabbergasted! The client had precisely pegged Lina in more ways than I was willing to come clean about! Mussolini had been bolstered by underlings giving him a false impression of his own cleverness, power, and success. The previous night, Lina had been given a prize. In her thank-you speech she'd called out the names of the people who had helped her, all of them underlings and all males.

After months of missed appointments, and Lina's delaying tactics, I finally had a look at the books. As I had begun to suspect our profits had arranged themselves in the black hole of Lina's pocket. Uneasiness churned in my gut that she had squirrelled away our money on personal projects with the aim to cut me out of any compensation. "New projects? Without me?"

She squirmed as if trying to dislodge a church mouse from

her underpants without using his hands. "You're busy and you are making plenty of money. You don't need this hassle."

Why did her answer make me feel I was the kid getting kicked off the sports team. I was aware I could sell my shares to the highest bidder, but the thought sickened me. "You want to dump me, the person who financed us and gave you your start?"

She glared at me as if she wanted to impale me on a pike. A look she'd perfected recently to counter anyone who faced up to her with unpleasant truths. "You'll get your legal investment back. This is business, that's all," she responded disdainfully touching her glass of champagne to her lips.

"Wow," I said. "I'm impressed by your incredible generosity! You want to repay my years of devotion to *The Magazine* by giving me back my original investment. You must feel very proud of yourself."

For twenty years I had watched her body transform and swell in direct relation to her sucking up people's talents before discarding them without the least consciousness of vampirism. Her eyes followed every flicker of my eyes as they moved disapprovingly over her ruined body: her ankles and legs, still slim, created the top-heavy silhouette of a mushroom, or more to the point, Humpy Dumpty.

xxx

To the outside world, my life looked like a fairytale story of success, and I admit it was. But after the betrayal of both Arthur and Lina, the moody grey stones that held up my faith in people crumbled. My fault, of course; I had been drinking green smoothies naively believing in the basic integrity and innate goodness of the people I loved. Green smoothies or not, I should have known better.

I hear you, dear reader, you are wondering how I had become so successful in such a competitive fashion world. How I'd been able to help finance both *The Magazine* and Arthur. Obviously working with Lina was not my principle activity. After my early years with Ungaro, somewhere between Ginsberg's *Howl* and the Beatles' *Sgt. Pepper's Lonely Hearts Club Band*, the fashion world began to transform. The existentialist somber colors metamorphosized into the amazing hippie movement.

Suddenly it was all mini-skirts, free-flowing original fashion designs in exuberant designs and colors. The young no longer wanted to dress like dowdy parents but even parents no longer wanted to dress like parents.

After being fired from Ungaro my intention was to open a boutique and start my own fashion line, but as a single woman I needed a male guarantor for the rent. Imagine that! Women weren't considered responsible enough to pay their rent. That was not just a French custom. A friend of mine in New York had to get her criminally convicted boyfriend to guarantee the rent when she opened her styling company. In a moment of optimism, I'd asked my father to be guarantor. Not even an abandoned daughter could have imagined he would replied: "I would not do that even for my best friend." Wow. If I needed an arm or a hand up, I was looking to the wrong guy. As hard as his refusal was to stomach, the curve ball that hurt the most was being prioritizing as worth less to him than his best friend.

My only option was to freelance; to spice up and breathe new life into other people's collections. And for me that was as easy as shedding last year's skin and renewing it in synch with my intuition and my gut instincts. As it turned out working for various companies in my home studio, was a good option. It gave me the chance to spend the early years with my daughter.

And so, it went until few years later, when after dropping Sarah off at school, I'd stopped at La Chope, a café on the Place de la Contrescarpe for a coffee. The intense blue of the sky filtered through the lattice of dark trees on the square like a Magritte painting. Sylvia, a headhunter, plunked herself down next to me and asked, "Do you want a full-time job? Something special. Just up your alley." She handed me the details: Designer wanted to take charge of prêt-a-porter collection for Chloe.

"It sounds like they want someone more experienced."

"Sounds like they want you."

A few days later I'd climbed the stairs to a spacious first floor workroom/office with a packet of sketches in my design case. Gaby, the sleek blond director of Chloe, was wrapped in a silky, pale blue bodysuit the color of her eyes. She leafed through my drawings and put aside her preferences. She threw me an enquiring glance and asked, "Would you consider working for us full time? Overseeing pret-a-porter collection?"

"My designs aren't too radical?"

With the irresistible smoothness of a steamroller, Gaby said, "We need something special. And I believe your designs will sell."

Chloe's new prêt-à-porter collection was aimed at attracting a following of young hippie buyers. They had hired a gung-ho team mostly collectively dedicated young people who worked long hours and almost never saw the light of day. Few jobs provide such palpable pleasure as working in the fashion industry, few are as exhausting.

A couple of months later, I received a summons. "Run upstairs, the big boss is waiting." Jacques, the financial director, sat at his desk. His encouraging smile did not relieve my panic. "Sit, young lady," he'd said motioning me to a place among the chartreuse cushions. He smoothed my nervousness by praising my work, calling me a great asset to the company and original talent. "I've been watching you. You're doing well. And now my dear, next week you'll be running off to Italy, buying some of that lovely Italian fabric for the new collection."

The French system set up for working mothers was meant to keep the fairy tale afloat and it was easy to find a qualified person to look after Sarah while I was absent. Sarah often claims she brought herself up which was probably how she remembers her imperfect childhood. But whose childhood is perfect? I think it was more she thought of me as irresponsible and wanted me to grow up. At times her eyes would fill with more than a healthy pinch of mistrust as she attempted to teach me that I couldn't be both a child and a mother. Given half a chance even today she s reverses our roles with her as the parent trying to set limits to my impetuous nature. I can't help giggling at her endlessly warnings, "Don't talk to any strangers," or "Be careful crossing the street."

xxx

The train to Como slid through Swiss tunnels under snow-capped Alps, passing towns set in a picture book landscape. It rattled its way through rocky gullies down to Lake Como, the center of the Italian fabric industry. The lake surrounded by steep shrouded mountains, soon disappeared around the curve of the hills. Birds chirped in thick vegetation which covered fences, houses, and even statues. Walled gardens, churches, and villas clung in clusters on the lakeshore. The Cathedral bells chimed out the hour much as I imagine it had done in the early seventh century when the Como silk trade started. That story is told brilliantly in Manzoni's book, *The Betrothed.*

The spontaneity and originality which had characterized the trends for the last ten years had begun mutating, going retro with tarty sexiness. This unashamed nostalgia for past decades became more about proposing rather than imposing. My first visit was to Mantero Seta, whose offices are situated in a fantastic turn-of-the-century Art Nouveau building. Ricardo, the owner, greeted me with a nod. I said I wanted a Pre-Raphaelite look, something straight out of Burne-Jones and William Morris. He returned with an armload of perfect fabrics. Then suggested we add an extra color, deepen the background, and treat the fabric with a special softener, all for a few extra cents. That reminded me that René Ungaro had mentioned how accommodating the Italians fabric houses were.

My next visit was to Seteria Ratti. Mr. Rati, the charming talented, controversial owner, was the black sheep of the Italian fabric houses. All due to his lack of family connections in the industry. His unexplained sudden wealth was a hot topic of speculation. As a resistance fighter in the Second World War, he had been in the group who captured Mussolini. The rumor was that he had recovered compromising letters between Mussolini and Churchill and had sold them to England.

After I had made my choice among the many sample lengths of paisleys and tiny flowers in floaty, diaphanous cotton voiles so light the slightest wind might puff them away, Mr. Ratti pulled me aside. "Before you go, I'd like to show you something." He returned with an armload of lightweight, jersey prints, in psychedelic pinks, oranges, and lime green. Perfect fabrics for the tunic tops over the floor length palazzo pants that I had in mind.

On my return to the Paris studio and the arrival of the samples an odd paralysis for anything but creating the collection took over. On the day of the défilé, I felt like a child on

Christmas full of expectation. After the deluge of clapping, and shouts of "Bravo," Gaby had congratulated me. "You have caught the spirit of the times and the potential for sales is promising." As we headed for the bar to drink to future success, it was then Gaby introduced me to those two German designers, Arnold and Bob who later became my friends. Arnold chirped "Love your designs! Perfect outfit. Perfect Summer of Love stuff. Your outfits will turn the city streets into a spectacle!"

"Hard to top your collection!" I responded. They had created quite a sensation with their high-camp glamorous designs.

Chapter 21

Got ice water in my veins
I would be crazy if I took
you back

It would go up against every rule
You left me standing in the doorway
crying Suffering like a fool.
Bob Dylan

By January in 2021 the Covid pandemic rules had tightened and no one was allowed to go more than a kilometer from home. And only to shop for food and take medical tests, facemasks on and permission papers at the ready. To my surprise my doorbell rang. There stood Adrienne, a kindred spirit and member of the survivor's club of dumped women. She plunked herself down on my sofa, lit a cigarette and took a long drag while attempting to suppress a giggle.

I frowned. "What's so funny?"

"A trauma today is a joke tomorrow. A good friend will pick you up when you fall, but your best friend will laugh and fill you up with champagne. Time to celebrate." She pulled out a bottle, popped the cork and poured us two glasses. "You gotta admit Arthur's claim this floozy vampirized and bewitched him belongs in the slush pile. What's for sure is she's a super good actress to have convinced him she has the hots for him. As good as any of them cinema gals. But she's not gonna stick around unless she's getting something out of it, cause sex with an old guy is more like cranking a pump than pleasure."

Cheers!" I said. "All this crap called love is nothing more than a grab-bag of assorted emotions with a label stuck on it. A one-way ticket to a state home for the permanently bemused. Let's forget whores and egoistic guys who think we are there to have and to hold when *they* feel like it. Let's drink to three unusual men who believed in the supernatural. Arthur Conan Doyle who wrote Sherlock Holmes spoke to them through mediums, Alan Turing the inventor of the first computer believed in telepathy and Winston Churchill who claimed he saw a ghost while visiting the White House after the war. He'd taken a bath, had a few scotches and was smoking a cigar as he entered the bedroom. Standing there was Abraham Lincoln." I started giggling. "Apparently unflappable even while completely naked, Churchill said: 'Good evening, Mr. President. You seem to have me at a disadvantage.' The spirit smiled and vanished."

Adrienne chortled. "Wow! Believing in them ghosts is

healthier than backing an old horse who comes in lame after losing their balls to a groupie. Or my partner being turned into a criminal by a Senegalese floozy." Tears sprang to her eyes. "Some blokes can't keep their dicks in their pants. They'll shag anything what moves. It's an arrogance thing. Arthur is just another rat looking for holes, but so far, he hasn't managed to defraud you. Dan got the Circus we had created despite being condemned for forging checks!"

I poured us another glass. "Yeah, guys think we are replaceable prop to their leading role. I'm amazed that those bald-headed men and big beer guts still believe they are attractive to women. Only gay guys stay in shape cause guys don't fancy those big beer guts," I said with a giggle.

She gave me one of those French shrugs expressive way of saying, not worth talking about. "Like Arthur I'm a slow starter. I always knew I was an artist but not sure what kind of artist. I didn't even get what you were talking about when you told me to stand up to patriarchal oppressors. I'm embarrassed it took me so long. I used to laugh at men's sexist jokes. I'm done with that and done with men talking down to me, over me, ignoring me. When I speak up, they call me a feminist as if feminism is a dirty word."

"So, you finally got a pair of glasses. About time!"

Adrienne, like a lot of French women had been completely unaware that in the 1960s the male-controlled press was trying to shame us into silence by calling us angry man-hating lesbians? "Do you remember saying: I think this strident feminist thing is a multi-layered ironic joke! If I was a man, and sometimes I feel like a man, I'd want to know what all this feminist man hating is all about."

She laughed and poured us the last of the champagne. "I forgot what a frightful memory you have. I have no memory of that, but it sounds like me. All the same I was a sexually liberated woman ahead of my time, now I'm a liberated feminist who owns her erotic self. When I tell my lovers I'm seeing other men they say, 'Great! Who needs commitment!' Then after a few weeks of fun they get angry, actin' like they have sexual rights."

I fell about in stitches. I'd always wanted to turn the tables on men's illusions. "Virginia Woolf said, for most of history,

Anonymous was a woman. When she was honored by Oxford University, she'd asked to visit the library. The authorities said: *Not without being accompanied by a man.* Yeah, like women can't be trusted, with their inferior minds they might smudge or steal books like undisciplined kids. Unbelievable!"

Adrienne laughed as she staggered to the door. "And our feminist hangovers are not going to emancipate us from the wrath of grapes."

xxx

Oddly enough, when I look back at those youthful years of the 1960/70s it is less a case of nostalgia than gratitude for those optimistic years when we believed we could change the world. I had protested for peace and a better world on the Paris barricades with Adrienne, in May 1968. But I'd optimistically hoped it would bring women more equality and consideration. It was the same old story: we cleaned up and made sandwiches while the guys made speeches. Adrienne asked why we needed equal rights, we did exactly as we pleased. We did, sort of. We had jobs, paid rent, and managed not to piss everyone off too much, so we could continue doing what we wanted to do. That was not the same as having the right to do it. We were even criticized by women for not being clever enough to manipulate men from behind—a criticism not just from uneducated women. Even today, the patriarchal backlash is alive and kicking, ready to rescind women's rights, ready to stuff us back into Ikea boxes as optional jigsaw pieces to fit with men.

Germaine Greer, a sexually liberated feminist, magically turned many a woman into a feminist with her book *The Female Eunuch*. She had also vivisected Norman Mailer on a TV program, when he had asked in an exasperated voice: *What do women want?* She snapped back, *Whatever it is we're asking for, it isn't you, honey.* Yoko Ono was just as clever with her song: *Yes, I'm a witch, I'm a bitch, I don't care what you say. My voice is real, my voice is truth, I don't fit in your ways.*

Sure, French men had been in favor of contraception, national nursery care and the right to abortion when they slipped up. That suited them! Equal pay for equal work, no way. And as Adrienne had correctly predicted emancipation bought women extra burdens and few masculine privileges. Women mostly have the crummy jobs men don't want while they still carry the burden of looking after the children and running the house.

I pulled out my sketch book to see what I'd written when I'd first met Adrienne.

Dec 5, 1960.

I was drawn to Place Saint-André-des-Arts, that odd, shaped Parisian area near Saint Michel, by the sound of bongos and guitars. The French accent of the attractive young singer made the words of a well-loved cowboy song slightly unfamiliar. Intrigued by her androgynous exterior, I threw a few francs in the hat and suggested a drink at the café on the corner of the Boul' Mich'.

She'd offered me one of her strong Gauloise cigarettes. "You don't look like one of them American girls, here to pick up French guys cause you're too puritanical to be sensual at home. You're more like one of them Saint-Germain existentialist types."

I'd laughed and admitted I was Canadian commonly known as unarmed American with health insurance.

"That just shows you! I'm the heavy, jumping to conclusions, talking like I know it all. A sort of inadvertent subversive living a sort of painful comedy." She smiled and admitted she'd memorized that phrase because it gave her an identity cover after she'd fallen out with her French middle-class family over the Algerian War. With an ironic grin she said her disappointment was that her rebellion hadn't ended the war.

A bubble of exhilaration surged through me that I'd likely met a soul sister with a unique sense of comedy and taste for absurdist adventure.

xxx

Sept 5, 1961.

As we sat one day drinking a glass of wine in the Beat Hotel Adrienne said, "Anyone from the outside world would be thinkin' this here hotel is a rest home for escaped loony-bin inmates. You see all them young Arab boys traipsing' up to William Burroughs's room?"

What did it matter if Burroughs spread his dollars to the poor for services rendered. I had been amused when a friend mentioned he visited Burroughs and his room had been completely empty except for a bed, a desk, a typewriter, and six ashtrays with six joints burning in them.

Suddenly fed up with the sleazy crowd around us I suggested we set off for Girodias' club where there was always an interesting mix of artists and literary celebrities hanging out for the free champagne and smoked salmon. Girodias the Olympia Book publisher had begun by printing pornographic books for American GIs at the end of WW11 but was now famous for publishing books that censorship lawed banned in other countries.

Except for our fondness of bohemian bars and playing hooky from routine, Adrienne was in many ways my opposite. I came across as a novice in an upside-down world auditioning to be an artist, while she the heavy, living life as if she was acting in a movie. Wherever we went, men's eyes fell on her. "Ignore the night slummer," she would whisper, a smirk on her face. "Just straight guys with wives tucked away in suburbia, looking around for something a bit trashier and tastier than what's offered at home. She admitted she'd flirted and slept with every type of man she'd lusted after and didn't get in school because she was too tall, too awkward, and too bossy. "Men were created for our pleasure so why not indulge?"

To put it frankly, I preferred to skip the casual feast because it wouldn't relieve my famine. I was a sucker for romance.

"Romance, bullshit! She protested. Possessive love is *the root of all evil*. Women end up in suburbia with kids while their guys go off whoring. Who needs it?"

Chapter 22

It ain't no use to sit and wonder why, babe
If'n you don't know by now
And it ain't no use to sit and wonder why, babe
It'll never do somehow
Bob Dylan

Our habit of talking on the phone every night and the frequent email exchanges with Arthur were not conversations of two people together, but people who'd spent two decades together and for a moment are able to feel close again. At times I thought he wanted me to beg him to come back but that would have been too humiliating. Especially as I suspected it was not over with this floozy and that he wanted to come back simply for his financial survival.

Feb 2, 2021.

Dear Katherine.

I am facing up to my mistakes, admitting failure, and trying to find a way to go on. I am wrecked by the knowledge that I am inadequate to fix things, my limitations plain for all to see. The fact is this perverse relationship lasted a very short time because of your fundamental importance to me. Of course, you know I was immediately attracted to your intelligence and delighted by your beauty, your looks! You are the only woman who has ever help. me. I ought to have been more aware of that. That's the fool I have been.

I didn't "toss you aside" as you often say. This is self-pain, masochism. It was my failure. My failure, do you understand? Try to see it as my perverse and unresolved relationship with womankind. You are a sexually healthy, normal woman; this was a perverse and ultimately destructive relationship. It was darker than I had ever dared to go, and I am fortunate to have withdrawn from it! I saw this relationship leading to self-destruction. It is easy for our imaginations to condense it if the ultimate endpoint is orgasm. But human beings don't want just orgasm, they want to be loved.

In recognizing my cruelty and unkindness, I am not irremediably condemned for it if I act in the future with kindness and love. Even if the other does not forgive me, the eternal Spirit does. I understand hurt, I was very hurt by Ciguapa defrauding me of my assets but after all these years I have come to see it in shades between black and white. I do think Christian teachings are very practical, useful. I don't know of any other religion which teaches forgiveness. I understand Christian morality (which is love) as the supreme intelligence. Love tells us that we can be cleansed of our guilt, and our cruelty towards others if we are prepared to forgive those who have hurt us through egoism or even deliberately.

To feel you are being good by forgiving negates the action. Patasola showed me real hypocrisy. Her conviction was that she was saintly and Christian, but she was unchristian in actions. The surest route to evil. Isn't that what Jesus says again and again in the gospel about the Pharisees? His severest condemnation was not for the whores and murderers but for the religious hypocrisy of the self-righteous.

Love Arthur

xxx

Feb 3, 2021.

Dear Arthur

That great German philosopher Nietzsche, so defamed because his sister altered his work to conform to Nazi doctrine said he would only believe in a God who knew how to dance. I prefer to dance rather than accept all this claptrap about the sexual and spiritual unity you claim you had with Ciguapa and then Patasola. A bit sick, but it does make a good story and well worth a laugh.

Also, a laugh that you seem to think I am hurting myself by not forgiving you and that I might even end up burning in hell if I don't. I cannot reset my emotional counter to zero. I cannot stomp on my own justified resentment for your benefit. It is contrary to sanity. Seeking forgiveness is equivalent to seeking a pardon. When bad behavior is not met with negative consequences, it is in effect, condoned. The best I can do is to accept your actions were flawed and those of a confused man. We can't change the past; but we can learn acceptance. Sadly, acceptance does not follow a nice predictable path as it depends on what must be accepted.

You say this affair is over. It is remarkable how many times you have told me this and in the next instance you have slipped right back into to it. Addicts quit all the time and then shoot up because they are weak. I would like to believe you are no longer the besotted man in the basement reading the Bible with a doll you've dressed up in your mother's clothes. Or is it Ciguapa's clothes? Only time will prove to me that you are being truthful.

Emotions are a complex stew of the ingredients and very difficult to sort out. You call my need to understand raking over old coals. You say it exhausts you emotionally. But I need to know *why you valued our years together so little?* You say you are haunted by the "who am I" because you don't understand why you acted the way you did. Who knows what any of us really are? A seething mass of carbon, mostly doing a foxtrot? The winner gets to be considered a human being; the loser is likely to find no one at home when he comes knocking.

Katherine

xxx

Feb 4, 2021.

Dear Katherine.

I know how shaken you have been, and I realize it will take months, maybe years. Maybe it is impossible to reconstruct. I realize you are still bitter— understandably, but that can pass. I thought I was being responsible in leaving you and of course it was the opposite. Paradoxically, I lied all my life. I lied to lie, I lied to escape, I lied to be loved, I lied out of fear. I was often confused about what I wanted and thought, mistakenly, stupidly, lying would cause less pain. I should have learned the lesson that it would end by causing more pain.

I'll be very frank. It is certainly over with her but that doesn't change the echo-effect in you. You're right, we won't return to the earlier relationship; in some ways it could be better. Me the optimist. There does not seem any point in it being otherwise. Little steps over the coming years may go a long way. Real deep happiness is possible between us, troubles and sorrows are in our heads and can be dispelled. I did not leave you as men and women leave a couple, I was not tired or angry with you, I enjoyed our life and loved you. I was torn away, bewitched by my own deep contradictory fantasies and pathological ghosts of "religious-sexual" polarity, which she incarnated.

I never think of her! I cannot even understand the bewitchment! It was a madness, like being overcome by my own confused emotions and fantastic imaginings. In reality I never left you, so please drop the term "dumped" which does not approximate the experience on my part, even if you felt it like that. As you said, let's get out of this bottomless swamp of hurt and confusion and relate afresh as two persons who do care about each other. I am willing to do whatever necessary—to go on faith that we can find the resources to remake our partnership even though your family and friends reject me.

I am terribly lonely and regret it all. I find it unbearable to live alone and to come to terms with my life after this horrible trauma. I do believe great fiction approaches these psychic matters, as in Strindberg's tormented play Dance of Death. My character in my autobiography is close to me, as you have often pointed out. The novel is quite self-penetrating, but despite my introspection, it served no purpose. It didn't change me. Rather I continued as always with the same misjudgments and illusions, but now this destructive trauma has changed me. It hasn't happened in one blinding blow, but I have never experienced any turn-around, or any sharp change as complete as now.

I told you the other day that God our Father has become an intimate reminder that there is the deep reality in thought and love that underlies our existence despite the superficial rationality and simplistic materialism which appears to govern our lives. Our minds are far more than the simple mix of rationality and unconscious drives and fears and anxieties. That is why the "our" of the Our Father prayer impresses me so deeply. Maybe it sounds like piety, but it is a psychic truth the sense of isolated self is an illusion. We do not pray as isolated individuals but as beings together. You said forgiveness isn't possible, acceptance is. The reality of Redemption and Atonement is that only forgiveness can free us.

Love Arthur

xxx

Feb 6, 2021.

Dear Arthur.

If I tried to explain the magic of our years together it would not do justice to the reality of those warm, loving, enchanted years. I wonder if I will I ever stop thinking about the times when the rain poured down and we cuddled and made love and talked through the long nights. Will I ever wake up and no longer miss your limbs entangling with mine? Will I ever stop thinking of things that might turn you thoughtful or make you laugh?

It didn't matter to me that you lived your life and worked as if you were in a dinghy with a leak, likely to sink unless I was there to keep bailing you out. All I asked in return was a safe place to lay my head. A place of trust, a place where the earth would not split open under my feet. You claim you weren't aware of my fragility hidden under my strong exterior. Maybe only Jews who also struggle to build a solid ground beneath their feet can understand my kind of fragility.

Like them I toiled to save myself from falling into that
great empty space waiting to suck me down. I know—
it's called insecurity. Pathetic really. I feel like a fraud
because I believe only Jews have the right to feel this
kind of insecurity.

Katherine

Arthur was touched by Katherine's words. Touch by how she
criticize him yet was sweet about it, He'd always loved that little
flash of sarcastic mischief in her eyes when she had a go at him.
She was his muse, and he missed her counsel and sacred flow
of words. The previous night he dreamt he heard Katherine's
voice close by, felt her warm breath. She was propped up like a
stuffed doll on the sofa; a tiny murmur, "Water" escaped her
lips. He rushed to fill a cup and put it to her lips, talking to her
all the while with great tenderness. Like a flower refreshed, she
shook herself and stumbled across the room murmuring,
"Why?" He wanted to take her in his arms and whisper the
answer, but he couldn't answer. He didn't know why he had
pulled up his roots in a state of elation. Nor why he had pursued
an objective not only questionable, but the prize illusory. From
his tortured position on the cross, he felt each nail as
punishment. He awoke will tears filling his eyes.

Initially, his living alone had liberated him from the stress
of Patasola's bipolar ups and downs and her untenable outbursts
and unpredictable inarticulate pronouncements. And yet it
wasn't easy for him to toss aside the emotions that had entangled
him as if they were a pair of badly fitting trousers. In a moment
of weakness, he had once again, given in to temptation likely to
cause further bruising. He had invited Patasola for Saint
Valentine's Day to spend a month with him.

Sitting at his desk he began to write, the words came
effortlessly with *Renounce* and *Free yourself* as the chorus. It
had a prophetic quality, not a farewell to Saint Patasola who he'd
once thought of as his religious guide, but a farewell to Patasola
the wicked temptress who had been mutilated by an axe because
she lacked compassion for the suffering of others.

He pulled his trousers over his pajamas, seized his
overcoat, and grabbed his scarf and boots. In less than a minute

he was on his bike wobbling along the canal under the bright moon, the ground iron hard with frost. As he freewheeled into a mean wind, he felt absurdly euphoric, laughing to himself as he steered around the frozen puddles that bordered the canal, the ice crusts rupturing under his tires like drum skins whispering in his ear. He had never loved Katherine as much as he now missed her. He longed for her, the way a person too long in the wilderness hungered for contact with another compatible soul.

He had no illusions; he couldn't just pop back into her life and yet it seemed the only intelligent thing to do. Nothing was more normal than that they should venture out, once again, as pals. The next day the weather worsened with the wind shifted to the north-east but that did not deter him boarding the train. Rain and the fog filled the air and turned Paris into a city of shadows as he stood for a moment at Katherine's door, calling up his courage to press the bell.

xxx

I looked out eagerly then reeled back as if what I was hallucinating. I thrust my head forward birdlike, trying to accommodate my eyes. "Arthur?" Never had I imagined he would materialize on my doorstep dressed in a pair of faded trousers and a jacket, his eyes desperately seeking, as if hoping to find what he had lost. Still blinking, I braced myself, surprised he could still make me dizzy. I waited for the violent spasms to stop as my mind flipped through all the possibilities, like cards on a Rolodex. I had not even a rough sketch of what I should do. I'd often pictured myself turning on my heel, leaving him standing, forlorn, and loveless, cursing himself for being such a fool. I wanted to hate him, but I only hate what he had done.

His lips trembled. "Just had to see you."

Something shifted: perhaps it was a collective passing of regret, for all the mistakes, for all his lies and broken promises. He held out a hand to me. His fingers warm and strong drew me to him and he kissed me. His lips were chapped from wind and sun, but agreeably soft. He no longer had the Weetabix beard, but he hadn't shaved recently which made his face rough to touch.

"You look so pretty but so thin, one would think there was a famine going on." He pressed another kiss against my forehead. "For months I have been living alone aware of my mistakes. I came to tell you how incredibly sorry I am."

Despite the resentment I'd built up toward him, what came was relief, swift and sudden, like a warm layer of honey around my heart. "So, the prodigal son returns from a long and perilous journey?"

He sank into a chair obviously finding pleasure in an encounter worthy of the language of the bible. "All these long months I've been writing you poems."

"Yet not sending them." My laugh was as brittle as gold foil being crushed.

"I'm sorry. It was selfish, but you had my emails..." His words trailed off as if not knowing how to continue. "Let's just say I think our friendship is too important to be discarded. The very thought is torment." He lifted his hazel eyes with a look so intense, it stole my breath away. "We've lost so much precious time and energy on trivia, let's now shout with joy for the beauty and mystery of Blake's angels."

I poured him a glass of red wine and busied myself with food. "Sit and eat, we'll talk." I caught a flash of admiration in his eyes, a sort of unfamiliar respect. I shook my head, convinced I was probably mixing up signals. I poked at my food while he ate with gusto almost falling asleep over his food.

I made up a bed in the guest room but too stressed to go to bed I sat listening to the sound of the rain and wind, mostly muffled by the shutters. I knew this moment would be tough. The question was not so much whether Arthur loved me—I believed he did. My regret was that I had not previously snooped into Arthur's private paper to find out the truth when my suspicions about his infidelity had surfaced. I would now not be so foolish.

Arthur's phone lay on the table. His password still the same, it opened to more porno photos, more exchanges of emails and voice messages with Patasola as recent as the day before yesterday. "Don't just come for Saint Valentine's Day, come for a month. I really want to see you, to hug you!"

Patasola replied, "Te quiero! Te quiero!"

Arthur replied, "Te quiero mas que alguna vez he amado an otra mujer. Tu eres mi vida mi alma."

I trembled, my thoughts splintering into a million pieces. The words ripped a ragged a gash straight though my heart. The man I'd loved for years, and years was saying he loved this groupie more than he had ever loved me—she was his life, his soul. I knew I would never be able to forget these words, they would taunt me until the end of my days. I did not want to hear more, but I was frozen into inertia, the phone, a red-hot poker glued to my hand. Arthur's voice continued, "Patasola I must talk to you about something very sensitive, I hope you'll understand. I have not thought or done anything in the last two months without praying and asking the Creator to guide me. Please understand me in this spirit. Katherine has accepted that I live alone. I talk to her around seven every day. Just routine, therapeutic conversations. She has been humiliated and betrayed, not only by my departure but because I did it so awkwardly. Come if you can tolerate these conversations."

My stomach muscles revolted, my brain in anguish. The ties that once bound me to Arthur, lay in shreds on the floor, dead things worn out by traitorous lies. He'd said he found her unlivable, the affair was over, and now he was pretending to be doing God's will by keeping in contact with me.

Cold dread crept across my skin as I staggered to my feet and dragged myself to the guest room. I placed the phone beside Arthur. With a start he awoke, at first not knowing where he was. A minute later he saw me and heard himself on his phone saying, "I sent a transfer of €500 on the 3rd of January, another of €500 on the 6th, but as for the transfer of €2,000, I forgot to confirm it. I'm sorry, now it is done."

Patasola's voice thanked him profusely followed by many more: "Te quiero! Te quiero!" The look he gave me was completely empty, as if he'd been awakened and ordered to enter a lookalike competition.

My distress hovered like a raw exposed halo of thorns around my head so tight I thought I would faint. I turned to leave the room but suddenly, as if I had been kicked in the stomach, I hunched over and hit the floor with a heart-stopping jerk. I struggled to get to my knees, but before I could, Arthur picked me up and carried me to a chair despite my crying, "Don't touch me."

"Please, just listen to me," he said holding on to me. "It's over with her! It is finished with her. I swear."

This rekindled my anger. "You lying bastard! You expect me to believe your badly imagined rubbish. I heard you say you loved her more than you ever loved any other woman—that she was your life, your soul."

He regarded me silently, pausing as if reflecting on his lies. "Those words mean nothing. It's over. I'm incredibly sorry. I don't know ..." he said slowly, waiting for whatever I was about to say, obviously knowing he had made a huge mistake to come when a few days earlier he had invited her to return. His lips quivered. "I came here wanting things to be different. To prove to you that I love only you. To prove that, mentally, I never left you." His eyes deepened to a hazel-grey color, as if some darkness in his soul was leaching into his eyes. "You are a part of me. I can't imagine life without you. You're my closest friend." He pulled me to him and tried to hug me.

A metallic taste flooded my mouth and my stomach heaved. I made a dash for the toilet to vomit out the shit spewing out of Arthur's mouth which must have been giving his asshole an inferiority complex. He handed me a wet towel. "I'm not lying, it's over; I just got sucked back in for a moment," he said avoiding eye contact. "I was lonely. I wasn't thinking straight. It's all fiction. I live in my imagination, in literary works. My life is fiction. I am my own literary fiction. But it's over, its truly over and finished. I knew that before I came here. That's why I came here."

My eyes told him it was too late; we were shattered; his contradictions had short-circuited, like a house at night when the lights had blown.

"Don't," he said.

"Don't what?"

"Look at me like you're wondering how you could ever have loved me."

That was exactly what I was wondering. "All this claptrap you spout is as plausible as a pig's glass eye. In truth this is another lying chapter in a shoddy story of her avarice and you a mere puppet spouting blank-eyed deceptions."

"Katherine," he said barely above a whisper, tears forming in his eyes. "I've been circling blindly like a man without a compass. You're my compass. You are the fearless one. Your help and dedication to my art inspired me. I orbited around you. You're my center." He wiped at his eyes. "I'm lost without you. You have no idea what I've been through these past months. I'm in so much pain."

Now he was the victim, pitching insincerity against equally insincere tears. A blatant illustration of a weeping man in a fictive drama he'd created. To me it wasn't a fiction, it was my life he'd carelessly played with. "Bigamy is having one wife too many. Enough is enough."

Moments after Arthur left my house, I looked at the glass of water I'd poured for him. My last offering of comfort from which he had taken a few sips. It was pathetic like telling someone I loved to go to hell and then worrying about him getting there safely.

Chapter 23

Drying in the colour of the evening sun
Like the nights when the northern lights perform
There'll be icicles and birthday clothes
And sometimes there'll be sorrow
Joni Mitchel

Karen Moller

It was as if Arthur was watching a film ten minutes after it had started because he was unable to work out the plot. He wasn't that he was stupid, he couldn't unwrap himself from the ancient folds of his erratic behavior. Not only had he burnt his chances again and again with Katherine, but worse he was unable to understand his own flip-flop actions.

Unlike love, his passion for this God-fearing superstitious primitive child, who had tiptoed out of the forest to embrace him, had evaporate when reality kicked in. For Patasola he was simply a business deal. This was not love, it was financial survival. The imbalance offended his *amore proper.* But that did not mean he was free of his obsession. His task now was not simple, not monumental, simply that he needed to be honest with both women.

Feb 26, 2021.

> Dear Patasola,
>
> I did not write you before, but I need to write now, to be clear after your last missive. I have already told you by letter and face to face that the word of God has taken possession of me. He told me to *renounce*—to separate myself from this carnal relationship as he has another will for me. It is hard to obey his command because I feel you suffer from this change in my intention. You have no blame, on the contrary it is you who inspired me to return to intense prayer.
>
> Love Arthur

xxx

Feb 27, 2021.

> *Dear Mr. Arthur.*
> *What you be tellin can no be right. God dinna say nothin to me. You be gettin wrong message.*
> *Patasola*

xxx

He shook his head. It wasn't usual that she simply ignored what he wrote, convinced that with her direct connection to God she knew God's wishes better than he.

He had once read that passions have terrible manners, they are uncontrollable, like children, or drunks, they are mad. The same could also be said for emotional vampires, they do not disappear with a sprinkle of salt or a garland of garlic. They don't leave when you want them to leave, they leave when they have finished gorging, as a starving person might gorge until their stomach splits.

To ease his mind, he wrote to Katherine not sure he would get a reply.

April 3, 2021.

> *Dear Katherine.*
>
> *I wonder where you are—I am thinking about your questioning, what did I mean by "changed"? In the airplane on my return to Madrid, in a sort of empty moment, I saw myself floating in a boat, facing the bottom of the sea. Upside down as my life. I realize how wrong and mixed up and stupid I have been. My psychic make-up made a complete about turn. I am not talking about my now extinct passion for Patasola, which I knew was extinct before I came to see you. What you heard on the iPhone meant nothing—it was the past even if it was recent. It was said in a moment of weakness and loneliness.*
>
> *I am now looking out of different eyes and seeing myself for the first time and not being pleased. Of course, no "explanation" can reconcile us, it was totally irrational, unthinking, breaking the deep bonds I had with you. That's why I call leaving you a catastrophe, temporary insanity. It happened due to this deep split in my own psyche. It had nothing to do with you nor my feelings for you. This is my attempt to tell you how I have now changed.*
>
> *Northern Catholics are quite puritanical compared to South American Catholics who do not suffer from this sexual/spiritual split. My entire*

272

boyhood I wrestled with these poles of Eros and spiritual mania, sexual desire, and religious transcendence. This uniting of the poles of "opposites" I had with Ciguapa were intensified by two with Patasola—both uniting but short-circuiting like an electrocution. This was a passionate affair, almost violently so, and although I did NOT decide to leave you when it happened nor did I want to, I was drawn deeply into it and eventually overwhelmed, the incident of infection playing a part.

I am now astonished how barmy I was over Patasola, it should have been a couple of f's as you say. This passion was short lived and lasted only a short time. I really believe I was bewitched literally by black magic crossing wires in my emotional and childhood hang-ups. I regret it bitterly. What an ass I was. Finally, I make no more promises or grand declarations, they have all been such a failure. It is normal you no longer trust me. I am deeply sorry for this last instance and the evidence that I was again not being honest with you. All of which I cannot undo.

Love Arthur

xxx

April 15, 2021.

Dear Arthur.

You have said many times this perverse relationship lasted a short time. That is not true! Sure, you quit living together, but your emotions continued to bounce back and forth for well over a year like a monkey on an elastic string. If you had any sense, you would have realized Patasola is a two-bit coin stuck in a machine running on OCD clichés, and you a puppet on a relentless rollercoaster of deceit.

I recently reread one of your short stories that Simon sent me about your desire to have another passionate affair similar to your neurotic passion for your ex-wife Ciguapa. The similarities between your youthful Eros/spiritual obsession for Ciguapa and your oldful Eros/spiritual passion for Patasola is amazing. All this claptrap about finding your Christian identity, simply an excuse to self-justify your corrupt psychic craving to be emotionally vampirized again by another pathological fit to your neurosis. Is it any wonder I remain skeptical that this present break with her is simply a flat tire?

Katherine

xxx

April 16, 2021.

Dear Katherine.

Love in friendship is the noblest emotion. It is rooted in "reason", but not the reason of the psychoanalyst, it goes deeper. I am convinced no matter how far apart we are, we are connected by a thread, or a tangle of cords regardless of place, time, or circumstances. You have been a wonderful companion and friend.

Borges asks the question: 'Are not the fervent Shakespeareans who give themselves over to a line of Shakespeare, are they not, literally, Shakespeare?' Because you understand and love the literary world, I want to share this perception with you on how we find it terribly difficult to quit our roles, even for a moment, because they are sewn into our beings, our lives. We know it, but we forget we are possessed by these roles. We play out, like Shakespeare's "players", and even as we become aware and condemn certain follies, it is enormously difficult to detach ourselves from this "fatality" written into our genes, our drives, and our emotions. The suffering, the cruelty is "real" but if we step back from the stage, to take off the actor's costume and recognize the role we are playing in our "theatre", it suddenly dwindles.

This is the conclusion I had arrived at in my Autobiography—but it did not help my character to escape his condition. I remained that same child who loved and feared his mother—always misbehaving and so always guilty. Weeping over my guilt and transgressions. This I understand as the "spiritual" person. I'm not claiming holiness or purity or

274

wisdom, just a sane, difficult, withdrawal from the role that has been assigned to me or we have assigned to ourselves through life's experience.

In any case, this is the step I am taking. This is the best thing I can share with you now. I am telling you because this is the deep lesson why Shakespeare overarches our human stage, our history. His vision—endlessly quoted, 'All the world's a stage, and all the men and women merely players' is profoundly revealing—more so than Plato's cave.

If you don't mind me saying so, because you have mentioned this, you have a very different role: rejected and abandoned especially by the father, but also by the mother—you fear rejection. You set out brashly to conquer the world to prove that you were worthy. This role made my leaving you for another woman that much more painful. Your suffering is as much to do with this deep childhood wound to your soul as to my mad Billy Goat leap. What you finally must recognize, is that my leaving was not a rejection of you but a throwback to my own multiple illusions. That's all. I want to tell you very clearly that you have always been a kind and delightful companion.

Love Arthur

You might think, from what Arthur says, my father was an insensitive asshole. He was more an insensitive sociopath. Yeah, dear reader, I like throwing around that sort of terminology because it feels empowering, even though I only half know what I am talking about. What is true is that my father likely suffered from, a mild form of Asperger Syndrome, characterized by difficult social interaction. Certainly, Asperger Syndrome is prevalent in many members of my family. It didn't make my father a cruel man, it made him a flawed parent. My first rejection was when he shouted: "Stop bothering me," then gave a slap to a three-and-a-half-year-old child which sent me flying across the room. All because I was tugging on his leg, begging for his attention as he hung over my baby sister's crib, cooing that she was so pretty, she was his favorite. I was too young to formulate it at the time, but I recognize now as the moment heartbreak entered my little girl's world. It left scars that never fully healed.

The second trauma was my father's belief women weren't worth educating. When I refused to accept the shitty role, I was being designated, he discarded me not only from the family but from his responsibility. Being abandoned in ninetieth century Jane Austen's time would have been a disaster. I would have had no choice, but this was the 1950s and a different world.

April 23, 2021.

Dear Arthur.

George Bernard Shaw said: "Life isn't about finding yourself. Life is about creating yourself." Yeah, kind of the opposite of your *just the way I am.* I'm impressed you think you can now *step out of the role, you have assigned yourself and recognize it is your "theatre".* Remarkable if you can at your age!

A recent 60-year scientific study concluded that by the age of seven a child's particular neurosis, large or small, has already begun to find anchor. By that age I was already a cauldron of deep bubbly rebellion scrambling to keep patriarchic devils from pushing me up the spout or down the drain. Just kidding but it certainly felt like that. Rebels are not born, they are made.

In contrast, by the age of seven you had decided survival meant avoiding conflict, so evident in your delightful poetic description of yourself: *I see myself as a small, feathered reptile not gifted with very big teeth and bright plumage racing along the prehistoric hidden pathways hoping to avoid confrontation with the larger nasty reptiles who might gobble me up.*

You say I feared rejection and abandonment but doesn't everyone? Rejection is a stealth bomb that scrambles emotions and destroys safety supports. It takes some kind of unique chutzpah on your part to suggest my failing health, loss of memory and grief were as much due to childhood wounds as grief over being dumped. Do you believe without my early wounds, I would have just shrugged my shoulders and gone on my contented way!

Since you are in the mood to analyze, let me draw your attention to your dual identities, particularly evident in your writing. The Doctor Jekyll/Petite Prince wants to be protector of women and gallant hero ready to sacrifice himself for gentle creatures. The prince is easily offended because in confrontations he simply gives in which call into question his masculinity. The Mr. Hyde is the raging apocalyptic Billy Goat, a greedy self-obsessed passionate animal who goes after what he wants regardless of the collateral damage. He is perfectly personified by Neil Cassidy in Kerouac's *On the Road*. More surprising is when the Billy Goat betrays, the Petite Prince considers himself the victim.

Katherine

xxx

May 13, 2021.

Dear Katherine.

I do recognize these dual traits in my temperament— they are powerful components of who I am, which carry both positive and negative consequences. My task now is to acknowledge the power that I have over these traits and address the areas in my life I have put at risk. This simple realization has changed how I see others seeing me, and changed how God sees me.

Seriousness is the key after having always been frivolous most of my life. People, we, I, even you sometimes do crazy things—inexplicable things because reason is only a small part of our mental emotional make-up. I did not mean to lie to you but in this shadowy contradictory zone of consciousness and emotions I both wanted to reconcile with you and wanted to continue with her. The blatant contradictions and those hurtful conversations overheard by you are owing to that mixture of fearfulness and the wish to have it all. I have lied and

277

*deceived women most of my life out of guilt or
fearfulness (yes, mostly the latter, unbelievably)
beginning with my mother!*

*Call my going off as temporary insanity, a sort of
emotional intoxication, an erotic storm and try not to
give it more significance! The guilt, the sorrow, the
self-examination has been so soul scraping that
everything has now changed in my awareness.*

*I am thinking about what I have been saying to
you about renewal of our partnership, I confess I am
not sure how, but I really think sweetie that we can
make something really fine, whole, clear, and
beautiful because I believe we have so much to share.
Love is like the wind, you can't see it, but you feel it.
The best thing to hold on to in life is each other.*

Love Arthur

xxx

May19, 2021.

Dear Arthur:

Mae West makes me laugh. She says: *When women
go wrong, men go right after them*, like dumb dicks.
To laugh at this tragedy, is the only way to bear it. No
matter what changes you claim in your character you
are unlikely to overcoming the dualities of your
Rapunzel nature. In the fairytale *Rapunzel*, is not
particularly weak or evil, but he uses lies to keep
others imprisoned to his greed and is himself
imprisoned as you are by your weak about faces. You
were obviously making it up as you went along,

Katherine

Month after month my friends said just tell Arthur to f-off.
The question has always been what did *I* want? Certainly
not for Arthur to just slip back into my life in his old twenty-
year unromantic thoughtless role, where he took me for
granted. Wide eyed optimism may be empowering but it is
far from infallible. No way do I want to be sitting at home
on Saturday night, with Arthur writing in his studio while I
read or watched TV even if it was a good film or

documentary. I want to be in it—well not actually in it, but out there being part of what is happening as I had been before I met him.

For centuries, love and romance have been endlessly explored as themes by writers and poets: Sappho to Shelley, Byron, and Browning, and all those in between. Not to mention Shakespeare or Jane Austen and Nicolas Sparks as well as the hundreds of romantic films. Aren't romantic expectations with spontaneous gestures of affection and emotional support considered a normal part of any love relationship? Guys might believe in romance, yet they are mostly incapable of being romantic in daily life. Could Arthur be romantic? Would he buy me flowers when he rarely bought me flowers—he did twice in twenty years. Actually, it is not about flowers it is about gestures that make one feel loved. He says he is no longer interested in sex and yet in my experience he was rarely affectionate except when he wanted sex. Why can't guys just be affectionate, period?

We women spend a lot of time thinking about what will please the men in our lives or what they might find amusing. I thought about Arthur constantly: I bought the type of food he liked to eat and clothes I knew he would like to wear. I'm not saying women are perfect, no doubt we like to think of ourselves as Wonder Woman, not just sidekicks to Superman or Batman. Even in romantic moments, most men have stomped unconsciously all over my emotions by saying or doing something unromantic. What is doubly sad, rather than apologize they excused themselves by saying, *don't take it personally, it's not my thing.* Yet romance is everyone's thing. It's what we all want. Don't we?

I'd always hoped the guys who courted me would write me romantic letters, but they never did. Mostly their letters were about what they wanted to do to me sexually and that includes the letters I received from Arthur. His current emails since he dumped me are the closest thing to romantic letters that I have ever received from any man.

Arthur can't help his lying, it's compulsive. From a young age, he had slipped in and out of relationships, leaving or being left, but never long without a woman. His endless declarations of love for me now, are I assume, the same words he spouted out to Patasola. All driven by his fear of being alone.

June 26, 2021.

> *Dear Katherine,*
> *I have tried several times to be honest with you, and I failed dismally. I was in two minds—telling lies to both, convincing myself I was telling the truth. What happened to us is simple. I was intoxicated by a woman. She was toxic. Her behavior was shocking, violent, but it took until now to break with her completely, like an addict, I kept reverting. That is why there were those three false attempts at reconciliation, they were not deliberate. I was confused. I did realize quite soon, the relationship with Patasola was intolerable, (the calendar time has become vague). Everything with her was about extreme emotions, screams in the Antwerp apartment and blood everywhere (she cut herself) when I told her, to her great surprise and anger that I needed time to myself.*
> *I have now broken with her in a most definitive and violent emotional break. I wanted to put this relationship with Patasola on a different footing, to resolve things in the friendliest of ways. Friendly was not her intention. She not only presented me with a heavy invoice for a panel she had put together for me, she insisted her name should be appear jointly with mine on the panel. To be fair that would have meant putting your name on the twenty-one panels you had previously done for me, as a gift of love.*
> *When I told her we could only be friends and that it would be a non-carnal relationship, she roared like a lioness and hurled insults. She became bitter. More than bitter. This person, who had claimed she loved me as she loved God now called me every name not in the scriptures. Her hysteria, almost*

insane rage was terrifying in its dimension. Enough to punch holes in my entire life. She became Lucifer or more precisely Lilith, the female demon who lays upon men like a mold turning them to dried husks after draining them of their resources and energy. She was ready to kick me, beat him, literally slice me to shreds. Unrepealable insults. I turned my back and walked away and never spoke to her again. I have ceased to think of her except to remind myself she is human, a confused and dark person I need to forgive.

Love Arthur

xxx

June 27, 2021.

Dear Arthur,

You now claim you have stood up to Patasola and have broken off with her. If true, remarkable, it would be a first. I think it is true to say you have never stood up to anyone ever. Even allowing that you are now telling the truth that this affair is over, something you have been saying for months.

I had hoped you would rent an apartment in Paris to see if we could rebuild some sort of partnership but was just another of my disillusion. No matter how tempting the view in the rear-view mirror was, you always intended to move to Madrid. You said it was for your career or as you prefer to put it, because you are better known there. For all your previous denials, this is your first attempt to be honest with me. To admit you moved to Spain because you intended to carry on some sort of relationship with this woman you so bitterly criticized. It makes me realizes I must set some firm boundaries. Boundaries are not steel doors slammed in a person's face, but rather, a firm way of saying we will see.

Katherine

xxx

May 20, 2021.

Dear Katherine,

Absolutely! This is on your terms. Everything is on

your terms. Look sweetie, I want your happiness, whatever shape that takes. Isn't that what it is to love someone? I was an old fool thinking a younger woman could possibly see anything except € in me. No fool like an old fool. I realized finally how mercenary she is.

I'm sorry that I protest when you start talking about my past acts. I want you to know it isn't because I am trying to forget it or discard my actions. I am not trying to evade responsibility. I am ashamed. The only ridicule or humiliation is for me. I realize you need to work through things. I was assuming too much. Of course, I understand you need to protect yourself.

If I sometimes speak of it as a mad act, I do not absolve myself, it's more I cannot understand how unconscious I was. I can only approach self-understanding by searching into these tensions and oppositions of my character: my own contradictions and my repeated patterns of behavior. Those deep half-submerged drives in my character, while I have dissected them before, they only became clear recently. That is as much as I can understand of my behavior.

Look, sweetie, we don't even have so much time to waste! Let's be happy and just drop all the misery, no need to waste the beauty that is here, hidden but there! We can still have fun and enjoy much together if you allow it. I am glad you are settling into more of a sociable mode that you always wanted, surrounded by friends, and a loving family. Many people must envy you. You take care of yourself, be well. I do love you and care about you! Good night, sweetie—a bear hug.

Love Arthur

xxx

May 26, 2021.

Dear Katherine

I have been wanting for a few days to tell you the following – it is insistent, so I've decided to write this out of sadness. I know it may mean nothing to you. You always speak of being 'dumped'. I realize that you are using the word because it expresses the *misery and sense of worthlessness you felt. But strangely, Katherine, I didn't dump you—in a sense I didn't even feel I was leaving you. I realize that sounds absurd because it is what you experienced. What I mean is that in my mind I was carried away by an illusory passion by her, but really more than 'by her', by my own perverse fantasies repeated over decades. In simple words I was not thinking, I want to leave Katherine—what was filling my imagination was I am going after this female mystery, this lure. If I had asked myself, "Do I really want to leave Katherine?" it would have been real, but instead I was entwined in a witch's net fascinated by a specter. I recognize that in those last months we were together I'd stopped being aware of you as I followed this phantom. My mind was clouded in darkness, consumed by the phantasm of I, and the thought that I could keep it hidden from you.*

Love and friendship are rare and beautiful things and an important variable in the happiness equation. Love is not exclusive to a couple, in a way it may even be less pure because of the jealousies, the resentments just beneath the surface. My mistakes, my self-deceptions have become crystal-clear to me as they never were. You are in my heart like you always have been. It is true when I say mentally, I never left you; I was under a shadow. I realized it quite soon. Far from just moving on, I think of you constantly. I believe with all my soul that love is the eternal value that binds us together. You gave me great beauty with your love, and I remember it with deep emotion. I chose to live in Madrid because I assumed there was no chance you would forgive me— that 'it' would hang over us for the rest of our lives like a dead albatross.

Going to confession has made me know myself. I have to live alone and come to grips with my own slippery soul.

Love Arthur

Chapter 24

There's a lover in the story/But the story's still the same
There's a lullaby for suffering/And a paradox to blame
But it's written in the scriptures/And it's not some idol claim
Leonard Cohen

There are no firmer grounds for friendships than between people who love the same books. Books *cemented* my friendship with Simon. I assume we will be friends until one of us dies or he goes off on a crazy drunken tangent and calls me a feminist bitch one time too many. These days we mostly communicate by email where he comes across as witty and coherent. Face to face he tends to hijack the conversation. A man talking to himself will listen for hours. And yet, his endless monologues do have a point if one has the patience to keep listening.

Simon is the brother I always wanted. He became part of my adopted family at my young age of twenty. I had already a few adopted fathers. I'm not sure these men saw themselves as brothers or father figures. Men don't think that way. No matter how old a man is, he still sees himself as a spring chicken and potential lover. My first adopted father was a cultivated Hungarian refugee. He owned the coffee shop where I hung out during my Art College years. Another was a Frenchman, a charming, funny cultivated intellectual type, exactly the father I would have like to have had. I met him while standing in a queue in a Paris post office, trying to collect my returned letters. I'd been out of Paris for more than a week attempting to earn a few dollars by selling encyclopedias to Americans. The Beat Hotel owner was convinced I would not return, (expatriates often just disappeared) she had returned my letters and packed up my belongings. I found myself room-less.

This newly adopted French father figure mentioned he had an extra bedroom in his apartment in Montparnasse and invited me to stay. Not in the least worried where this might lead, I headed off with him to his apartment. Of course, this was before all those films about dumb-assed students being enticed to apartments and getting murdered by serial killers.

Aug 6, 2020.

Dear Simon,

I guess what we all want is for life to be full of general okay-ness. Certainly okay-ness has nothing to do with the horrible jolt of Arthur walking out the door and leaving me an iPad full of masturbatory porno photos he'd exchanged with a Columbian groupie. Boys will be boys, so they say, but who would believe an 84-year-old would go through a belated mid-life crisis.

No matter how I wrap it, Arthur's dumping me, after a four-day sex orgy with a groupie he hardly knew, sent me into cuckoo land. Yeah, sounds like a joke but the real joke is that weirdo sex and religion played their part, as does this vulnerable man's deluded belief this Patasola, the age of his granddaughter, is madly in love with him.

I had become so invisible to Arthur in these last month's I was surprised to see myself in the mirror. Did I learn something, and I guess I did. Craziness exists. Don't let your happiness depend on somebody or something you may lose.

Love Katherine

xxx

August 10, 2020.

Dear Katherine,

Theodor Reik wrote an insightful psychological treatise about why we inflict pain and suffering on others. He said the tragedy of old age is not that one is old, but in thinking one is young we repeat our follies. According to him even the wisest men make fools of themselves over women, while foolish women are wise about men.

Breakups are unpleasant no matter what, but slightly less unpleasant if you don't take them as a personal indictment. Don't demean yourself. In knowing you, Arthur knows he is as lucky as I am to know you, for sure. You exist even if Arthur is not there to admire you. If you ran his story past younger women, well if you ran his story past just about anybody, they'd laugh at Arthur's belief this young woman is after him because she is in love with him. What a dreamer. Another important point: a coup de foudre is never about "falling in love"; it is simply sexual attraction felt by two people. We old Anglos sometimes admit this leads to a quickie, at best a fling. Passions stand men on their heads. Male status, pride, and dignity revolve around what other men think of us. I am not capable of self-delusion in matters of love. I have never been able to put one over on a woman without "paying the price".

It has always been the tradition that a man gives his money to the woman. This is straight from the horse's mouth...unless he's a ponce or a pimp. You are unusual in that your background showed you it was a man's world and you decided that was not how it was going to be for you. You made your money through your great talents, which extended to everything a man, could do and more. And you did it entirely on your own merits, rather than on the coattails of a man.

Love Simon

xxx

Oct 24, 2020.

Dear Simon.

To say I have not been well is an understatement. According to the therapist, Arthur's dumping me a second time caused my brain to wipe the traumatic event, from my memory. Invisible wounds are the deepest. They hurt more than anything that bleeds.

Emily Dickinson, one of our favorite novelists said: hope is the thing with feathers that perches in the soul, and sings the tune without words, and never stops at all. Hope is an ennobling symbol of survival but a flimsy defense against waiting for memories to return with answers. A bit like Samuel Beckett's waiting for *Godot*, who rarely arrives.

I remember you once said new love drives out old love and since I have no intention of finding new love (enough is enough) it's likely I will stay in love and continue to live with the horror of abandonment and unfamiliar circumstance. In the *Myth of Sisyphus* Camus argues that abandonment is equivalent to unfamiliar circumstance. Something you in particular understand, with your having been abandoned by your mother at the age of two and thrown into unfamiliar circumstance.

Love Katherine

xxx

Oct 16, 2020.

Dear Katherine,

We have been true readers all our life and fully recognize the enormous debt we owe authors. Your daughter even accused us of mistaking literature for life. Arthur, by comparison, is a fictional character. His story is never ending and repetitive like that passage about his ex-wife's protector. The woman saying—what will I do without my protector? It rings a bell because it was in Arthur's earlier book about Ciguapa. A question the writer Anaïs Nin must have asked herself—confronted by a younger man who wanted her, she cleverly managed to be kept by both. With hindsight, Arthur must see his dive into the bushes with Ciguapa, to avoid being spotted by her protector, as a bit troubling. Especially when it comes to her explanation that her protector, who keeps her in some great style, "does not have sex with her". Only a very naïf lad would believe that one. But it was believable in his story. A beautiful fable. What it does is inspire you to write (which a writer is always waiting to happen).

I have no idea how my world could be turned upside down if I received this kind of passionate attention from a woman. It makes me feel I am not living out my fantasies, and I am only eighty-two! I'm jealous I don't have the money for a porno-groupie who would save this nation's most desperate bachelor from the bother of having to use my own imagination.

I remember telling a story about going to bed

with a young woman in Portsmouth (actually, it was in a caravan on Portsdown Hill). I'd just come back from Paris, and I heard her say, as she undressed, I don't want anything continental, Simon. This is a story I've told many times for laughs but only to men. Now in old age I realize I could have sat her down on the bed and asked her, what exactly she had in mind.

Love Simon

xxx

Oct 30, 2020.

Dear Simon.

Arthur never admitted to himself that Ciguapa lied to him. I suspect he would not have held it against her just as he probably doesn't hold it against Patasola that she lives off immoral earnings. What Arthur won't admit, because it is too humiliating, is: *this affair is a financial deal for her and is not about her being madly in love with him.*

Arthur is easily picked apart by wolves who find him fertile ground in which to plant their teeth. He is a sucker for a sob story, and this Latino has a good one: a pitiful barefoot childhood in the Pampas of Columbia, abandoned in the street at the age of three, later raped and made pregnant. Manipulators are good at making up stories. I have to hand it to her for her having managed to edge her way into Spanish artistic circles even if it was by sucking up to old guys.

Love Katherine

xxx

Dec 25, 2020.

Dear Katherine,

Happy Christmas. How about this for a coincidence. You know I have a granddaughter who lives in Brooklyn. She's a dancer and I try to send her anything with a Brooklyn connection. I gave her a subscription to the Brooklyn Rail, which you probably know is a pretty good cultural online mag. Blow me, down! They sent some guff to me, which I looked at... and found a couple of stories by Arthur

*which describes him driving-off in your car because
he was dreaming of his ex-wife. (I felt stunned by the
detail of him driving off in your car). For Arthur to
have written this is worth a follow-up. This story is
inviolable to this sort of treatment, if examined
through one's own sense of reality. Arthur first
dreams of his real mother who he replaces with
Ciguapa, a woman the age of his mother. The fact that
he denigrates his ex-wife is strange, as if he wants to
be let off the hook for dreaming about his dead wife
after years of suffering terrible strife with her. The
story ends, and he's living alone in an empty flat in –
dare I say Antwerp? My first thought was how do I
tell Katherine? I can't. So, I'm sending you a copy of
this short story.*

Love Simon

xxx

Jan 13, 2021.

Dear Simon.

Arthur's short story in *Brooklyn Rail* is quite a
revelation. As you say, this prediction of what was to
happen has a paranormal quality. Thank you for
finding and sending this story. It has given me a new
perspective on the whole unfortunate mess and
enabled me to see this event as an accident waiting to
happen. Arthur's ex coming back in his dreams was
obviously a deep craving festering in his physic—a
craving to indulge in another passionate vampiric
relationship before he died.

The short story made me realize there is no set
map for life—mine, yours, or anyone's. From the
moment of birth, our lives become entangled in a
cocoon of papered over cracks. Hence for Arthur
what happened in one compartment did not conflict
with what happened in another. To him I am a
fixture, a permanent part of his life like a mother,
sister, or brother. Now relegated to Ciguapa's old role
as the dumped woman he claims he still loves.

We are expected to forgive a sinner who believes

his lies just as fans forgive the scam-bag Trump? Forgiveness does not follow a nice, predictable path. Nor does it fix anything or grant immediate peace. It's all a bit airy-fairy because some days I forgive him, then after a bad night I unforgive him. What I try to do, is accept him for what he is: a crazy, messed up fully human guy, a more messed up version of ourselves. As you say, a fictional character, whose life is more a series of short stories, or rather a collection of work in progress.

Love Katherine

xxx

Feb 1, 2021.

Dear Katherine,

I think my discovery of Arthur's story in the Brooklyn Rail brings a focus to these events you could never imagine otherwise. That is what literature is able to do. Arthur is a good writer, and this short story is certainly the best I've read of anything he's written. You and he are bonded, that's why you suffered so much from not knowing why or what was happening. (Neither did Arthur.) Hindsight is something that can cast the original event in a deeper light. This short story is truly an eye-opener. I could see at once why you found your way to a more interesting interpretation of the situation between you and Arthur. One that I would not have seen without reading what you wrote.

Here's a bit more you should know which will throw light, I hope, on the bizarre tone in which I wrote to you. What I first questioned after reading Arthur's story—when was this story written? You must have been puzzled by what I was suggesting... that Arthur had "imagined" the scenario of his break-up with you and had secretly published the story, Poe-sequel, psychic horror-story. Age comes into this; me usually thinking be careful what you put into words when you pass eighty. You need the Other Person to be impossibly understanding of who you are in case

293

you are talking utter bollocks. I am so relieved, Katherine, that you are that strong friend, who has never openly shown you are upset by some of the things I say. Your good heart and good head make for a formidable combination. What's brilliant is (as you say) his story removes all self-criticism since nothing you did plays any part in the real story.

I must say what you tell me about Arthur's ex-wife is utterly fascinating and sent me straight to Google. Her picture reminded me of Anaïs Nin— there is a video about her, and the art foundation her daughter's inheritors set up. It struck me as having cost quite a bit of money to make. All this posthumous promotion is as if she's a "write-in" candidate as a "missing female artist" who was in a world, too fixated on "male artists." Especially, since her Wiki-life story plunks her amid a starry galaxy of famous painters. The story becomes interesting only because Arthur is in the public domain. I must say, there must be a more mundane explanation as to why she never sold a painting!

Love Simon

xxx

March 20, 2021.

Dear Simon.

Despite Ciguapa living to be almost a hundred years old she was not a very committed painter and never had exhibitions. She produced fewer than a hundred paintings, very few of them of any quality. So, it is hard to claim her as a *"missing female artist in a world too fixated on male artists"*. As you say, interesting only because of Arthur is a poet in the public domain and a reference figure in his connections to other poets from the 1960/70s.

Love Katherine

xxx

March 22, 2021.

Dear Katherine,

We writers Ma'am, as Disraeli the then prime

minister of England said to Queen Victoria, 'are only interested in revealing good stories based on life' and this "story" is a profound one. Arthur is lucky he married a writer! Some pretty big things have happened in our lives, and I really think literature has well-equipped us to leap into the writer's pulpit. Wouldn't anybody who discovered they had a different name for the first eighteen months of their life?

Arthur is firmly a 20th century romantic type. The ins-and-outs of his psyche follow his fiction and make a great story for someone who is a romantic. One does not need to make up stories when one's own version is there to be written. The whole situation is grist for the writers' mill. You become Arthur's literary exorcist if you write about his belief, he was vampirized by his first wife and then by the witch Patasola which adds a fascinating element of drama, a much better story than you could make up. As you say, a comic story of a tragic protagonist bedevil in late life by desire to live another fiction before he dies. You have the armature of a good book, and you will do it without regret, which is (in retrospect) TRULY Brontean because you could not possibly know "why" without reading his story in the Brooklyn Rail, *just like the Brontean heroine never does!*

Arthur is a pretty fantastic poet, a sophisticated, intellectual narcissist but as a writer he can't be judged by convention. In his sixty-year writing poetry/singing career, he has continued to document his salacious fantasies. I think you will agree there is therapeutic function to narrating a traumatic event and the relief it brings the survivor. Arthur's story provides a good excuse for you to pundit away like only you know how! Be fair, and honest, and honor the love, mistakes, and beauty that you created together.

Love Simon

xxx

April 16, 2021.

Dear Simon.

Arthur is a *20th century romantic type* in the abstract literary sense of Russian writers in the eighteen hundreds. Like Tolstoy who wrote one of the greatest love stories he was incapable of *being romantic in life.* There are similarities between Tolstoy's religious crisis and Arthur's spiritual crisis—it sent them both slightly mad at least for a while. Arthur says: *The electrifying wires of opposites, sex and religion crossed, and I suffered a profound spiritual crisis. It deluded me into believing this godly creature had intimate exchanges with our high and mighty God.* Don't laugh. He actually said that!

Tolstoy writes: *Faith came to me; I believed in the doctrine of Jesus, and my whole life underwent a sudden transformation. What I had once wished for I wished for no longer and I began to desire what I had never before desired. What had once appeared to me right, now became wrong, and the wrong of the past I beheld as right.* Tolstoy then draped the crucifix around his neck and declared he was saved. It was no laugh. Neither Arthur's nor Tolstoy's manic love of God changed either of them for the better. After vowing to embody his Christian intentions Tolstoy became deceitful, committed adultery, and treated his wife without Christian kindness.

Love Katherine

xxx

May 1, 2021.

Dear Katherine.

I am about to leave here and go to London, so just a quick note about recent film footage, I saw of modern-day vampires in heavy eyeliner and Punk ghost skeleton outfits, standing around drinking small amounts of one another's gore juice. An attempt, I imagine, to convince the public that vampirism is a flourishing social phenomenon, instead of it being a tiny subset of goths running around creating a certain amount of anxiety trying to be intimidating.

Old age may be delusional but not for the artist! All the fuss about the American painter de Kooning (see his story online) was because he refused to speak to anyone in his last years. He just carried on painting. I like to believe in my advanced years that I have become a true philosopher. No competition from Bertrand Russell, our great English philosopher who at the age of ninety-seven, suggested expanding the circle of our interests, making them wider and more impersonal, until bit by bit the walls of the ego recede, and life increasingly merged into universal life. I love this optimist, but I can't help wondering what he is talking about.

Love Simon

xxx

June 12, 2022.

Dear Simon.

Age does slow one's thoughts, maybe a good thing in some cases. Arthur says he had an epiphany and that gave him the courage to tell Patasola they could only be friends. I presume she was astonished that an old guy was leaving the jacuzzi party before he'd handed her all his worldly goods.

All worthy of Augustine's tribulations. Arthur for months had claimed he freed himself, or rather reason freed him from his obsession, which he refers to as a *female mystery, a lure, a specter that entwined him in the devil's net.* He now calls it madness and \ which confirm Dostoyevsky's brilliant words: "*Lying to ourselves is more deeply ingrained than lying to others.*"

Charlie Chaplin said: *Life is a tragedy when seen in close-up, but a comedy in long-shot.* To appreciate the comedy of Arthur's madness is to blend time and tragedy together. This is not meant to make fun of anyone ... except myself. So just for a laugh I am sending you this brief synopsis of this Boulevard comedy. Here we have the husband Arthur, a brilliant, intelligent man who loves to discuss ideas. After a four-day orgy with an uneducated religious groupie half his age, his imagination takes fire, and this aging cockerel convinces himself this young chicken is not only in love with him, but since she has a direct connection to God, she will help him recover his Christian identity which he somehow lost. Unable to confront his wife of twenty years, he leaves her an iPad of porno exchanges with this groupie and takes off in his wife's car.

After doubts about his unhinged decision, he tries to rekindle the partnership with his wife but in a moment of weakness, he brings the groupie with him but hides her in a hotel room. Which of course is discovered because no way is the groupie going to let the fish she's caught reconcile with his wife. Still hoping for a reconciliation, he separates from the groupie and tells his wife he is going to Madrid to return her possessions and clarify things with her. Instead, he invites her to the Canaries suggesting they can marry there. At this point your realize \ life does not imitate art; it often imitates bad television, and certainly this tale would only be successful if the protagonist administered a dose of cyanide to the guilty party. And only if like Paul Auster's grandmother, the betrayed wife got off the rap because the judge decided the sinner merited his punishment. This is not a joke. Paul Auster's grandmother did kill her husband and the judge did let her off the rap.

Arthur says he will write about his flawed and fractured obsession when he is fully able to understand it. it could be just as fascinating as his *Autobiography* if he drops the title, *Hitler's Baby Girl* a title he chose because of Patasola belief Hitler would come back to save the world. Arthur wasn't just sleeping with the enemy he was having sex with a Nazi who claimed Hitler was a good Christian who thought it okay to torment and kill people because God was on his side. A better title would be *Angel of Satan. Or Angel of the Abyss.*

Love Katherine.

xxx

June 14, 2022.

Dear Katherine.

Epiphany is a very special word that has never lost its meaning, since it acquired a personal meaning, thanks to James Joyce's use of this word in Ulysses. I am more than happy to be writing to you on this glorious morning, here in the Mayfield Valley, especially after having slept on your brief synopsis. *I am glad you can laugh at this ridiculous scenario, a scenario familiar to many couples. There's nothing like a good dose of another woman to make a man appreciate his wife but that does not mean the bridge will mend.*

What is incomprehensible in your case, there was no lack of love, nor lack of friendship between you and Arthur, which normally creates unhappy marriages. You've known what it means to be friends with your lover—to come home to a person who'll give you a little love, a little affection, and a little tenderness. In my case, at the end of my marriage, that meant my going to the wrong house.

Old friends have mysterious bonds. It's rather interesting to be in touch with someone in your past who still has a great memory for the tiny details one no longer remembers. Whenever I look at a pile of paper (all covered in words) I do think it is because I know you, any of this exists (whatever it is). I find the only "writing" I do is emails like this. I feel better this is so.

Love Simon

xxx

July 5, 2022.

Dear Simon.

Normally, vampires "bite" their victims and turn them into vampires but apparently emotional vampires can transfer their toxic traits to their victims. Patasola dragged Arthur into her funhouse of distorted mirrors and apparently, so he claims he resisted her perverse sexual/religious fanaticism.

No one can go through being dumped and feel free of blame because who is blameless? Despite our having all the compatible ingredients to make marriage work, Arthur simply drew a mental curtain around our life as if going off with another woman had nothing to do with us? Our compatible partnership slipped away as carelessly as the sea wipes the beach clear of all trace of our having visited it.

Friendship, mutual respect and feeling at ease with your ex is complicated when starting from a place where justice and fairness has been turned on its ass. Melinda Gates says, it is worth a try although it may not always be friendly.

Had I never met Arthur I would have missed the experience of finding a cuddly feminist mascot—a sort of thinking woman's teddy-bear. I admit all creativity is to some extent a desire to fix oneself and writing about this trauma has been therapeutic. As I wrote the darkness receded. It helped me see the situation from the outside, instead of only from the inside. Can I really blame Arthur for his desire to seize the chance to repeat his adolescent romance of Eros and spiritual passion, while he was still able to indulge. An interlude to avoid being the old guy he was swiftly becoming.

I imagine you nodding in agreement, thinking don't we all deserve to romp and hump no matter what age we are, even if we have to pay for it?

Love Katherine

Chapter 25

I hear the ancient footstepslike the motion of the sea
Sometimes I turn, there's someone there,
other times it's only me
I am hanging in the balance
of the reality of man
Like every sparrow falling,
like every grain of sand
Like a river flows surely to the sea
Darling, so it goes,
somethings were meant to be.
Bob Dylan

S*ept. 2, 2022.*
Dear Katherine,
This afternoon, more or less in the last stage of unpacking and organizing my new apartment—you know I have never been that conscious or concerned about clothes. I like a nice piece of clothing like the next chap, but I have never been focused on that. While unpacking all these beautiful shirts and jackets, I realized how each one you gave me was an expression of love. Of course, you have given me much more than clothes, but it's not about what you gave me so spontaneously and thoughtfully but that every gift was a gift from your heart. As I unpacked, my heart bled for my lack of awareness, for my ungratefulness—not for the clothing or your financial help but for your love! You are the only woman in my life who has given me anything! Even Ciguapa, what did she give me? I bought her an apartment; I made her a perfect studio, and bought thousands of dollars of paint and canvas but what did she ever give me? I won't even mention that other woman. A bad joke on me. Maybe God (the mysterious spirit) wanted me to see finally into the depths of myself.

I do appreciate and value deeply your help throughout the years and everything you have done for me. It was an immense gift! I did not mean to dismiss your generosity, which was given out of love. I knew if I were to begin earning real money I would naturally and spontaneously spend it on you with glee. The fact that I did not worry about money was huge. It is all the more obvious as now I do worry about money all the time!

I have been skewed left, right and center not only by Patasola but also by Alicious de Grande who has done virtually nothing for me yet continues to demand money for introducing me to promoters which leads to nothing.

Justice is not only about fairness, it is also about empathy and sympathy. A lover who does not identify with your feelings, or put themselves in your shoes, is not at one with you. Patasola did not empathize with me, so why did I go a step further and believe she loved me? I cannot understand myself. How I could have acted with such careless abandon? I have called it "madness" but obviously I am not "mad", but certainly there is some deep contradiction intrinsic to my emotional make-up throughout my life. It goes all the way back to my mother whom I loved intensely.

One evening at the age of twenty-one I packed up and left my family at the insistence of Ciguapa, who was almost my mother. Years later, I packed up and left Ciguapa for another woman. Suffering for doing so, and feeling like a criminal, I turned my back on Ciguapa whom I did love despite everything. Then you, the only really good and kind woman in my life. My heart bleeds for my moral obtuseness, for the hurt and pain I have caused you.

Even supposing that out of the goodness of your soul you can go on caring and writing to me you must question if you can you trust me. I lied repeatedly and yet as I wrote I had the conviction of truth that writing these lies brought to me. You are a writer; you know this only too well.

Katherine, be yourself, your strong, funny, clever self. You have such an ability to enjoy life, food, art, travel, intellect, friends, family. Let us talk and share and laugh, love is not chained to anything, or any circumstances! Darling, we are two creative and bold souls, so let's be creative together.

Love Arthur

xxx

Sept 10, 2022.

Dear Arthur.

Thank you for saying you appreciate my years of love and generosity. I do not want to criticize you after your warm words and your effort to ease my heartache. It is true if you had been financially independent, it would have eased many underlying tensions. You say *I knew if I were to begin earning real money I would naturally and spontaneously spend it on you with glee.* Actually, that is the most humiliating part. When you did have some money of your own, you spent it with glee on another woman who had more money than you.

Supposedly the most common reason couples break up is sexual incompatibility, differences in life goals, poor communication and lack of friendship and emotional intimacy. I would say despite having all the ingrediencies to make our partnership work our marriage we stopped paying attention to each other and it slipped away like quicksand.

Katherine

xxx.

Sept 15, 2022.

Dear Katherine.

You have this conquering, self-assured, bright open mind, that is the real you! So don't give way to self-inflicted pain. Don't go out into the garden to sing that rhyme about eating worms, as you did in childhood. You are a strong, daunting personality and you have a brilliant sharp brain. People take to you naturally because of your assuredness and open-mindedness. You are capable of so many things: designing, writing, recreating yourself, which is amazing!

I confess I am no longer who I was. I will not repeat the endless maternal/erotic/guilt vicious circle. I want to be straight and clear about my life and feelings. I see my "cowardice" of the past clearly, the "easy out" I took so many times, which does not mean I am free of them now or some of the sensibilities you do not like. I cannot throw myself happily into confrontations.

We are living separate lives, but we can be close. People may be physically together but emotionally separated, as we were those months after my four-day tryst with Patasola. I am deeply sorry about that. I hope to build a new understanding between us. All couples little by little develop habits and, yes, resentments, but if they want to, after a great shock it is possible to re-create lives and friendship (obviously not trying to reproduce the past). Of course, only if both want it. I know I do because I love you and share so much with you. Love is a matter of the spirit, in the simplest sense of that word, without mystique, just the disposition of the will and the heart. The essence of loving is to communicate and talk out one's soul. That is why I need to see you.

I have tried to find a way back to you—feebly at few times—back to our former life. I agree it was my own self-made blind alley and my paradoxical and flipflop decisions that prevented those reconciliation. I am not trying to justify myself. Nor to debate this with you. Just to explain what was happening in my own mind, which now seems dark and incomprehensible now.

I always felt very close to you, I don't understand why I acted with such unconscious egoism. I am deeply ashamed of my behavior towards you. These have been the worst years by far of my life. Never have I experienced such pain, self-contempt, self-blame, regrets. Your wish that this had never happened, which is exactly what I wish. I can't understand it any better than you, other than to recognize how easily I am taken over and emotionally vampirized.

Love Arthur

xxx

Sept 18, 2022.
Dear Arthur.

You think my family helps me fend off loneliness, but they are consumed by troubles of their own. Mostly they just want to know if I am okay enough for them to get back to their own pressing concerns.

Andre Maurois, that witty French writer who was Winston Churchill's interpreter and war liaison officer wrote in his wonderful book, *Les s\Silences du Colonel Bramble*—A happy marriage is a long conversation which always seems too short. You cut our conversations short. My bitterness is not a period at the end of a sentence, more a comma, a pause to await developments. You say you recognizes your Billy Goat passion was not love and yet it broke the bond between us when I heard you say you loved this other woman more than you ever loved me. That she was your life and your soul.

You say you are changed. But you should take a leaf out of Siri Hustvedt's clever novel, *A Summer Without Men*. It is not the sort of book you would normally read. I doubt you were even a fan of her husband, Paul Auster. The story she wrote is about an unfaithful husband who wants to return after his tryst with his secretary. His wife says, "Court me". Those words expresses exactly my feelings. Courtship is required. I thought you understood that when you made a few promises—when you said we would make a car trip around Italy, take a boat trip, spend time together. But each time we have seen each other it was only because you had an appointment in Paris and needed a place to stay. Instead of courting me you make me feel I am a pot on the back of the stove you are keeping warm for your future use.

Katherine

xxx

Oct 19, 2022.

Dear Katherine.

I have now finally torn through that net, and I see the obvious, with clarity. For two years and more, guilt and loneliness crushed me. In loneliness, the heart of life is missing. I have been in deep shock since I moved to Spain. I have not forgotten the beauties of our companionship. Now like an ice floe breaking up, I have been, unfrozen—an unfrozen block of ego: self-preservation, self-importance, and self-justification. I needed to be broken to see this, to be this. I am shocked by the clarity with which I see my behavior and unkindness. I never meant to hurt you but that doesn't change it.

I send you this story written by Mario Vargas Llosa (Peru, 86 years old) the winner of the Nobel Prize for Literature. His words are words I could have written. Like him I did not know the love I held, until I lost it. His story, with autobiographical overtones, was published in Letras Libres more than two years ago. It is the story of a disillusioned man who is reaching the twilight of his life, a man who regrets having left his wife for another. "Every night, it seems incredible, since I committed the folly of leaving my wife, I think of her, and remorse assails me. I think there was only one thing I did wrong in life: abandoning her for a woman who wasn't worth it. Every night I think of her, and I ask her forgiveness. I already forgot the name of that woman for whom I abandoned Carmencita. It was a violent and fleeting infatuation, one of those crazy things that destroy a life. For doing what I did, my life was destroyed, and I was never happy again. It was a crush on the pichula, not the heart. Of that pichula that no longer serves me for anything, except to pee.

Love Arthur

xxx

Oct 29, 2022.

Dear Arthur.

It is amazing this similarity between you and Mario Vargas Llosa. Both awakening from your bewitched state and ready to admit that once upon a time you had a good life and wish you'd known it sooner. I am also awakening to the reality that I might not get to spend forever with the man I care most about because you won't or can't make the effort to win me back. A partnership cannot be remade on a shit pile of broken threads; it needs reconstruction with new materials. No way will a patch and a few planks do. You don't seem to understand it is about my own self-respect. I need proof you do care about being with *me*, not just about the comfortable lifestyle I provided for so many years.

Katherine

xxx

Nov 25, 2022.

Dear Katherine.

I send you a goodnight hug on your birthday. Far from my moving on, I think of you constantly. I remember so much of our happy experiences together with love! It is simply untrue that "I didn't care", you must put all that shadowy image of me out of your head, it could not be more distorted. What happened to us is simple. I was intoxicated by a woman. She was toxic. I realize more and more how serpentine she is. It's a miracle I didn't kill myself because for an indefinite length of time, I was incapable of doing a single creative thing.

It is true when I say I never left you. I was under a shadow. I realized it quite soon, Patasola's behavior was shocking, violent, but it took months for me to break with her, like an addict I was addicted. That is why there were those false starts, they were not deliberate. In the end when it was too late, I broke with her in the most definitive and violent emotional break. I have never thought of her since except to remind myself she is a confused dark human I need to forgive.

I have been in deep shock for almost two years, overwhelmed with guilt and regrets over what happened between us. I am deeply ashamed of my behavior. Only a slow self-awareness and spiritual concentration helped me survive. My life, my mistakes, my self-deceptions have become crystal-clear to me as never before. For the last couple of hours streams of language have been breaking about me. In this concentration of fragments, a poetic language breaks through these conventional fragments of language. I write frantically not to lose that but in order to sleep. Everything I have ever known or loved is stilled as shattered crystal. These poetic out-bursts come from nothingness, blankness, a wall-like hole. It's as if I stand on the edge of a great shattered glass—the glass the experience and the perception of my life. That I am a nullity.

In Mass today I had an especially violent illumination, like headlights on a deer in the road at night. This is something I mentioned before, but here it is once more, without any softener, black on white. I have begun to think that finally in the hands of the Absolute Intelligence and Love, however mysterious and incoherent that may sound, I see my behavior with you as so brutal and insensitive that I can hardly recognize that it was me. I regret it with all my being. I don't even understand how I could have acted that way. It seems like another person. It was temporary madness. But sadly, it was me, at my worst. I do think that in part I was "ensorcelé" but of course still responsible. So not an excuse.

I have not forgotten the beauties of our companionship. Love and friendship are rare and beautiful things and an important variable in the happiness equation. Love is not peculiar to a couple; in a way it may be more difficult and less pure because of the jealousies and the resentments that may lie beneath the surface. I loved you and enjoyed so much with you, but I think also that I was semi-conscious, that my behavior made you unhappy. I hope, you are recovering your deep spirit now.

Love Arthur

xxx

Dec 11, 2022.

Dear Arthur.

I send you a hug on your birthday. Aging is full of irony, like checking the news and knowing there is going to be some new development we won't like. No doubt inside of every old person is a young person wondering what happened. Young people cannot possibly fathom what it means to cross the threshold into one's eighties as we edge towards our nineties. According to Camus: *Old age isn't life's parody. Life is life's parody.* We live in a society where the social pressures on us are not to grow old, yet the only worthwhile fight is against losing one's health. People assumed the old lose their brain power as well as their physical strength, some do but others like Warren Buffett at 94 remain as active and bright as ever.

I was not exactly unhappy with you, more disappointed because you had cease to be affectionate and treated me merely as someone who made the meals and paid the bills. We never when out to theatres, cinemas, or concerts or on holiday. It was all work and no play with endless expense on materials and no results. You ignored my advice and continued performing in mediocre venues that did not appreciate the uniqueness of your talents. After the Paris concert when success seemed within your grasp you sabotaged it by tying up with Alicious de Grande who aim was out to defraud you. A woman as self-interested as the groupie she criticized. Not exactly an ideal situation to make someone happy.

Katherine

xxx

Dec 24, 2022.

Dear Katherine.

I think one of the healthiest emotions in life is when we take a look at ourselves and find ourselves hilarious. Like the many times on an elaborate stage, I performed enthusiastically and repeatedly to a virtually empty theatre. Yesterday but more powerfully, I understood all this as never before. I could not until now attain this awareness because I had been too sure I knew what I was doing, imagining, and being—but I did not.

I am convinced, subject to creativity and inspiration, we invent our lives, just like the adjectives and verbs in a novel or the materials we use for artistic poetic creation. It has taken inner courage and faith for me to face my shadows and to become more conscious of what was really going on in my tryst with Patasola. I'm sure once I have figured out what happened, and I can't yet really figure that out, I will write my own account.

The mystery of age is a paradox and the tragedies of life have the potential to be comic stories with hindsight. I have been blocked by my awareness that this story could not possibly be written in a conscious 'novelesque' way. It is possible now because my ego and I have fractured, and I can see how the novel I have in the back of my mind could be written. It will include us, but it will be about far more than that. It will be about my spiritual journey through the wastelands of seeking, and being, alternately sought by, but quite often running desperately away.

I am simply a failed, broken human being. It is out of this brokenness I can create with the language of brokenness, a little like Gerard Manley Hopkins but from a different side of life and faith. In these last two years I have climbed far into my preceding life and my dark unknown self. No claim to any "spiritual" depth, on the contrary, just a disastrous look into my own chaotic life.

I know you are writing. I am ready to be your first reader, ready to accept your version of our story. I believe one can write their way through trauma with wit and intelligence no matter the tragedy. My taking the easy option as I have always done: Writing without publishing or publishing with anybody willing to publish me, was simply winking in the dark. I knew what I was doing but no

one else does.
    Love Arthur

xxx

Dec 25, 2022.

Dear Arthur,

I send you my best wishes and the hope the New Year brings you peace and success. Thank you for offering to be my first critic of this pepper pot tale of my pathetic indignity over being dumped. Can you really distance yourself enough from the tear-welling to be objective? Very difficult I would assume, even more difficult than it has been for me to re-story the past, fragment by fragment, while still trying to digest it. For every line I wrote a thousand lines were eliminated, each rendering provided a different lens into the past.

The great Renaissance writer Michel de Montaigne, who popularized essays as a literary form has been my guide. In his delightful patchwork quilt of words, he says his wild and monstrous plan was to present himself to himself. Certainly, writing this tale helped me gained a better understanding not only of myself but a better understanding of human weaknesses.

I like to believe I have present myself to myself, but if you read the text closely, I think you will find I have also presented you to yourself. Something which I would not have been able to do had you not allowed me to use your emails which show you as a flawed human being who makes bad decisions he regrets.

Despite your intelligence you remained as naive as a newborn babe. In your confused and vulnerable state, you are an easy victim to predators. Especially fake religious ones like Patasola, a woman not only willing to cross the boundaries of proper sexual conduct but one clever enough to lure you into her erotic embrace with the aim to gain dominance over you.

313

I like to think Henry James, who said he didn't regret a single "excess" of his irresponsible youth, would have told this nineteenth-century tale of a woman scorned by a flawed human being, with the sympathy and cynicism it merits.

Katherine

xxx

As a child I was intrigued by fairytales. They created a reality for my invented world where I played the orphan in enchanted woods and castles until I discovered Wonder Woman. My acts of rebellion were not heroism, they were more a way to take control over my fears and loneliness.

In the original fairytale the Little *Mermaid* by Hans Christian Andersen, the Little Mermaid visits the surface of the sea, on her 15th birthday. She is captivated by a desire to be human and have an immortal soul. In later versions of the *Little Mermaid*, this desire was transformed into a conventional tale of a desire for love and a life with the prince who she has saved from drowning. Yeah, right. Under patriarchal rules that's what she is supposed to want, isn't it? Pretty much the story of women's lives.

I wasn't thinking about immortality when at the age of 15 my father took me to Denmark, Hans Christian Andersen's birthplace, but was there that Sleeping Beauty was awakened, not by the kiss of the Prince, she was awakened by the world of art and my desire to be part of that world.

When the Little Mermaid asks the witch to exchange her tail for legs, the witch tells her she will have to give up her enchanting voice but worse unless the prince promises to be true, she will not have an immortal soul. She isn't listening just as I wasn't listening when my friends warned me that my family would abandon me if I disobeyed the rules set for girls. Nor was I listening later when they told me not to fall for a poet whose history of infidelity was as fickle as his finances. Yeah, I know, you can't teach an optimistic dreamer a new dance.

I now accept the Arthur's love was not mine to lose. I was his but he was not mine. I was the wrong princess for the prince's neurosis. A neurosis formed in Arthur's childhood by a predator neurotic mother and then the cunningly packaged predator Ciguapa, a mother figure in love with the son she never had. Once the pattern was set, he was ripe for the latter-day predator and gold digger packaged as a religious saint. I know what you are thinking—it was more a pitiful last grab for an erotic adventure with the child he never had. I am willing to concede that point but it is not the complete story.

The original version of the *Little Mermaid* is tragic and truer to life than the Disney version which has a happy ending. Ariel and her sassy crab friend, Sebastian, overcome the wicked sea witch (who changed Ariel into a human) and Ariel is able to swim off with her soul mate prince. In the original tale the Little Mermaid discovers how deeply a human heart can love and how a fragile ego can break when she is abandoned. At least the *Little Mermaid* did not suffer the agonizing pain of Arthur's indecisiveness. Nor did she hear him tell another woman he loved her more than he ever loved me.

When the prince goes off with another, the mermaid's sisters rise out of the sea and bring her a dagger to kill the prince which will enable her to become a mermaid once again. But the Little Mermaid cannot kill the sleeping prince. She loves him too much and wants his happiness more than she values her own. She throws the dagger and herself into the sea and disappears into the foam just as dawn breaks.

Obviously, I didn't die, but it was hard to stop glancing back at the past which was slowly becoming watery ink. It is in our human nature when we read stories of broken love to disparately want a happy conclusion, where *true love saves all and people who love each other get back together and live happily ever after.* A bit like movies where best friends fall in love. Does it ever happen? Isn't that the Disneyland version, as fake as the idea of people falling in love, marrying, and living happily ever after when most don't?

Put yourself in my shoes, dear reader, and tell me how you think this story should end? Obviously, it's not going to be the Disney version. If you want a surprise twist at the end of this sorry tale, I expect it will be the result Arthur's extremely poor memory. (He claims it's not poor memory, simply that he keeps it uncluttered for poetry and necessary knowledge).

Most of his relationships with women, were accidental because *he almost always got the wrong woman.* It was not unusual for him to discover a telephone number in his pocket with no memory of how it got there. Many a time he told hilarious stories of telephoning a woman thinking she was a voluptuous blond Italian, only to be dumbfounded when a boyish dark-haired Brazilian showed up. Or after making a date with what he thought was a sexy gallery owner, he was astonished when a young peasant girl arrived, who he could not even recall having met. These accidental meetings did not in the least deter him from seducing these women and developing a relationship with them. Circumstance he accepted as fate, as one might in a romantic novel. Some of these affairs lasted a couple of years.

Now with Arthur having suffered real loneliness for the first time in his life, the surprise twist at the end of this story will be when he finds another telephone number in his pocket. And if the woman who shows up is at all acceptable, I presume he will ask her to marry him.

And me? I will continue to live in the back pages of this book, frozen in halted breath awaiting readers to give my words a second life. My last words are Elvis's words: **Darling, so it goes, some things were meant to be** or rather some things are just what they are.

Other titles by BLKDOG Publishing for your consideration:

Britannia: The Wall
By Richard Denham & M. J. Trow

THE END OF ROMAN BRITAIN BEGINS.

The story opens in 367 AD. Four soldiers - Justinus, Paternus, Leocadius and Vitalis - are out hunting for food supplies at an outpost of Hadrian's Wall, when the Wall comes under attack.

The four find their fort destroyed, their comrades killed, and Paternus is unable to find his wife and son. As they run south to Eboracum, they realize that this is no ordinary border raid. Ranged against the Romans at the edge of the world are four different peoples, and they have banded together under a mysterious leader who wears a silver mask and uses the name Valentinus - man of Valentia, the turbulent area north of the Wall.

Faced with questions they are hard-pressed to answer, Leocadius blurts out a story that makes the men Heroes of the Wall. Their lives change not only when Valentinus begins his lethal sweep across Britannia but as soon as Leo's lie is out in the world, growing and changing as it goes.

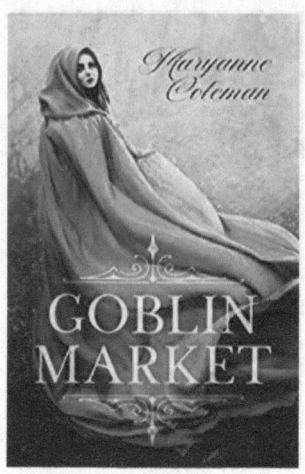

Goblin Market
By Maryanne Coleman

Have you ever wondered what happened to the faeries you used to believe in? They lived at the bottom of the garden and left rings in the grass and sparkling glamour in the air to remind you where they were. But that was then – now you might find them in places you might not think to look. They might be stacking shelves, delivering milk or weighing babies at the clinic. Open your eyes and keep your wits about you and you might see them.

But no one is looking anymore and that is hard for a Faerie Queen to bear and Titania has had enough. When Titania stamps her foot, everyone in Faerieland jumps; publicity is what they need. Television, magazines. But that sort of thing is much more the remit of the bad boys of the Unseelie Court, the ones who weave a new kind of magic; the World Wide Web. Here is Puck re-learning how to fly; Leanne the agent who really is a vampire; Oberon's Boys playing cards behind the wainscoting; Black Annis, the bag-lady from Hainault, all gathered in a Restoration comedy that is strictly twenty-first century.

Fade
By Bethan White

There is nothing extraordinary about Chris Rowan. Each day he wakes to the same faces, has the same breakfast, the same commute, the same sort of homes he tries to rent out to unsuspecting tenants.

There is nothing extraordinary about Chris Rowan. That is apart from the black dog that haunts his nightmares and an unexpected encounter with a long-forgotten demon from his past. A nudge that will send Chris on his own downward spiral, from which there may be no escape.

There is nothing extraordinary about Chris Rowan...

EST. 2019

BLKDOG

www.blkdogpublishing.com